THE CATCH

Other Books by Archer Mayor

THE CATCH

A Joe Gunther Novel

ARCHER MAYOR

St. Martin's Minotaur
New York

This is a work of fiction. All of the characters, organizations, and events portrayed in this novel are either products of the author's imagination or are used fictitiously.

www.minotaurbooks.com

ISBN-13: 978-0-312-38191-2
ISBN-10: 0-312-38191-3

First Edition: October 2008

10 9 8 7 6 5 4 3 2 1

To Nancy, with love and thanks

ACKNOWLEDGMENTS

No Joe Gunther book would have ever come into existence without the advice and expertise of dozens of people, and *The Catch* is no exception. I always hope that I honor the time, effort, and input that such kind folks so willingly give me by reflecting with some accuracy their contributions. That having been said, I know I stumble regularly. With that in mind, I thank those below, and so many others, while accepting full responsibility for any gaffes my readers might encounter in the following tale.

Mike McGonigle
Nancy Aichele
John Martin
Darrell Crandall
David Dent
Bill Parker
Marci Sorg
Janet Champlin
Ed David
Harry Bailey
Castle Freeman
Julie Lavorgna

Steven L. Waterman
Phil Crossman
Jim Acheson
Ralph Bridges
Brian Smith
Kathryn Tolbert
Phil and Sue Peverada
    and family
Chris and Lisa Montagna
Ray Walker
Paco Aumand

Brian Andersen   Eric Caron
Harold Polley   Paulina Essunger

Also:

The Maine Drug Enforcement Agency
The Maine Marine Patrol
The Maine State Police
Maine Public Radio
The Vermont State Police
The U.S. Immigration and Customs Enforcement
The Vermont Forensic Laboratory

THE CATCH

CHAPTER ONE

Deputy Sheriff Brian Sleuter was looking for a better country/western station when the Toyota flew by, spraying a few roadside pebbles against the front bumper of his cruiser.

"Jesus Christ, Bud," he said softly, turning on his headlights, putting the car into gear, and hitting his blue lights—all in a single, well-practiced gesture—"why don't you flip me the bird while you're at it?"

He fishtailed into the road from his hiding place, his rear tires spinning before gaining purchase, and took off down Vermont Route 7 with a burst from the Impala's built-up engine, the Toyota's rear lights already fading fast into the late-night summer darkness. This stretch of road—straight, isolated, and well paved—was a magnet for speeders.

It was long after midnight, and Sleuter had been waiting patiently for just such an opportunity. In the split second that his well-trained eye had glimpsed the interior of the car, illuminated only by its own dash lights, he'd caught sight of two people, both young males. That, combined with the Toyota being older, dark-colored, and nonde-script in appearance—and that it was headed south from the direction of Burlington and possibly Canada—helped him think he might be about to tag his first drug runner in five weeks.

That had been way too long for a certifiable, self-admitted Type-A personality like Brian Sleuter. He saw himself as a man on the make, and the faster that he created a name for himself, the sooner he could move up to some outfit like ATF or DEA where he could really throw the book at the bad guys.

The Toyota grew in size before him as he pushed the accelerator to the floor. Official police denials notwithstanding, high-speed run-downs had their thrills. The engine's unleashed roar, the sudden blurring of scenery on both sides, pulsing to the strobe bar's steady beat, heightened the defiant, indomitable sense of superiority that washed through Sleuter every time he put on his uniform. He'd been told that wasn't a good thing—that it ran counter to the whole professional, courteous, protect-and-serve bullshit the boss spouted at monthly trainings—but he knew what he knew, which was that a gun and a badge made for a good argument in a fight, and that he had no interest in being a social worker.

Call him a jackass if you had front teeth to spare, but at least he was no loser.

The Toyota began slowing down, pulling over to the side of the narrow road. Ahead of them both, a pair of headlights crested a distant hill, aiming their way. Sleuter instinctively charted their progress, as he was simultaneously watching for any suspicious activity from the Toyota, but all the on-comer did was slow as they always did upon sight of the blue lights, before sliding by timidly as Sleuter angled his cruiser to a stop behind his quarry.

He hit the spotlight switch by his left window, freezing the car before him in a blinding halo, and removed the radio mike from its cradle.

"Fifty-one — Dispatch."

"Fifty-one. This is Dispatch."

"I'm Seventy-five Massachusetts passenger Romeo Foxtrot Zulu, Three Eight One, a mile or two north of the Route 17 crossroad on Route 7."

"Ten-Four, Fifty-one."

At least Dispatch was on the ball, Sleuter thought as he opened his door, not shooting the shit with someone or taking a leak, as usual. He glanced at the camera screen glowing high and near the center of his windshield, to make sure the icon representing his body recorder was on. He wasn't a huge believer in high-tech gadgets — he hated computers, for example — but he'd won more than one case in court because of voice and image recordings.

He emerged from his car and paused, studying what he could see of the two men caught in the harsh glare. Unfortunately, that only amounted to the backs of their heads. He needed to know what their hands were doing.

He circled around to the rear of the cruiser, keeping out of his own lights, and closed in on the Toyota from its right side, thereby avoiding being seen in the driver's outside left mirror — the place most operators checked to monitor an officer's approach.

When he came even with the car's right-rear bumper, knowing he'd entered the cruiser's camera frame, Sleuter did one more thing out of long habit: he reached out with his left hand and pressed it against the metal of the vehicle. This strict official protocol, a gesture born of painful past experience, reflected how many times cops had been shot and/or killed during a stop, and their evidentiary fingerprints later found on the suspect's car.

Each time Sleuter touched a vehicle this way, he did so consciously, as aware of the bet he was hedging as when he donned his ballistic vest before every shift.

He stopped again to scrutinize what he could see of the interior of the car, and to add to the discomfort of its occupants. He also glanced around quickly. There weren't any trees along this stretch — it was open, rolling countryside, cupped between the Green Mountains to the east, and the Adirondacks across Lake Champlain to the west. At night, that made it overwhelmingly black and vast and helped make Brian Sleuter feel like the most exposed object for miles around.

Returning to the task at hand, and secure that he'd seen no obvious signs of danger from inside the passenger area, like the glint of a gun or a suspicious posture or movement, he turned on his small, powerful handlight and shined it directly into the car, starting with its rear seat.

Again, he saw nothing untoward.

Both heads swiveled in his direction as he walked up to the passenger window and tapped on it with his light, standing even with the back door to make of himself a harder target. The window whirred down.

"Hey, there, officer," the driver spoke across the chest of his companion, who merely stared ahead after the briefest glimpse in Sleuter's direction — an immobility Brian found telling.

"Evening," he answered. "I'd like to see your driver's license, registration, and proof of insurance."

The driver, a young man with a mustache and a silver post twinkling in the nest of his left eyebrow, smiled and nodded. "Sure thing, officer." He reached over and opened the glove box before the Sphinx-like passenger.

Sleuter followed the man's hand with his flashlight beam and watched it fish among an assortment of documents and food wrappers, eventually finding a wrinkled envelope and pulling it out. The driver extracted the requested paperwork and handed it over.

Sleuter glanced at the Massachusetts license he held in his left hand, having wedged his light under his left armpit—thereby keeping his gun hand free at all times. "This your current address, Mr. Marano?"

"Nah. I moved. The right one's on the registration. I'm still getting the license changed."

Sleuter nudged the passenger on the shoulder. "How 'bout you? You got any identification?"

The passenger finally looked up at him fully, his expression tense. "I didn't do nuthin'."

"Didn't say you did. Got any identification?"

The man hesitated. He, too, was young, like the driver, but sported a goatee and no piercings that Sleuter could see. He did, however, have the edge of a tattoo poking just over the top of his T-shirt. It looked like part of a snake. He was also sweating, which Sleuter found noteworthy. It was summer, fair enough, but that didn't have the same meaning up here as it did farther south—the nights generally ran cool, just like now.

"Sure. No problem," the man said and reached for his back pocket, lifting himself off the seat in the process.

Sleuter stepped back, watching them carefully. Every nerve in his body told him he had something cooking here, people with criminal records at least, and probably more.

He took the other man's driver's license when it was handed to him and repeated his earlier question: "You still at this address, Mr. —" he paused to read, "Grega?"

"Sure," Grega answered, once more looking straight ahead.

Sleuter paused a moment, considering his approach. What he was hoping for was a consent search. What he knew he should request was backup. But he was reluctant to pursue that. If this panned out the way he was hoping, he didn't want to share the credit.

"What happens when I run you two through the computer?" he asked. "I gonna find anything?"

"Not me, officer," Marano said with his quick smile. "You can check all you want."

"Yeah," Grega answered more ambivalently. "Check all you want."

Sleuter nodded, mostly to himself. Those were pretty standard responses. And didn't mean much. People either thought that out-of-state records didn't cross the border, or that Vermont cops were too dumb to even operate a computer. Or both.

"Okay," he told them. "Stay put. I'll be right back."

"Take your time, officer," said Marano, his courtesy tinged with contempt.

Sleuter backed away, keeping his eye on the car as he went, not fully turning away until he felt he was safe. As before, he circled the rear of his cruiser to regain his seat, still not wanting to give his suspects the slightest flash of his silhouette.

"Fifty-one—Dispatch," he radioed after closing his door behind him.

"Dispatch."

"You have a twenty-eight? Twenty-seven, RO."

Dispatch gave him the registration first, as requested. "Massachusetts passenger Romeo Foxtrot Zulu, Three Eight One, is a 2004, two-door Toyota Solara, color black, registered to James Marano and valid until 2009." She gave him the address in Boston, on Dorchester Avenue—nicknamed "Dot Ave" among cops, and infamous as a drug and gang hotbed. It matched what appeared on Marano's registration.

"The twenty-seven," she continued in the same flat voice, referring to the registered owner's—or "RO's"—operator's license, "is valid in Massachusetts. No priors in Vermont."

That was the first layer, and usually the most useless. Sleuter opened his mouth to ask her to dig deeper when he simultaneously noticed two things that made him abruptly straighten in his seat— the passenger in the Toyota was no longer visible, and there was a sudden movement to his left.

But that was all. The bullet entering his temple put an end to everything else.

CHAPTER TWO

Matthew J. Mroz left the restaurant where he'd enjoyed dinner, stepped out into Rockland's Main Street, and took in a deep lungful of warm evening air. His last name rhymed with "morose," not inappropriately given his profession, but it had been chopped down to Roz by his associates, who were prone to catchy monikers.

Mroz was a drug dealer—successful, ambitious, ruthless, and careful. Originally from Portland, Maine—the state's largest city— he'd migrated down the coast to Rockland several years ago, recognizing the crowded nature of his birth town's illegal marketplace, and also that the products being sold there—largely the cocaine and heroin so trendy in the states just south of them—were overlooking a far hungrier clientele.

Early on, Matthew Mroz had come to understand that, on a per capita basis at least, Maine had one of the largest prescription drug abuse problems in the country.

In his eyes, the least he could do was to serve a pressing social need. In so doing, he'd become wealthy, influential, and popular—at least in specialized circles. He'd also become a source of keen interest to competitors and the police, which helped explain the presence by his side of a bald, muscular, unpleasant-looking man named Harold, who at the moment was checking up and down the street through squinted eyes.

Harold had more than enough to scrutinize. Rockland was a large town—a ferry boat port servicing several Penobscot Bay islands; the primary urban hub for a cluster of nearby communities like Camden and Rockport, whose genteel configurations shied away from some of Rockland's more practical, grittier offerings; and the host of some small but locally significant industrial enterprises like a harborside petroleum storage facility, a marina, and a large quarrying operation.

More to Roz's interest, however, was that Rockland was also a magnet for touristy transients—complete with recreational appetites.

"Where to?" Harold asked, content for the moment that no black helicopters were hovering overhead, and no people like him hiding among the throng of summer visitors.

"The Oh-So-High, moron," Mroz said simply, invoking his nickname for one of the motels where he routinely conducted business.

Harold nodded silently, having already guessed the destination and being used to the abuse. He'd been working for Roz for three years by now and had established a rhythm of what he chose to hear and what he didn't. He let his boss pass before him, so he could guard his back while watching ahead—what he considered good protective behavior, even though he was shy any professional training.

He could handle himself—had on numerous occasions. But Harold was a realist, and knew he was more thug than bodyguard.

On the other hand, that's how Roz used him—as a two-legged pit bull. He just would have preferred not being spoken to as such.

Which wasn't to say that his patience was unlimited.

They proceeded down the street between the phalanx of red-brick buildings reflecting downtown's muscular commercial past. Rockland had been a minor powerhouse once, much more than it was now, even in these tourist-driven times. No Portland, of course, but still a significant influence in Maine's development. Now, erst-while businesses from fishing concerns to boat building to shipping and the like had been replaced by boutiques, restaurants, art galleries, and gift shops.

Matt Mroz's Oh-So-High motel wasn't of that ilk. Less flashy than its waterfront counterparts, it was set back, down a side street, and sported a straightforward, pragmatic demeanor—parking lot, two rows of stacked rooms girdled by a running balcony. No gym, no pool, no in-room movies, or "Magic Finger" beds. Just the basics. It was, to be fair, not the first stop for travelers hungry for salt air and enchanting views. Commercial drivers used the place for its intended purpose, others for its discretion and anonymity.

"Same room?" Harold asked as they left the sidewalk and entered the parking lot bordered on three sides by the motel's monotonous door-and-window facade.

Mroz eyed him sorrowfully over his shoulder. "Jesus, Harold. That's the whole point."

Harold had his doubts. It seemed to him that conducting business from the same location every time might be exactly the wrong thing to do if you didn't want to be surprised. But that was Roz's hang-up—"Safety in familiarity," he'd said, or something like that. Harold always figured it was because Roz had been kicked around as a kid or something. In any case, it made life a lot easier for Harold—not only did it mean fewer places to check out in advance, but in this instance, it meant that Harold could set things up just as he wanted.

They climbed the exterior metal staircase to the second-floor balcony and proceeded to a room located at the very far end—one that Mroz kept rented on a near permanent basis.

Harold removed the key from his pocket and slid it into the lock as Mroz stepped back to lean against the railing.

"Be right back," Harold told him, as always, before slipping inside to check the place for safety.

Mroz nodded comfortably and turned to gaze out over the parking lot—the only available view. The light was fading, the clouds were a salmon pink from the setting sun, and the heat of the day had dropped just enough to imbue the air with a soft warmth usually associated with picnics and strolls in the park. Life was pretty good.

Harold stuck his head out the door. "All clear."

Mroz left his perch and passed into the familiar room, virtually a home away from home, given the volume of business he did here, especially at this time of year.

It wasn't anything grand, of course—the usual assortment of cheap furniture, bad artwork, and poorly addressed rug stains. But it gave Mroz a sense of comfort and stability, and considering some of the places he'd been, it was even a step up.

Harold was at the window, peering out. "He's coming."

Mroz was sitting on the edge of the bed. "Don't know what I'd do without you, Harold."

Harold ignored him. The man approaching the motel was a regular, in his thirties with thinning blond hair and a nervous manner, who kept justifying his visits by referring to various ailments.

A couple of minutes later, there was a timid knock on the door. As always, Harold opened up, keeping the customer outside while he checked around. He then motioned the man inside without a word, his tough-guy demeanor firmly in place.

Mroz was still sitting on the bed. "George. How're you doin'?"

"Not too good, Roz," their visitor said. "Back pain's been acting up."

Mroz laughed. "I don't give a rat's ass, George. Don't you get that? How much do you want this time?"

"Ten might do it," George said softly, reaching into his pocket.

Mroz stared at him for a moment before giving a silent nod to Harold, who crossed over to the closet, removed a paper bag, and counted out ten OxyContins from an orange plastic pill bottle. He poured those in turn into a small white envelope and handed that to his boss.

Mroz waggled it back and forth between his index and thumb, eyeing George thoughtfully. "What do you think? That a thousand bucks you got in your hand?"

George looked confused. "Isn't that what you said? One hundred each?"

Mroz stuck out his hand for the money. "That's what I said—I'm running a special all this week."

"Is it going up?" George asked, taking the envelope in exchange.

"Call me when you're in need again, George," Mroz told him. "I'll tell you then."

George nodded a couple of times, fresh out of conversation and now distracted by what he was holding.

Mroz shook his head—the sad but sympathetic purveyor of balm for the needy.

"Get out of here, George. Enjoy the rest of your evening."

There was a momentary silence following George's departure. By habit, Harold never said much of anything, but Mroz was a talker, and incapable of letting more than a minute go by without saying something.

"Thousand right out of the gate. Could be a good night. I like 'em when they start strong like that. Puts me in a good mood."

"That's good to hear," said a male voice from the direction of the bathroom.

Mroz leaped to his feet, staggering slightly in the process. A man stood in the bathroom doorway, a gun in his leather-gloved hand. He was smiling slightly.

Mroz jerked his head around, looking for his bodyguard. Harold was standing at his post by the window, still watching for visitors. He turned and nodded to the man. "Nobody coming."

"What the fuck's going on here?" Mroz demanded of the newcomer. "Who the fuck're you?"

"I'm Alan Budney," the man told him. "His new boss."

Mroz glanced at Harold again, but without much confidence. "Harold?" he asked.

Harold merely shrugged and went back to studying the outdoors.

Mroz nodded, visibly weighing his options. "You want in on the action?"

Budney shook his head. "Nope. I want it all."

With that, he pulled the trigger, filling the room with a sharp, explosive crack and putting a hole in Matthew Mroz's chest.

The latter fell back against the wall and bounced awkwardly onto the floor, one hand on the wound, not saying a word. His eyes stayed glued to Budney's, but without purpose or reproach. If anything, there was a look of wonder on his face before all signs of life slipped away.

Budney wasted no time with Harold. He stuck his arm out, took aim, and squeezed off two quick rounds from across the room.

Harold wasn't as cooperative as his ex-boss. "You son of a bitch," he yelled, and launched himself at Budney, as if totally ignorant of the twin stains that had blossomed on his T-shirt.

Budney didn't hesitate. He fired twice more, hitting Harold once in the head. That dropped the big man like a dead tree, flopping him onto the bed where he stayed without further motion.

"What did you expect, you dumb bastard?" Budney asked no one in particular. He stared at both men for a couple of seconds, as if uncertain about what to do next. He hadn't anticipated the adrenaline now pulsing through him like an electric current.

He passed his gloved hand across his mouth, shoved the gun into his waistband, and walked over to the window to see if anyone was coming. When he'd set this up with Harold, promising him the world in money and influence, they'd arranged for a big enough break between scheduled customers for Budney to act freely and without interruption. In the same vein, Budney had rented both the room next door and the one below—under assumed names—just to make sure the gunshots wouldn't be easily overheard. The pacing of Mroz's client list, however, had been Harold's department.

Budney looked nervously out across the parking lot, half expecting a cordon of police cars and SWAT members to be ringing the motel. But there was little going on—a young couple crossing the lot, hand in hand, some traffic driving by in the street beyond.

All looked peaceful and serene, in total contrast with the contents of the room.

Budney opened the door slowly, pulled his shirt over the gun butt, stored his gloves in his back pocket, and stepped out to enact the next phase of his plan. He didn't bother collecting either the cash or the drugs. He preferred thinking that, at this point, that smackat of small potatoes.

CHAPTER THREE

Joe Gunther rubbed his eyes, blinked, and briefly turned away from the crime scene lights and the long row of parked, strobe-equipped vehicles. He gazed at the rising sun, barely backlighting the tops of the Green Mountains in the distance, but already tinting the tall grasses of the open, rolling fields nearby with the first strokes of dawn's blush. It was a time of the day he'd especially cherished as a boy, when he'd arise from his bed to share breakfast with his benignly taciturn father before the latter headed out to tend to the crops and animals.

It was an appropriate remembrance, and not solely because of the sunrise—the area around Vergennes was ancient farm country, some of Vermont's most productive. Joe had been brought up on the other side of the state, but the effect was similar if a bit more spectacular here, and he was too tired to be picky.

He shut his car door and turned to his reason for being here. A sheriff's cruiser was positioned by the side of the road, in standard patrol stop presentation, its nose slightly angled toward the center of traffic, as if ready to leave at a moment's notice. Officers placed their cars that way partly for protection as they got out to approach whomever they'd stopped.

There was irony in this instance, though, since it looked like the cop had never left his vehicle.

But that was a first impression, and Joe knew better than to rely on it. In his decades as a police officer, even far from the urban mayhem of New York and Boston, Gunther had seen his share of either straightforward murderous encounters, or others intriguingly cloaked in misdirection or obscurity. He'd learned that each could first appear as the other.

Nevertheless, this did not look like a slam dunk. There was too much about it that smacked of complication.

He sighed gently. He liked complications, or at least working his way through them. A methodical man—some even thought a little plodding—he had a dogged, nonflamboyant, almost Old World style. He was courteous and considerate, hardworking and slow to take credit—the inveterate team player. Which helped explain his present position. Joe Gunther, after leading Brattleboro's municipal detective squad, seemingly forever, was now the field force commander of the Vermont Bureau of Investigation, the state's relatively new major crimes unit.

But he felt a true weariness with the nature of this call. Murders in Vermont were few, averaging perhaps seven or eight a year—rare enough to make it standing protocol that he be called to the scene regardless of time or location. But the killing of a cop? That was virtually unheard of—a once-in-a-decade event, at least so far.

As a result, Gunther knew that the entire state would be watching every detail of this one—and that every news outlet would be hoping to dog his heels.

Which still didn't fully address the heart of his melancholy—Joe Gunther was a combat veteran, a lifelong witness to violence, a man whose entire professional life had been devoted to cleaning up in the wake of human bedlam. He'd seen brutality and the threat of death visit not just his comrades and the general population, but members of his own family. And yet he still couldn't adopt the commonly held belief that such acting out was as natural to human beings as sex and the need to eat. Killing remained for him a gesture bordering on lunacy.

A square-built, plainclothes detective with a sandy crew cut split away from the group clustered around the cruiser and approached him. "Anyone give you the lowdown on this, Joe?"

Joe shook his hand. Michael Bradley was the squad leader for the VBI Burlington office, some twenty-five miles away, and thus, under Joe, the senior investigator here. "Hi, Mike. Long time. Just that a deputy had been found, an apparent homicide."

Bradley nodded. "Right—Brian Sleuter. Five years on the job, good record of arrests. Aggressive, ambitious, aiming for the big leagues somewhere—some say anywhere, since he was supposedly frustrated with the sheriff's department. It's looking like he might've been surprised on a traffic stop."

Joe was looking past his colleague's shoulder, taking in what he could see of the crime scene, along with the various uniforms and faces. Gunther had been a presence in Vermont's small law enforcement community for long enough to have at least met most of its senior members. Thus, he could already see some of the entanglements he'd soon be delicately sorting through. Mixed together, if not precisely mingling, were the state police, the sheriff's department, the Vergennes police, the state's attorney, the medical examiner's lead investigator, and at least a couple of others from Mike Bradley's office. And that, he knew, would be just the beginning.

"We know about the traffic stop?" he asked Mike, redirecting his focus.

"From Dispatch only, right now, but Sleuter did have his video running, so that ought to help, assuming he had a tape in."

Joe eyed him carefully. "We haven't looked at that yet?"

Bradley smiled. A veteran himself, late of the Burlington police department—the state's largest—he wasn't given to being flustered. "It's a cop killing. We're taking our time—within reason."

"Right," Joe agreed.

Bradley laughed gently as a follow-up. "Meaning we're about to pop the trunk, if you're interested."

They began crossing over to the group around the car. "What did their dispatch have to say?" Joe asked.

Bradley pulled out a notepad for reference. "A black, '04 Toyota Solara, registered to James Marano, from Massachusetts—Dorchester Avenue address."

"He was the driver?"

Bradley shrugged. "Sleuter asked for the twenty-seven RO, so presumably the owner and the driver were one and the same. And no," he added quickly as Joe opened his mouth, "I don't know if he had a passenger."

They reached the group and Joe began exchanging handshakes. It wasn't many years ago that the VBI hadn't existed and that the state police would have been running this scene. The initial transition—and the sometimes attending resentments—had been

partly overcome by the VBI leadership resolutely avoiding the limelight, entering cases only when invited, and referring to their agency
as a support tool only. But that went only so far. Every time Joe entered a case, therefore, he paid homage to the past, respected sensitivities, stressed his helpful role, while yet—with as much subtlety as
possible—essentially taking over the investigation.

For the moment, however, most of that didn't matter. Here—
now—he was surrounded by fellow cops, all of them concentrating
on the murder of one of their own.

Bradley nodded to a crime lab tech, whose team had cordoned
off the cruiser. The woman, looking like a futuristic model at a car
show—clad in a white Tyvek suit and isolated from the crowd behind
a "Crime Scene" tape barrier—opened the vehicle's trunk to reveal
its contents, familiar to every patrol-trained officer in the crowd. Facing them was the standard collection of first aid kit, traffic cones, an
officer's shift bag, and a shotgun case. More pointedly right now,
however, was a small steel cabinet bolted to the trunk's back wall—
the video recorder.

With her gloved hand, and using Brian Sleuter's key, the tech unlocked the recorder's security door, revealing a standard VCR control panel. She pushed the Eject button, extracted the tape, and held
it up to the artificial light.

"About halfway unreeled," she announced, handing it to one of
her colleagues on the other side of the barrier.

"You going to check that out here?" Joe asked him.

The man smiled helpfully. "I can. I have a player in the truck. I
know how much you guys want to look at it."

"I'd appreciate it," Joe encouraged him.

"Follow me," he said simply.

A small herd fell in behind him as he trudged toward the large crime lab truck parked somewhat precariously along the grassy ditch separating the macadam from the miles of surrounding fields that were slowly emerging from the darkness. Technically, there was a pecking order involved in who participated in a high profile investigation. The county sheriff had officially requested VBI assistance, rubbing in the state police's awkward second fiddle position. But Joe didn't want any such political smog in the air—not when he still had no idea whose resources he might need—so he remained silent.

The crime scene tech, however, looked over his shoulder at the sound of so many feet behind him. "It's a tight fit back there," he warned.

A state police lieutenant suggested, "How 'bout one rep from each agency?"

Satisfied, Joe let them mutter through that one on their own, sliding up alongside the tech instead and sticking out his hand.

"Never had the pleasure. Joe Gunther. VBI."

The tech's eyes widened as he put his gloved hand into Joe's. "This is an honor. I've heard a lot about you. Ed Needles. I just joined the lab about six months ago—from Natick, Mass."

"Welcome on board. How do you like it?"

"Good bunch. The facility's a little funky, compared to what I know, but I like the people. No politics; straightforward; well trained. I got no complaints."

They reached the back of the truck, equipped with a set of wooden steps, reminiscent of a ladder propped against a gypsy's caravan wagon. It was immediate proof of the lab's touch of practical funkiness. In single file, the chosen few tromped into the truck's resonant box and marched toward the front, where the wall above a counter was festooned with a battery of rack-mounted electronic gadgets, including a TV screen and several computer monitors.

Without ceremony, Needles slapped the cassette into a VCR and hit the Rewind button. After a couple of attempts to locate the beginning of Sleuter's last stop on the tape, the tech hit Play and took a half step back so everyone could see.

The confined space, claustrophobic and rapidly too warm, fell completely silent aside from the tinny voices emanating from the TV. They all watched, transfixed, as the cruiser's camera revealed—in color and in surprisingly sharp detail—a dark Toyota pulling over to the side of the road. Brian Sleuter's voice was heard talking to Dispatch, along with her response, as Joe noticed Mike Bradley beside him pulling his pad from his pocket and starting to take notes.

"There are two of them," a voice whispered toward the back of the tightly packed group.

Sleuter approached the Solara from the right, staying out of the glare of his own take-down lights. In a gesture that sent a chill down Joe's spine, the deputy quickly placed his handprint on the car's back end.

"Good work, Bri," murmured his boss, the sheriff. "We'll nail the bastard with that."

The conversation with Marano and Grega came over the speaker, and Bradley began writing in earnest. They'd get a copy of the tape eventually, but no one wanted to lose any time. Chances of solving a homicide fade almost exponentially with every hour that passes, and no one had known about Grega before now. Dispatch had never been told.

The tension rose as Sleuter left the side of the car with the documents he'd collected. Once more, he circled his own vehicle, disappearing from view, reappearing only by proxy as the camera shook, announcing that he'd settled back behind the wheel.

There was the sound of the mike being unclipped from its holder, followed by Sleuter's routine inquiries about Marano, the driver.

"Oh, shit. Look up," urged a voice behind Joe. "Look in front of you."

Before them, unnoticed by the deputy, the back of Grega's head slid down out of sight, followed by the Toyota's passenger door opening just wide enough to let a body slip outside. Everyone leaned forward, as if entering the TV screen would afford a better view of what might be occurring. In the blink of an eye, they caught the briefest glimpse of Grega's shoulder as he crawled across the very front of the cruiser, trying to avoid being seen, and then—almost immediately—a loud shot made them all jump in surprise.

"*Jesus*," someone exclaimed.

There was another pause before Grega ran back across the screen, no longer concerned about discretion, the same documents visibly clutched in a red-stained right hand.

"Son of a bitch took back the twenty-sevens," Bradley said, no longer writing.

Joe nodded, watching as the Toyota's brake lights flared briefly, to be instantly fogged by twin spurts of gravel and dust as the front tires spun out, accelerating away from the road's shoulder.

"Not to worry, Mike," he said quietly. "We'll get them." He pointed with his chin at the TV screen, adding, "And with this, we'll make it stick."

CHAPTER FOUR

Y ou hear about Matt Mroz?"

Greg Joseph glanced across the front seat of the unmarked car at his passenger. "Roz? No. What about him?"

"Somebody capped him last night—single round to the chest."

Joseph whistled softly. "I heard about a shooting—didn't know it was him. Jeez. That'll shake things up. That was a double, though, wasn't it?"

Kevin Delaney nodded. "Yeah. His bodyguard caught it, too. It'll be in the papers later this morning."

"Damn. Who do we have working it?"

"Stevens."

Joseph didn't react, at least not so Delaney could see. But he was envious of Phil Stevens, with whom he'd graduated from the academy. The Maine State Police's CID unit handled all homicides outside of Portland, Bangor, or Lewiston—city departments that investigated their own—and Phil had been with them for three years already, while Greg was still stuck in the boonies of Aroostook County, damn near inside Canada.

He wasn't underworked—no cop in Maine could claim that, the state being so huge and the number of cops so small—but there were definitely some assignments hotter than others.

This one was a dud, even though Delaney was okay. As Northern Division commander of the Maine Drug Enforcement Agency, Delaney could've been a snotty jerk. But he was a regular guy. The MDEA was an elite outfit, which gave them the option of being a bunch of obnoxious hot dogs. And although they did have a cowboy now and then, they generally made an effort to not piss off too many people.

Greg stared glumly out the window at the drizzly night, resigned to his fate. Maine was New England's largest state by far, thinly populated with just over a million people, and so vast that cops like him, isolated in the northern reaches, could well be the only law enforcement for an area the size of a large township, depending on the time of day. Older veterans spoke of having had patrol areas of fourteen hundred square miles back in the day, which wasn't so long ago.

Delaney reached for the binoculars resting on the dash, fitted them to his eyes, as he had several times already during the two hours they'd been sitting here, and watched the border crossing ahead. It was like a scene from *The Spy Who Came in from the Cold*. They were stationed in Fort Kent, pulled over by the edge of the U.S. side's parking lot, waiting to find out if a tip Delaney had received would pay off, although Joseph didn't actually know that for a fact. He'd been left in the dark, as usual.

"They know who whacked Mroz?" he asked, returning from his ruminations.

Delaney spoke while still holding the glasses. "Nope. Not a clue. Nobody heard anything, nobody saw anything, and nobody's talking—at least not yet."

He sat forward slightly, and Joseph held off speaking, trying to interpret the other man's body language before looking himself to see what was going on, half expecting to see an East German spy sprinting for freedom on a bike amid a hail of bullets. Of course, there was nothing aside from a van with U.S. plates, stopped at the entry gate for a routine interview. Joseph figured all this had something to do with drug smuggling—that much was a no-brainer—but it didn't explain Delaney's presence here in the middle of the night. The man was a supervisor—a nine-to-fiver—someone who normally came out for major cases only.

"Anything?" he finally asked as the van rolled away without mishap, passing by them forty seconds later, carrying a woman with two sleeping kids in the back.

Delaney replaced the binoculars. "Nah."

He didn't look particularly disappointed—mostly thoughtful.

"What exactly are we looking for?" Joseph asked. "I was just told to keep you company watching the border. They didn't seem to know why."

The MDEA man shifted in his seat so he could both look at Joseph and yet still be attentive to the checkpoint. "Yeah. Sorry about that, and I really appreciate the backup. None of us really knows what's up. It's too early yet."

"But it ties into Mroz getting killed? I thought you didn't know who did that."

"We don't, but like you said, it's guaranteed to stir everything up. Roz was big on prescription drug imports, along with a lot of other stuff. With him gone, it's open season on his organization, or on somebody coming up with something new."

Delaney pointed at the checkpoint in the distance. "We got information that Roz's primary contact in Canada was coming over to find out what to do next."

"Who's that?" Joseph asked reasonably enough.

But his passenger shrugged. "Don't know. Just that he was arriving tonight, through here. Supposed to be driving a van like that last one."

Joseph was nonplussed. It was a shot-in-the-dark—so, how to explain a supervisor riding shotgun?

"Sounds a little skimpy," he said diplomatically.

Delaney laughed before displaying why he might have achieved his rank. "So, what's a brass hat like me doing out here in the middle of the night, right?"

"Well . . ."

The other man waved Joseph's embarrassment away. "Don't worry about it. Greg, right?"

"Yeah."

"Couple of reasons: On the type-A, gotta-get-out-and-play side, it's been a while since I've done any fieldwork, my wife's out of town with the kids, and I have a light load on my desk at the moment. On the more serious side, Roz's killing is a big deal, and most of my guys are out right now trying to find out what's going on. Maine's filling up with prescription drugs, and we still don't know how the product's getting to market. I mean, yeah, there're a few crooked docs and pharmacists out there, like everywhere else, and some pills getting diverted between point A and point B—wherever those happen to be. Also, a lot of mules're crossing the border, either body packing or squirreling stuff into spare tires and car cavities.

"In fact," he interrupted himself with a broad smile, "we got one guy who was shooting pills across the St. Croix River in hollow aluminum arrows to a buddy on our side. Good thing he didn't kill him—that would've made for an interesting autopsy.

"Anyhow," he resumed, "none of that explains the quantities we're seeing, which're big and getting bigger."

"Maybe the Hell's Angels?" Joseph asked, referring to one of Canada's largest reputed drug-handling organizations.

But Delaney made a face. "They don't fool with prescriptions much, and the geography is off. They're stronger above New Hampshire, Vermont, and points west."

He stopped talking and reached for the glasses on the dash again. Joseph followed his scrutiny and saw another van, like the first, stopped at the checkpoint.

"I like this one," Delaney said, binoculars still in place.

Joseph shifted slightly in his seat and rested his left hand on the steering wheel. "What's your pleasure?"

"We follow him," Delaney answered. "At least till I can get a team to relieve us. That's why I asked for your unmarked car, so we don't spook him."

Keeping his lights off, Joseph started the engine. After another minute of observation, Delaney exchanged the binoculars for a cell phone. At the border booth, the van pulled away and began heading their way. As it passed by, Joseph saw a single, heavily bearded male at the wheel, his eyes fixed straight ahead. Joseph waited a few seconds before unobtrusively swinging in behind.

Delaney held the phone up to his ear after speed dialing. "Cathy? Kevin. We picked him up . . . Uh-huh . . . Fort Kent . . . Hang on a sec."

He looked out the windshield for a moment as the van ahead turned onto Pleasant Street and, shortly thereafter, crossed the connector bridge onto Route 161.

He returned the phone to his ear. "Yeah—161, to Caribou, I'd guess. Then, who knows?" He followed that by giving her a description of the van, its Quebec registration, and the driver, adding, "Call Customs and get the name this guy used at the border. Probably bogus, but it can't hurt." He wrapped up by arranging for a spot just north of Caribou where a substitute tail could replace them behind the van.

"Who was that?" Joseph asked, comfortably situated among the thin traffic flow trailing the van.

"Cathy Lawless," Delaney told him. He'd always enjoyed that name for a cop. "My Number Two."

Joseph nodded, having heard of her. "And you really think this guy will lead you to something?"

Delaney absentmindedly clipped his cell phone back onto his belt, his eyes straight ahead. "What I *know*," he said, "is that whoever whacked Matt Mroz wasn't screwing around. What I *think* is that we may all be in a knife fight to beat the band, if more like-minded people join in."

He sighed, paused to rub his cheeks with both hands, and added, "And given the stakes, that's what I'd be betting."

CHAPTER FIVE

Joe Gunther pulled into his driveway off of Green Street and
killed the engine. He sat there for a minute, letting the gentle summer breeze carry the scent of newly cut grass into the car's interior.

He loved this house. He'd only lived here a couple of years,
renting, in fact, and recognized that calling it a house at all was a
stretch, since it was technically a carriage house attached to the
rear of a monstrous Victorian pile. But within that latter aspect lay
the charm he so enjoyed—it was small, tucked away, quiet, and
faced only a small lawn and some trees, smack in the middle of
Brattleboro.

Given the world he was regularly exposed to, it truly qualified as
a retreat.

He got out quietly, careful not to slam his door, even though the
town around him was already bustling, it being late morning by now.
But he'd been up for twenty-eight hours and his brain was still functioning in middle-of-the-night mode.

Not that he could take a break quite yet. He'd only dropped by to shower and change clothes before going to the office to meet with his team and discuss the case. Cop killings with two suspects still on the loose were not given the standard treatment—nor did they permit much sleep.

He crossed the driveway, unlocked his front door, and let himself in, smiling as he read a Post-it note stuck to the hallway mirror at eye level.

"Beware—naked woman in big bed."

His priorities shifted, ever so slightly.

He slipped his shoes off, noticing for the first time Lyn's own under the hall table, splashed some water on his face at the kitchen sink around the corner, and—drying off with a hand towel as he went—climbed the narrow, low-ceilinged staircase to the tiny bedroom that had been tucked under the hand-hewn roof rafters above.

The note told no lies. The bed was big—or seemed that way in this setting—and its current occupant was certainly naked. In the gloom provided by an almost completely effective blackout curtain, Joe saw the slim, athletic shape of a woman stretched out diagonally across the mattress, her breasts and stomach exposed by a sheet half tossed aside in midslumber.

This was Lyn Silva, whom he'd met a couple of years ago on a case in Gloucester, Massachusetts, and who'd since moved to Brattleboro, opened up a bar, and become his lover, his sounding board, and his best friend, all in one.

He sat gingerly on the edge of the bed and admired her for a few moments. Her long hair was spread across both the pillow and half her face, reminding him of paintings he'd seen in museums. She looked serene and beautiful and almost unreal, at odds with what

Joe knew of her biography, which was typically full of life's mishaps and surprises.

In those ways, Lyn was simply a variation of Joe himself—he, a lifelong cop and childless widower; she, a single, working mother of an adult daughter. She was neither extraordinary nor exotic, which was perhaps what made her a little of both in his eyes, he who had grown tired of extremes.

"Hey," she said in a near whisper.

He smiled in surprise, not having noticed that she was studying him as well.

He leaned forward and kissed her, his nostrils filling with her warmth.

He pulled back just enough so that he could speak. "How long have you been asleep?"

She smiled. "Trick question. What time is it?"

"Eleven-thirty."

"About seven hours. Not bad. I wanted to see you when you got back, so I came here instead of my place."

He kissed her again. "I'm glad you did."

She reached up and touched his unshaven cheek. "Was it bad?"

"Yes—a cop was killed. We don't know who did it yet."

"Oh, Joe. I'm so sorry."

"So am I."

She kissed him gently before asking, "Did you get any rest at all?"

"Not yet, and I've got to keep going. I just dropped by to freshen up and change my clothes." He looked at her and added, "I am really glad you're here." He brushed one of her breasts with his fingertips—the hint of a caress.

She smiled up at him and swept the rest of the sheet clear of her body. "Since you've got to take your clothes off anyhow, would you like to stretch out for a couple of minutes?"

He laughed. "I would, in fact."

The southeast office of the Vermont Bureau of Investigation was located on the second floor of Brattleboro's municipal building, one flight above the town's police department, where Joe Gunther and two of his three-person team had worked before VBI's creation. Those were Sammie Martens and Willy Kunkle, who, despite distinctly different temperaments and styles—and a history of having growled at each other for years back in the PD days—had since become among the unlikeliest of couples. The unit's third member was Lester Spinney, a gangly ex-state trooper who commuted every day from Springfield, Vermont, where he lived with his wife and kids on Summer Street, an address that generally described his disposition. To say that Spinney and Kunkle were a study in contrasts was to put it lightly, meaning that every once in a while, Gunther had the urge to shelter the former from the latter's excesses, although Spinney had never requested it. Spinney was the least flamboyant of them, but the best grounded and most thoughtful—qualities Joe valued highly, even if they were only rarely heeded by the other two.

Over the years, Joe had grown to know these people like family, trust them with his life, and believe absolutely in their abilities— which was a good thing in Willy's case, as he owed his continuous employment to Joe's many interventions on his behalf.

All three of them were in their small, cramped office when Joe walked in—about twenty minutes later than he'd intended.

"Hey, boss," Sammie said from her desk, her expression showing concern. "How're you doing?"

Willy was not so conciliatory. "He's better off than the other guy. They got a line on the shooter yet?"

Lester merely smiled sympathetically and nodded his greeting, to which Joe responded in kind.

"I'm fine," Joe said, putting the small backpack he used as a brief-case on top of his desk. "Thanks for asking." He sat beside the pack, dangling one leg, and looked at Willy. "And they're working on that."

Willy was all but barricaded behind his desk, which he'd placed diagonally across one corner of the office, so he could face out as if ready to take fire.

"I bet," he snorted. "This is about drugs, right? The paper just said nobody was talking, even off the record—that'll probably change in the next five minutes."

Joe tilted his head equivocally. "Maybe. Most likely. What we know so far is that a Massachusetts Toyota Solara was pulled over by this deputy late last night—for what reason is anyone's guess. The deputy—Brian Sleuter—was a hotshot, with a good arrest record, including a lot of drug busts.

"The car contained two men: James Marano, the driver, and his passenger, Luis Grega. We got an almost instant hit when we issued a BOL on the car's registration, that it had entered the U.S. from Canada at the Highgate checkpoint about ninety minutes before it was stopped by Sleuter."

"Drugs," Willy said again. "I knew it."

Sammie gave him an exasperated look from across the room.

"What about the U.S. side of the equation?" Lester asked quietly. "The Massachusetts address attached to the registration?"

Joe nodded. "Dorchester Avenue, south Boston."

"Drugs," Willy repeated in a bored voice, rolling his eyes.

"Shut *up*," Sammie told him.

"Marano's the resident of record," Joe continued, knowing better than to pay attention. "We've asked the local cops to just keep an eye on it for the time being, not to bust anyone, and to identify everybody's comings and goings, if they can."

"Good luck with that," Willy commented. "Those jerk-offs can't identify their own children, unless somebody pays them to do it—if you get my drift."

Lester laughed. "Never a problem getting your drift, Willy."

"Were there any other hits from that Be-On-the-Lookout?" Sam asked.

"Not so far," Joe answered. "The Toyota pretty much vanished, as far as we can tell. We did a complete records check on both men. They have extensive criminal histories." He nodded to Willy, adding, "Which are mostly centered around drugs."

"Which one's the shooter?" Willy asked, finally contributing to the conversation.

"Sleuter had his cruiser camera on," Joe told them. "On tape, you can see Grega, the passenger, slip out the side door and work his way back between the vehicles. You lose sight of him there, but then you hear the shot and see him running back to his car, his and Marano's paperwork in hand. We interviewed some of Sleuter's fellow officers to learn his habits during a traffic stop, and supposedly he always attached the paperwork to a clip he'd mounted especially to his steering wheel. It would've been no challenge for Grega to see what he needed right after shooting him in the head."

"I'm guessing he never got a ticket started?" Lester asked.

"Apparently not. Again, on tape, this whole thing takes a few minutes only, from start to finish. Sleuter had both men's twenty-sevens, but he never got the chance to even finish Marano's record check, much less start on Grega's. If it hadn't been for Sleuter's body mike, and that Customs got the names of both occupants at the border, we wouldn't have Grega's ID at all."

"Can we milk the border crossing angle somehow?" Willy asked suddenly, as if out of the blue.

And therein lay just one example of why Joe worked so hard to keep Willy on his staff. He smiled broadly. "God, I hate to say this, but great minds think alike. I contacted ICE in Boston, and have an appointment this afternoon. The border involvement is custom-made for us to hook up with them and get the biggest bang for the buck, at least in terms of law enforcement muscle."

"Meaning you like the Feds?" Willy asked, as if arguing against himself.

"Plus," Joe added, "They've been decent in the past, creating task forces instead of running over us. And I know the SAC personally. I think that—and the fact that this is a cop killing—will help grease the skids."

Sam glanced at her watch. "When's your meeting with them?"

"Three hours, and I need a driver if I want to be coherent when I get there. You available?"

He knew she was. He could tell it from the way she'd asked the question. There was no "Number Two" agent in this office—not officially. But all of them acknowledged the almost father/daughter connection between Sam and the boss. It made sense to everyone there that if Gunther had anyone accompany him on this trip, that person would be Sam.

"You're not letting the Burlington office handle this alone, are you?" Willy asked, not miffed at being passed over, but not wanting to be left out altogether.

"Not a chance," Joe reassured him. "This is the first cop killing we've had in years where we didn't have the bad guy in custody right off. By this afternoon, everyone and his uncle's going to be crawling over this, from the press to the politicians to every cop in the state. Mike Bradley was with me this morning. I want you two to coordinate with him—even drive up there in a couple of days to help them create a command center, if necessary, and to keep ahead of the stampede. We want to see if either one of these bad guys had any local connections. It's anyone's guess right now if they were just driving through the state, or had a specific reason for being here. Also, Willy, I want you especially to take a close look at Brian Sleuter—more than just a once-over—just to find out what kind of cop he was. Right now, we're going with the random-traffic-stop-gone-bad scenario, but there's always a chance that somebody knew somebody else here, and that all this is a disguised hit."

Joe stood up, then paused to add, "But keep that part under your hat. I don't want any pals of his to start circulating that we think he deserved what he got. We'll have enough sensitivities floating around without that."

Willy gave him a mocking salute. "Yes, oh leader."

Sammie rose also to join Joe as he headed for the door, glancing at her partner as she passed his desk, "You are such a tool," she told him.

Willy laughed. "Love you, too, darlin'. Should I stay up tonight?"

"Yeah." She laughed back at him. "That way, you'll miss me even more."

CHAPTER SIX

ICE stood for Immigration and Customs Enforcement, which made sense, since it was comprised of the old Immigration and Naturalization Service and part of what used to be U.S. Customs. But few people missed that the end result was possibly the most self-enhancing acronym in law enforcement since SWAT. There was at least a cynical suspicion—among doubters of big government in general, of course—that INS and Customs had been lumped together during the great Homeland Security shuffle solely so that a few cops could wear hats and jackets straight out of some fictional, way-too-cool, Saturday morning cartoon.

The Boston ICE office was run by a Special Agent in Charge, or SAC, none of which had much meaning to anyone outside the federal system. But to its denizens, such distinctions were weighty matters and played a direct role in pay grade, seniority, and the likelihood of advancement. All cops were obsessively cognizant of their benefits packages, union provisions, wage variances, shift schedules, and retirement dates, among other bureaucratic minutiae. But Feds in particular, Joe had discovered, put the average focus on all this to shame. They tended to rigorously track not only their own statistics but those of their coworkers, with the keenness of horse bettors studying the dailies.

ICE was headquartered in two downtown Boston buildings—the Tip O'Neill, on Causeway, and—much to the irritation of those who regularly traveled between them—the neighboring JFK Building. Sammie Martens, having chauffeured Joe here once before, parked in the basement of O'Neill.

Joe was a frequent visitor; Vermont being thinly populated and a border state made it a target for those smugglers moving people or product into the U.S. covertly. And, more recently, with the advent of the VBI and its statewide major crimes charter, it had actually become practical for Gunther and a few others to become deputized to ICE.

During this process, Joe had met and become friends with the improbably named Rufus Cole Botzow, the SAC who ran the Boston office.

It was Botzow they were here to meet.

The building was urban blandness personified—a sensation only heightened after Sam and Joe left the elevator and were ushered across the threshold of the ICE office, and herded through a maze of chin-level cubicles, most occupied by people either studying computer screens or talking quietly on the phone. Lacking was any sense of a high profile, hard-hitting bunch of action junkies. The men and a few women they passed appeared to be merely casually attired office workers, looking as if their only concern was finishing the day without stapling their thumbs or getting caught in traffic on the way home.

To Sam, who'd never made it upstairs on her first visit, the overall effect was a little disconcerting. Joe, on the other hand, was quite comfortable with it all, anticipating the turns as they wended their way toward the corner office.

Rufus Cole Botzow was a large bald man with remarkably bushy eyebrows, who came marching out of his lair with a broad smile and an extended hand as soon as he caught sight of them through his extensive inner glass wall.

He brought them both into an office personalized by service plaques, a row of hanging law enforcement baseball caps, photographs of grinning, armed people in military fatigues, and a display of children's art, mostly magnet-mounted to the front of several filing cabinets. It was the cave of a man who'd experienced a broad sampling of life's offerings, some of them a little dicey.

Botzow waved them to a pair of comfortable seats and settled himself behind a paper-strewn desk, also decorated with memorabilia.

"Damn, Joe, it's been a while. I can't even remember when I last saw you. A year?"

"Almost." Joe smiled back at him. "You came up to hunt deer in New Hampshire and took a detour to visit."

Botzow laughed. "My God, you're right. No wonder I spaced that out. Didn't see a goddamn thing on that hunt. I thought about shooting a parked car, just to say I hit something."

Gunther gestured at the walls surrounding them. "Would've been a little hard to explain, mounted here."

Their host shook his head. "I don't know. I've got so much crap already, a car on the wall might not even be noticed. Why'd you drop by, Joe? All I know is that it's got something to do with that deputy's death you e-mailed me about."

"The shooter's driver lives at this address." Joe placed on the desk a printout of what they'd gathered so far on both Marano and Grega. "We think Grega pulled the trigger."

Botzow looked sympathetic. "Jesus—tough break. Not like that happens much in Vermont, right?"

"Not much," Joe admitted. "We had a cop killed in a hit-and-run a few years back, but the guy was caught right off. It turns the whole state inside out."

Botzow was nodding. "Right. Still, it's a homicide."

Joe held up his hand. "I know, I know, and ICE doesn't do that. We understand that. There is a border involvement, though. This car was fresh from entering at the Highgate checkpoint."

Botzow read the two printouts, speaking as he did so. "That's interesting. They stop them there for any reason?"

"No. They passed right through."

The SAC lowered the paperwork and studied him, his next question floating unasked between them.

Joe pointed at the printouts. "Keep going. Eighty percent of their involvements are drug-related. I'm betting you have at least one of them in your databases."

But Botzow replaced the sheets flat on his desk, smiling. "Bullshit—you already *know* that much. You're hoping we have an open case that'll actually mention one of them."

Joe returned the smile and shrugged. "That would heighten your interest, wouldn't it?"

"And maybe make it official?" He shrugged. "Could be. Hang on."

He rose from his chair, circled the desk, and left the office. Sam turned to her boss and half whispered, "What d'you think?"

"He hasn't thrown us out yet."

When their host returned a quarter of an hour later, he merely leaned against his own doorjamb, his hands empty, and asked, "What d'you want from us, assuming we want to play?"

Joe and Sam exchanged glances.

"To be part of the team that knocks on the door of this Dot Ave address." Joe patted the printout resting on Botzow's desk. "I am still deputized with you folks," he mentioned for good measure.

The SAC pursed his lips thoughtfully. "I think we can improve on that, especially since we don't know where this might lead—how about forming a task force?"

Joe raised his eyebrows. "What exactly did you find out?"

"Luis Grega is suspected of killing at least one dealer in Canada, and he's mentioned in a couple of our ongoing smuggling cases. Best of all, he's now in this country illegally. Let's just say for the moment that we're very interested in meeting him—and the Canadians are flat-out eager. But we haven't had an angle on his whereabouts until now."

"Cool," Sam murmured.

Botzow laughed. "Yeah. I agree."

He bowed slightly at the door, gesturing them to precede him out. "Let's meet our guys who kick in doors for a living."

Later that night, Joe and Sammie, clad in borrowed ballistic vests and stuffed into the rear of an overcrowded, anonymous delivery van, sat and waited for instructions, reduced for the most part to glorified onlookers.

It had been an educational few hours. From the SAC, they were introduced to the DSAC, his deputy, and then taken to meet the group supervisor, or "group supe," overseeing the Drugs-and-Gangs squad, who in turn brought them before the special agent running the actual case in which Luis Grega was a source of interest.

This last person was named Lenny Chapman. A tan, athletic man in his mid-thirties, Chapman had worked for eight years with a midwestern municipal police department, which made him kindly disposed to the likes of Joe and Sam. During the briefing that followed and the subsequent strategy session with the ICE entry team—who would do the actual forced entry so popular on TV—Chapman made a point of deferring to the two Vermonters, asking for their opinion and input, and making sure they felt as much a part of the team as everyone else.

It was quite a team. Each participant seemed relaxed while at the same time exhibiting a real keenness to get going. Sitting among them, Joe was reminded of a pack of bloodhounds, penned up for too long in the kennel.

Now that they were finally on stakeout, though, the mood was different still. From bloodhounds, most of them had become something less definable—predatory, but not as suggestive of raw impulsive energy. There was a watchful, almost patient tension in the van that Joe could see most clearly in Lenny Chapman, who'd positioned himself closest to the rear door and sat there, half crouched, a radio to his ear, waiting for the entry team's surveillance crew to give them the go-ahead. Joe watched the young man's profile, barely visible in the half light leaking in through the tinted windows, and studied the way his jaw slowly and methodically worked the piece of gum he'd slipped into his mouth just before heading out.

This, Joe imagined, was a man who made a point of keeping his emotions under control.

He glanced at Sam and saw a similar eagerness in her body language—the proverbial spring under restraint. She and the Lenny Chapmans of the profession thirsted for events like the one they were now facing. And Joe had to concede that he'd once shared their enthusiasm—a long time ago.

He shifted his gaze out the window beside him. This section of Dorchester Avenue was a tired, depleted, run-down place, populated with a mixture of peeling, clapboarded duplexes and larger, stained brick apartment buildings whose very blandness suggested illicitness.

He didn't doubt that his sheer exhaustion was exerting an influence on his mood—he'd only had two naps in two days, one on the drive down and the second, shorter still, just before this, but nevertheless, his notion of joy was no longer being poised for action in a blighted urban landscape.

He wondered if his priorities hadn't evolved—that he'd segued from the pure pleasure of chasing people down and locking them up, to something harder to define—perhaps a growing interest in pondering their motivations. Right now, for example, watching the street under the sterile glow of the overhead lighting, he remained focused on bringing in—or down—a cop killer. But he was equally mindful of what might have prompted Luis Grega to turn a traffic stop and, at worst, another dance with the judicial system into a cold-blooded homicide.

Joe was conscious of an evolving bafflement on his part, not unlike that of a trained but wearying combatant, who was fighting an urge to stand up in midbattle simply to ask what the hell was going on.

These were not ruminations he shared. Ever.

Lenny Chapman turned toward the small, tightly packed group and raised his radio slightly, as if it had become a pennant to follow.

"We're set. Surveillance has confirmed both targets. The entry team is positioning. It's rock-and-roll time, ladies and gentlemen."

CHAPTER SEVEN

There was no more meditating on Joe Gunther's part when Lenny Chapman gave them the signal to move out. Old soldier that he was, he hit the rear exit of the van like a paratrooper hurtling through the side dive door of a plane, as adrenalized as his younger companions.

They ran across Dorchester Avenue, shadows on a gloomy street, startling a couple of passersby, barely catching the attention of another, and took the entryway stairs of a dilapidated apartment building, two at a time.

Chapman led them all the way, speaking rapidly into his radio, coordinating with the black-clad, armored entry team already ahead, who, by now, had broken down the door of James Marano's apartment and charged inside.

However, Joe, Sammie, and the rest of Chapman's team, assigned to take over from the entry guys and effect the arrests, never made it to the third, top floor. Midway there, Chapman held up his hand

and stopped them dead in their tracks, listening incredulously to his radio.

"Shit," he said, turning toward them, "they've flown. They had a hole in the wall to the next apartment, covered by a dresser."

That was all Joe needed to hear. He turned on his heel and started pounding back downstairs, Sam instinctively in hot pursuit.

"What's up?" she asked, breathing hard.

"Simple," he answered, hoping not to break his neck on the dimly lighted stairs. "They planned this out. They live on the top floor. That means a roof escape. The ICE guys're already behind them. We should try to cut them off."

Either satisfied with this, or still working out what he meant, Sam didn't respond. But Joe could still hear her boots banging on the steps close behind him, joined, he noticed, by others. It seemed he wasn't alone in his thinking.

Bursting out onto the street, Joe immediately led the way across before swinging around and studying the building they'd just left.

Panting by now, he pointed to both sides, just as Chapman and a couple of others also appeared on the stoop. "Two alleyways," Joe told her. "You take the right; I'll take the left. Check for anything like a fire escape or maybe a jury-rigged bridge or a zip line, running to the next-door building."

As he spoke, he was already moving left, shouting over his shoulder. Across the street, Chapman saw what they were doing and got on his radio to get an update from upstairs.

Joe ran back across Dorchester, aiming for his alleyway, and was intercepted at its mouth by one of Chapman's men.

"You have a flashlight?" he asked him.

The man dutifully pulled a small halogen torch from a holder on his belt.

Joe pointed upward. "See if there's anything connecting the two buildings."

The special agent looked at him. "We got the fire escape covered. It's in the back anyhow."

Joe simply took the light from his hand. "They would've known that. If they knew enough to knock out a wall, they didn't stop there."

He played the beam between the buildings. Sure enough, as bright as a shaft of sunshine, the underside of a broad, pale, yellow pine plank was reflected back at them, running from the roof of Marano's building through a window of its taller neighbor.

"That's it," Joe said, returning the light and running for that neighbor's front door. "Third floor—one of the apartments at the end." He paused only long enough to call out for Sam.

The lobby door was half open, on a busted hinge, eliminating the need for a key or someone to buzz them in. Joe glanced around quickly, saw the staircase leading up, and headed for it, hearing multiple footsteps pounding along in his wake.

As he took the stairs two at a time, pulling himself along by the banister, he used his other hand to pull out his gun. From being last man in line earlier, he was now at risk of coming face-to-face with a certified cop killer.

But his exposure was short-lived. Against Sam's and Lenny's youth and motivation, he didn't have a chance of leading any foot pursuit for long. By the time he'd reached the second-story landing, all three of them were looking like a Ben-Hur chariot race, metaphorically wheel-to-wheel. Joe was bringing up the rear only about ten steps behind.

Chapman, at least, had the courtesy to say in passing—even if he wasn't breathing hard—"Nice move, Joe. Quick thinking."

Quick, perhaps, but not perfectly timed. Above them—appearing and vanishing so fast it seemed more like an apparition than an actual sighting—the outline of a man peered down at them, followed by the slamming of a door.

The three cops saw it at the same time, since they were all looking up the stairwell for something to happen. Chapman was the one to yell out, "*Federal agents. Do not move,*" albeit to no avail.

At the third-floor landing, they barely paused at the door to the hallway beyond. Chapman kicked it open, huddled just inside its protective angle, and then, pointing his gun where he looked, he quickly risked a glance in both directions.

A shot almost immediately reverberated down the hallway. No bullet hit nearby.

"You okay?" Sam asked.

"Yeah," Chapman answered. "Looked like Grega, shooting from an apartment at the opposite end of the corridor from where they crossed on the plank. They must have multiple hideouts, all strung in a line. He's probably the one we saw."

"Any sign of your entry team?" Joe asked hopefully.

Chapman gave a very quick update on his radio, heard someone say, "We're on the bridge now," and then turned to Joe. "We're running out of time," he said.

He then did as Joe might have once—clipped the radio to his belt, took his gun in both hands, quickly checked again outside, and, getting no explosive response, slid fast and low into the hallway. He began jogging toward the apartment where he'd last seen Grega—Sam and Joe in close backup.

Joe was not a happy man. Keen as he was to take Grega, the risks of running down a hallway full of closed doors—any one of which could open behind them—seemed ill advised at best. Sadly, however, that had suddenly been rendered moot. Now, it was all about backing up Lenny Chapman, and keeping everybody alive if possible.

At the apartment door in question, Chapman jumped to its far jamb, flattened against the wall, waited a second for Joe and Sam to position themselves opposite him, and then pounded on the door from the side.

He didn't get to say a word before two more shots splintered the door where his hand had been, the rounds thudding into the wall across the way.

Simultaneously, a door far down the hallway opened to reveal two members of the ICE entry team, at last arrived from their travels across midair. Joe was relieved to see Chapman motion to them to join their understrength trio.

As the entry team leader drew near, he cocked his head toward the bullet-punctured door. "Wild guess—you want us to kick that in?"

"You're good, Arnie," Chapman complimented him, fading back with the two Vermonters.

The team quickly positioned itself, destroyed the door, and charged into the apartment, shouting at the tops of their lungs, Chapman, Joe, and Sam hot on their heels.

The place was obviously specifically used for this purpose—a backup residence with minimal furnishings, a thick layer of dust, and a window leading out to the fire escape. After ensuring that the apartment was clear, everyone hit the escape ladder, half heading down, and the other half going for the roof. Joe joined the upwardly bound, betting on a runner's primordial instinct to head for the high ground.

His choice proved correct moments later. Their quarry, in a mirror image of his brief appearance at the top of the stairs earlier, once more stuck his head over the edge of the roof and looked down at them. Only this time, he was armed.

"*Gun*," shouted one of the people at the front of the line.

But there was nothing anyone could do with such short warning and in such tight confines. The shot cracked out, accompanied by a blinding flash from the gun's discharge, and Joe heard one of the leaders grunt and drop back onto the next person in line.

Without hesitation, several answering shots came from the group, and there was an almost mad rush to get by the wounded man, and the one tending to him, in order to reach the roof. Joe and Sam were now third and fourth in line.

What they saw as they cleared the roofline was wondrous and hellish, both. Under a star-speckled dome of night sky, its bottom circumference ringed by a muted blaze of surrounding city lights, a single man stood in the middle of the roof, his gun blazing in random directions as he twisted and turned, slapped by the bullets of the ICE agents hitting him.

Crouching beside the top of the ladder, Joe watched as the silhouetted figure finally stopped its mad dance and dropped into a heap like a puppet with its strings cut.

"My God," he heard Sam say behind him.

Joe rose and slowly approached the fallen man with the others, all of them still with their guns out and ready.

But there was no movement. Caressed by the nervous hoverings of multiple flashlight beams, the body lay covered with blood, contorted as if stung by a thousand volts of electricity.

"That one of them?" someone asked.

Joe considered the question, suddenly realizing its significance. In this neighborhood, the dead man might have been anyone with a gun and a criminal record. Not to mention that, aside from a couple of indistinct half sightings, there'd been no solid identification of either Marano or Grega ever since the surveillance team had given the go-ahead.

Lenny Chapman appeared beside Joe, he having opted to join the team going down the fire escape. He had a photograph in his hand.

"Let's see his whole face," he requested.

One of the men in black reached out and twisted the body's head around while another steadied a light on it. Chapman crouched and held the mug shot up.

"It's Marano," he announced after a brief pause.

"What about Grega?" Joe asked in the following quiet.

Chapman looked up at him and shook his head. "He was with this guy in the first apartment—we have confirmation of that. We also know that two men used the bridge over the alleyway. But I and the others saw someone jumping from the fire escape and taking off below. I'm only guessing that was Grega."

He stood up, put the mug shot back into his pocket, and stared down at James Marano, adding, "Regardless, it looks like Grega beat feet. Your cop killer's still on the street."

Joe considered that. "Maybe," he agreed. "But we still have the apartment to go through. Could be we'll find something there."

Chapman turned slightly and gazed out over the vast cityscape all around them, glimmering like a distant grasslands fire. Far off, they could hear sirens.

"Good luck with that one," he said.

CHAPTER EIGHT

Kevin Delaney exited his car, waited for the traffic to clear, and crossed the street, carrying a cardboard tray full of coffee cups. He'd caught a few hours of sleep at home after Cathy Lawless took over the tail he'd established last night at the Fort Kent border crossing.

But now it was morning, his curiosity had gotten the better of him, and despite the paperwork waiting at the office and the exhaustion still scratching the back of his eyeballs, he was in the border town of Calais, almost two hundred miles from Fort Kent. That's where Cathy and the source of their interest had settled down for the time being—in a small shopping mall consisting of several stores and two modest office buildings.

He'd heard back on his inquiry to Customs about the van driver's name—Eugene Didry. This he'd passed along to Cathy, even though it had resulted in no hits anywhere, implying that it had been stuck onto a well-forged passport.

Delaney opened the back door of a delivery van and stepped inside. The air was stale, warm, and unpleasant.

There were two people—a man and a woman—sitting in chairs mounted to the floor, facing a row of equipment attached to the wall, along with a long tinted window looking onto one of the office buildings across the parking lot.

The woman's face lit up at the sight of the tray. "My savior," she said, reaching for one of the cups as Delaney reluctantly shut the door behind him.

"Hey, Dave," he addressed the man, "want some coffee?"

Dave Beaubien, Cathy Lawless's MDEA partner, reached out, took a cup, and nodded once. "Thanks."

Delaney smiled to himself. As far as he could tell, that constituted a full sentence for Dave—the definition of a man of few words. Of course, being partnered to Cathy almost guaranteed not getting a word in edgewise, so perhaps it was all to the good.

"Anything?" Delaney asked Lawless.

She finished taking a long swig of her coffee before answering. "Christ, that hits the spot. Nope. Not a thing. Didry—or whatever his name is—has been inside for about ninety minutes now." She interrupted herself long enough to point at the parking lot. "That's his vehicle over there. Of course, that doesn't mean he didn't sneak out the back and take off. Wouldn't be the first time."

Her boss raised his eyebrows. "You suspect that?"

She took another swallow before answering. "I don't know. There're just the two of us here."

Delaney nodded at that and changed subjects slightly. "Makes you wonder why he entered at Fort Kent, just to drive all this way to another border town within U.S. lines."

"Doesn't make me wonder," Cathy said brightly. "He's been meeting people along the way."

Delaney's eyes widened slightly. "Do tell," he prompted her.

She turned to her partner. "Dave—you got that list?"

Beaubien wordlessly handed her a spiral notepad. She, in turn, passed it to Delaney, explaining, "Four meets, each at the towns listed, each town being a past entry port for drugs that we know about. The people listed are either guys we saw come out and talk to this character, or they live in the houses he entered. Either way, every one of them has a history with us."

Delaney studied the list, recognizing everyone on it. These were not nickel-and-dime players. More to the point, they'd all been linked, circumstantially and not, to Matt Mroz's now leaderless network.

"You get a good picture of Didry?" he finally asked. "We'll need to send a copy to the Canadians—see if anyone there can give us the guy's real name."

Instead of answering, Dave merely patted the long-lens camera on the counter beside him.

"Yeah," Cathy added, "except that Didry has a beard as big as it is phony. I'd be amazed if his own mother could pick him out of a lineup."

Delaney gazed thoughtfully out the window and mused, half to himself, "What the hell is going on in there?"

Alan Budney was also at a window, peering out discreetly—in an vacated, second-floor office of the same run-down mall in Calais where the MDEA team was running surveillance from the parking lot.

"That them?" Budney asked. "The white van with the tinted windows?"

Eugene Didry, whose real name was Georges Tatien, rose from his chair and crossed the room nonchalantly.

"*Oui*—that is them," he said in a thick Gallic accent.

"Who are they? DEA?"

Tatien shook his head. "*Non*. I do not think so. DEA is almost invisible in your state. That is MDEA, I think. Very good, but too thin with the personnel."

Tatien eyed his American counterpart from up close. He'd been waiting for Budney for well over an hour, sitting patiently in his chair. Timing was routinely approximate in this line of work, so he hadn't expected a precise arrival. But he also hadn't expected the kind of person now before him. Drug dealers weren't all the losers and idiots that cops liked to portray, nor were they the smooth, well-tailored sophisticates of the movies. But they did tend to fit an overall style—a little reckless, a little careless, often addicted to the product they peddled.

Budney seemed the exception. When he'd entered the room, without apology, he'd asked, "You Didry?" After Tatien had admitted as much, Budney had followed with, "I'm assuming you were followed; did you make the same assumption?"

It had been a deceptively elegant opener, especially to a traditional philosophe like Tatien, who shared the French fondness for oblique and indirect allusions. With one seemingly simple inquiry, Budney had questioned Tatien's intelligence, ability, poise, and observational abilities—not to mention his trustworthiness. It had been economical and intuitive, reflective of a possibly intriguing brain. A satisfying beginning.

Unless, of course, Budney had intended none of it.

Georges Tatien, born rich, well educated, but too much of a risk-taker to follow society's narrow rules, had opted for a life of courting danger in exchange for large amounts of easy, untraceable money. It gave him the thrills of the demimonde that so horrified and tantalized his peers, along with a lot of extra cash with which he did as he pleased.

There had been frightening moments. Drug dealers were often unstable, unpredictable, and unreliable—quick to blur the distinction between loyalty and self service, and easily coerced by the police into betraying their colleagues. But therein lay a large part of the attraction for Tatien—he could flatter himself with having a psychological acuity that would keep him safe from the dealers and ahead of the police.

Thus, Alan Budney's unconventional icebreaker had come like a tonic at a time when Tatien had become bored by the likes of Matthew Mroz—an egocentric hedonist with little imagination.

Budney finally turned away from the window to face the Canadian. "I hear you're a careful man." He jerked his thumb outside. "How careful have you been with them?"

Tatien returned to his chair. He liked this setting—a near-empty room, with a thin coating of dust over two metal chairs and a cheap desk. It was theatrically appealing.

"I have discovered," he answered thoughtfully, "that if I give the police a shadow to chase, it is better than allowing them to make something by themselves. Roads taken that are wrong are so much harder to drive in reverse. Do I make sense to you?"

Budney smiled and sat in the other chair, completing Tatien's picture of how this scene should look. "You're telling me that Didry isn't your real name," he suggested.

Tatien laughed softly and touched his voluminous beard. "As fictional as my whiskers."

"You've been in this game for a while, haven't you?"

Tatien nodded. "I have."

"You worked with Matt Mroz."

"I did that, yes."

"You okay with his being out of the game?"

Tatien's smile broadened. "I like that—instead of 'dead.' Very good. Yes, I am okay."

"How about your people over here? What about them?"

Tatien shrugged. " 'My people.' That is maybe not so true."

"That they're your people or that they're okay that Roz is gone?"

"Yes to both: they are not mine, and they do not care."

Budney considered that. He liked this man, whatever he might be called. He seemed careful and smart, and he'd been quick to respond to Alan's invitation to meet. He was also highly regarded in the business, although not by the moniker Didry, necessarily. That had been one of the most interesting things Alan had discovered—that "the Canadian" was most widely known simply as that, and not by any particular name. When they'd spoken by cell phone just a couple of days earlier, and this man had said, "I am Eugene Didry," Alan had immediately suspected otherwise, and hadn't cared. The Canadian was reputed to be The Man when it came to pharmaceuticals, and that's exactly what Alan wanted to discuss with him.

"Do you have any idea what percentage of his trade Roz did with you?" Alan asked.

Tatien made an equivocal expression. "I knew he did many things."

"Twenty percent," Budney asserted. "The rest was divided among weed, coke, meth, heroin, ecstasy, and crack, more or less, depending on availability and market demand. And he imported it from all over, from New York to Canada to Aroostook County."

Tatien didn't respond, figuring there was some point to all this.

"Any idea what his losses were to theft, busts, bad product, and everything else?"

"You will tell me?" Tatien prompted with a smile.

Alan rose from his seat and began pacing the room. "A full thirty-two percent. Incredibly sloppy. Half the time, he had no clue who had or was doing what."

"You are well informed." Tatien had no doubt whatsoever by now that Budney had either had Matthew Mroz killed or had done it himself. The man's tone of voice betrayed his pride and contempt. But Tatien found such hostility curious—for all of Mroz's possible faults as a businessman, he still had been making an extremely good living in a literally cutthroat occupation. In some types of trade, profit margins of ten percent were seen as exemplary; in a bad year, Mroz had to have been quintupling his outlay.

Budney stopped in midstride and stared at his guest. "I *am* well informed. I researched every aspect of his operation, talked to the people who made it work. I knew it a hell of a lot better than he ever did. I also figured out what he was doing wrong, and I know how to make it into something he couldn't have touched."

Tatien scratched an earlobe meditatively. "I am listening with interest."

Budney leaned forward slightly for emphasis, his hands on his hips. "You should be, 'cause I'd like to make you a key player instead of just another supplier. I believe that with your sources and my new distribution network, we can make Roz look like a sidewalk peddler, even in a backwoods, mosquito-filled, prehistoric swamp like Maine."

Tatien laughed, not only at the allusion, but at the sense of enthusiasm he was catching from this young man. For the first time in a long while, Georges Tatien thought he might enjoy himself once more.

He spread his hands out to his sides, as if in surrender. "You have a captive audience."

CHAPTER NINE

Lenny Chapman was at once angry and motivated. Shooting people on rooftops in Boston was bad enough, the standard joke about all the paperwork being only the half of it. This particular ICE office was a political hotbed, and he hadn't been here long enough, or kissed enough asses, that he was guaranteed a pass for all the bad press he knew would be churned up from within the office and the media combined.

Which didn't include the tensions surrounding the obligatory post-shoot investigation.

It behooved him to make the Dot Ave killing of James Marano the start of an investigative cornucopia so rich as to reduce the whole incident to a minor detail.

Surrounded by a small team hard at work dismantling the contents of Marano's apartment, Chapman cast a glance at Joe Gunther and his female sidekick, wondering if they were going to prove a help or a hindrance with his ambitions. Right now, given that they had started the ball rolling toward this mess, he wasn't optimistic, even while he was paradoxically grateful to them for flushing Grega out of the bushes.

He had another problem—time was short. There was going to be a critique of the evening's outcome, with everyone spending most of the night at the office, being scrutinized by people in suits who hadn't even been at the scene. Chapman wanted at least a vague idea of what Marano and Grega had been up to before he was forced to stop dead in his tracks and cool his heels for this bureaucratic circus.

"How did you get Grega's name in the first place?"

Chapman blinked at the still unfamiliar voice. Gunther was looking right at him.

"What? I don't . . . He was just mentioned in passing, at least initially." Chapman scratched his head, realizing he'd been caught daydreaming. "Let's see," he began again, looking away from the Vermonter and gazing at his colleagues, who were tagging, labeling, and photographing almost everything in sight.

"His name came up a couple of months ago. A snitch of mine was going on and on about how the Hell's Angels were losing their grip in Canada, and how other players were starting to horn in on their territory. He mentioned how his pal, Luis Grega, was making serious money running product across the border as a result."

"He was a mule?"

Chapman nodded, thinking back. "At first. Later, the same guy told me he was violent, upwardly mobile, and ambitious to make a dent in the U.S. That moved him up in my ranking, because he'd been caught here illegally once already and tossed out. If he was back and turning nasty, I wanted to grab him—and now had double grounds to do so."

Gunther asked, "Did your snitch say who he was working for?"

"No. It was pretty vague—mostly generalities. I remember him saying, too, that another trend was the growth of drug use in the boonies, and how cities were losing their appeal as the only places to make money. He was very upbeat and used Grega as an example of all boats getting a lift from a good tide."

Chapman read the look in the older detective's eyes and added, "Needless to say, I'll get back in touch with him and squeeze him harder."

One of the search team approached them with a plastic evidence bag. "Found a cell," he said.

Chapman's expression lightened. "Great. The lab should make some hay out of that. You finding anything else?"

The man made an unhappy face. "Be nice if these people kept diaries. Mostly, it's clothes and trash and drugs. A lot of cash lying around. There are some scraps of paper with scribbling on them— we'll have to take a closer look at that. See if any of it takes us anywhere. Otherwise, not much. I'm guessing this wasn't the only place they called home."

The technician held the cell phone up to the light so that Chapman could better see it, adding, "By the way, this is a throwaway, so don't get your hopes too high. Some of these guys use 'em for a single call before ditching 'em."

"I know, Larry," Chapman said, distracted and irritable. "Just let me know what you find."

"If anything," Larry offered.

"Right." Chapman turned away, pretending to look out the apartment's open door. "If anything."

Larry faded away. Chapman gave Gunther a half smile and

murmured, "Don't like him much; not sure why. He never gives me good news."

"It's early yet," Joe suggested hopefully.

Chapman reflected on his looming bureaucratic headaches and muttered, "Not early enough."

He suddenly faced Gunther full on, his expression much lightened. "They've got things under control here. What d'you say about chasing that snitch down I told you about? He *might* have more to say about Grega. Where's your sidekick?"

Gunther crossed to the doorway leading into the apartment's one bedroom and called out to Sam, who was watching the search there. She appeared at the door. "Boss?"

"Field trip," he told her, and pointed at Chapman, who was already heading into the hallway.

The three of them went downstairs, to the sidewalk and the hum of the surrounding city.

"We're going to see a man about a man," Joe murmured to Sam as they followed Chapman to an unmarked agency car.

Gunther let Sam ride up front, mostly so he could stretch out in the back, wedge his shoulder into the corner, and shut his eyes, if only briefly. His days of being able to stay up around the clock with impunity were long gone.

Chapman drove around for about half an hour, occasionally working his phone in an attempt to locate his target, before finally parking opposite a bodega in a neighborhood Joe didn't bother trying to identify.

"We have to sit here for a couple of minutes," Chapman explained. "So he can see us. Then we'll pick him up around back."

"This guy reliable?" Sam asked.

"Has been so far. I've been using him for maybe three years without a hitch. We started out because I had him by the balls, but he finally worked a deal with the prosecutor. So for the past half year or so, he's been giving me stuff for free. Claims he owes me for helping him out—guess it's all in how you look at something."

Chapman put the car back into gear and drove around to the rear of the building, into a small, fetid courtyard lined by blank brick walls and a row of evil-smelling garbage cans. He hadn't come to a full stop before a shadow appeared at the window across from where Joe was sitting, and the door flew open to admit a wiry, dark-haired man with wide, unnaturally energetic eyes, with which he immediately scanned the car's interior in a panic.

"Who're these guys, Lenny? I don't know these guys."

Chapman twisted around and patted him on the knee. "Easy, Flaco. I told you about them. They're out-of-town cops, from Vermont. They only want some information. I didn't even give them your name."

Flaco had to absorb that for a few seconds, staring at the floor of the car before finally nodding. "I heard about Vermont," he said.

Joe wasn't sure what to do with that but recognized it as a peace offering.

"Nice place," he said. "You ought to come visit."

Flaco cast him a quizzical glance before refocusing on the floor, as if doing so would make him invisible. "Thanks."

"We can drive or we can sit here," Chapman stated. "Your choice."

Flaco worked himself into the corner, as Joe had done earlier, but slid way down in the seat, so he couldn't be seen from the street. "Drive."

Chapman backed out of the alley and headed on a random drive around the area.

"What d'ya want?" Flaco asked from his corner, addressing the back of Chapman's head.

"Tell us about Luis Grega," Chapman requested.

Flaco's mouth opened. "Grega? Who gives a fuck about Grega?"

"Gee," Chapman reacted, yielding a little to the night's pressures. "Maybe *we* do, Flaco. You mentioned him last time we talked, remember?"

Flaco kept looking from one of them to the other, reminding Joe of a dog trying to decide who might hit him first. "Lucky prick—that's about it."

"Making a lot of good money?" Joe prompted him.

Flaco eyeballed him carefully, weighing the cost of addressing anyone besides Chapman. "Yeah," he finally conceded, adding, "Till lately."

"Doing what?" Joe continued.

That loosened him up a little. "What you think? Running dope. That's what he does. Shit, that's what we all do."

"Who for?"

"Whoever, man. It's a complicated world. Lotta people work for a lotta other people."

Joe heard Sammie let out an irritated sigh. But he kept at it. "We heard he was taking stuff over the border from Canada. But you're right. Sounds pretty sophisticated. Probably more than you could know about. Which is fine, of course."

Flaco straightened with outrage, momentarily uncaring who might see him from outside. "I know plenty. I didn't say I didn't know. I said it was complicated. Maybe I was making it simple for you."

"Easy, Flaco," Chapman cautioned quietly. "I could stop driving right here and let you out."

The skinny man looked around suddenly and slumped back down in his seat, suitably abashed. "I'm not stupid. I done good work for you, haven't I?"

"Always," Chapman soothed him.

Joe made sure Flaco could see him shrug nonchalantly. "Sounded like you were unsure, is all," he told him, "since you didn't answer the question."

Their guest pursed his lips, struggling with some inner debate. "What I meant is that a bunch of things have just changed, so nobody's real sure what's goin' on."

"Okay," Joe conceded, to help him save face. "Guess I got that wrong. So, what *is* going on?"

"There was a killing. Got everybody running around covering their butts."

Joe nodded. "Yeah. We know about that. Kind of put Grega in the hot seat."

Flaco paused in his continual scanning of their three faces to stare directly at Joe. "Grega? What's he got to do with it?"

Joe hesitated, rethinking. "Wasn't he pretty close to that shooting?"

"Nah. He was down here, after his last run."

Sammie spoke up for the first time. "Where was this killing?"

"Shit, I don't know those places. They got all sorts of funny names. It was somewhere up there."

"Where?" she repeated, trying to sound conversational.

He looked at her as if she needed therapy. "Maine. Where else?"

There was dead silence in the car as all three cops struggled to contain their surprise.

"Right," Chapman volunteered at last, retrieving the relevant tidbit from a different part of his brain. "Rockland."

Flaco brightened. "Yeah—that was it. What kind of name is that, right?"

"But still," Gunther persisted, "Grega was directly affected. You said he'd been making good money till lately. The Maine shooting shut him down?"

"Shut everybody down in that network—that's what I been telling you."

"Meaning it's all connected," Sam almost blurted out, "Canada, Vermont, and now Maine."

He stared at her for a moment. "Whatever. I don't know about Vermont, like I said."

"Let's back up a little," Joe suggested. "When Grega was making money, before anybody got killed, what was the setup?"

"Standard deal," Flaco answered. "He'd get a call, drive up to Canada, get the stuff, and drive it back."

"What kind of stuff?"

"Whatever's hot: coke, weed, pills, meth—you name it."

"How?"

"How did he do it? Depends. The weed's bulky, so that takes more doin'. A lot of the other junk, you can body pack or hide in your car or somethin'. When Customs started getting wise to the body packing, we went to usin' girls. And when they tumbled to that, it was pregnant girls, since they didn't want to feel them up or x-ray them." He laughed. "You can shove a lot of shit up there—know what I mean?"

There was no response. Flaco paid no attention. "Course, that's only if you use the official crossing points. There's the whole border, too—lakes, rivers, Indian reservations. I heard of those model airplanes being used, too. You know, remote control? It's not that hard, once you get the hang of it. All that crap about the border being monitored twenty-four/seven and a hundred percent is bullshit. They got a few cops running a crapshoot."

Gunther kept pushing. "But it all came out of Canada, regardless of what it was."

Flaco shook his head pityingly. "I been talking to myself here."

"Who's the supplier, then?"

His expression changed to something possibly more self-protective. "I don't know."

"You implied you've done this, too," Joe said. "Who did you see up there?"

Flaco glanced at Lenny Chapman.

"Tell him," Chapman urged. "I'm not here to jam you up. You and I work together, remember?"

But it was a nonstarter. "I don't know," Flaco said. "Honest. I don't think anybody knows. I did it a couple of times. Luis did it a bunch. Every time, all we got was the product. We'd be told to show up wherever and pick it up, and it would be there. Never saw nobody. I always figured we were watched, but maybe that was just the creeps, you know?"

"You knew Grega did it," Sammie asked. "You got other names?"

Flaco was already waving that away with his hand. "Nah, nah. Luis brought me in 'cause he couldn't do it a couple of times. I was like a subcontractor. I only knew him, and he said we might get in trouble even then."

"Meaning he knew more than you did," Joe said.

"Well, *yeah.* Plus, Grega's a bad man, on the move. Takes no shit. Rumor is, he's killed people, but what do I know?" Flaco finished rhetorically.

Joe exchanged quick looks with his colleagues. Chapman took that as an opportunity to aim the car toward a darkened parking lot under an elevated railway, speaking as he drove. "Right, Flaco, what do you know?"

He stopped the car and twisted around in his seat. "You been a big help, man." He reached back and shook hands. "Take it easy."

Flaco was nonplussed. "That it?"

"That's it," Chapman told him.

The skinny man hesitantly got out of the backseat, holding the door open for a moment to ask, "What was this about?"

"Jimmy Marano was shot to death tonight," Chapman said. "And Grega's on the run. You might want to watch your back. Somebody's shaking things up, and since I found you in under an hour, you might want to figure out who's calling the shots now, or they might find you next."

Chapman started rolling away before Flaco had even fully closed the door.

Joe leaned over and finished shutting it. "I'm with him, Lenny," he admitted. "What exactly did we get out of that?"

Chapman laughed as he picked up speed and reached for his cell phone. "I hope we got a rabbit to run," he said. "And with any luck, we should be able to track him as he goes. In Flaco's case, it's less *what* he knows and more *who* that counts. This isn't the first time I've used him to lead me to someone else."

He began giving instructions on the phone, ordering a tail on Flaco, "as tight as a tick." He turned to his guests afterward. "Flaco's never happier than when he shares bad news with someone. We've just got to hope that someone's connected to the fire we just lit under him."

CHAPTER TEN

D on't be an asshole. Pass the gravy."

Alan Budney stopped talking to his sister, reached out, and grabbed the small pot of gravy that his mother had just brought. He handed it to his brother beside him, eyeing his father at the head of the table.

"'Bout time," the older man said in response.

Alan ignored him, returning to his conversation.

He was at home—or what had been home when he was younger—where his parents still lived, by the ocean's edge, in Blackmore Harbor, in the heart of Maine's Down East seacoast.

The Budney place wasn't what Realtors envisioned when they touted "waterfront property" on their lawn signs, although, as pure real estate, it was worth a small fortune. From the outside, it was a workingman's multistructure estate, practically built, practically maintained, littered with the detritus of generations of mechanically oriented, machine-loving lobstermen. Budney's great-grandfather had built the original shed, leaving more room for the equipment and the shop than for living quarters. Succeeding family members had improved upon the overall, adding, remodeling, and expanding its components to better suit the multiple missions of home, boat dock, and maintenance yard.

The results weren't aesthetic, but comfortable enough in a cluttered, dirty, ramshackle way. None of the Budney women had been driven to plant bushes or otherwise improve the compound's exterior, and none of the men had ever applied their ham-handed artistry to the home's interior.

To Alan, the setting had only been a prison—a place of rigid, unforgiving rules, demands, and expectations he'd chafed against all his life.

"Hey, hotshot," his father called out, taking hold of the pot of gravy and spilling some of its contents across his mashed potatoes. "What've you been doing since you got out?"

Alan ignored him and kept talking, although his sister's face had frozen, her eyes fixed on their father. She had been one of the kids to choose the opposite course from Alan, catering to and caving under the Old Man's reign.

Alpheus Budney, universally called Buddy, was a bluff bully of a man, the grandson of a lobsterman, who'd known no other profession and aspired to none. Through times lean and flush—the latter of which had been the norm for several years—he had pretty much run his life, his business, his five kids and wife, and much of the village of Blackmore Harbor the same way, making him consistent if not considerate.

Over time, all of the kids had left the house except Helen, the spinster in training with whom Alan had been talking. Only Alan had left the calling as well, graduating from high school to go on to college, instead of joining his father, buying his own boat, or marrying into another fishing clan, as had every one of his siblings.

Alan, in many ways the most similar to their father, had always been the rebel. He'd been the one who, even while helping on the boat from the day he could handle a knife, had dreamed of a life off the water. While everyone around him seemed content to assume whatever role fate had decreed—and to count themselves lucky in the process—Alan had silently raged against convention. He admitted the money was good, the lifestyle reminiscent of the old cowboys, and the overall aura of the profession attractively renegade. The lobstermen of Matinicus Isle had an outlaw reputation so cultured and burnished, in fact, that they were known as virtual gunfighters—certainly appealing to someone of Alan's disposition.

But the appearance of the hardy, independent, sometimes rebellious lobsterman was also couched in the reality of horrendous hours, brutal weather conditions, constant danger, financial insecurity, and endless governmental nagging about when and how you could do what you'd been doing for generations. There was a true working-class ruggedness attached to the image, which, despite the current good money and high times, repelled Alan Budney. He aspired to a life of plenty, but he didn't see the point of almost killing himself to get it.

Also, of course, there had been his father. Not just a local lobsterman, but a highliner—a fisherman of legendary prowess—and, worst of all for Alan, the "King of Blackmore Harbor." Virtually every lobster fleet had such a leader. Their status was unofficial, although they were often selectmen or fire department trustees or headed the Veterans of Foreign Wars chapter, as did Buddy. They ran the gamut from being benign, avuncular sorts—evoking a secular priest from some Bing Crosby movie—to fleshing out the traditions of the worst petty tyrant.

There was little question where Buddy fit in.

And so Alan had gone to college, to his mother's joy and his father's disgust, although he'd just barely received a degree in chemistry. This he'd all but stolen through an alcohol-induced haze, aided by an undemanding curriculum and the general slackness of his teachers, one of whom he'd actually threatened in order to get a crucial passing grade.

For Alan had a cold-bloodedness that his father could only aspire to. Buddy was brutal and uncaring and selfish and self-interested. But a mercurial passion flowed through it all, both igniting his moods and rendering them less than lethal. Alan was all business. As outwardly charming as his father could be—almost seductive when he chose—he had no pressure valve to let off steam. As Matt Mroz and his bodyguard had found out, Alan kept his rage fully intact up to the end.

"Look, you little shit," Buddy now addressed him, still eating. "You sit at this table, you talk when you're talked to."

Since he wasn't about to get any further with Helen, Alan turned to his father. "What's up, Dad?"

"I asked you what you were doin', now you're out of jail."

"Considering options."

The older man raised his eyebrows. "Can't decide between cleaning toilets and picking up garbage? Go for the garbage. At least it's out in the open."

He burst out laughing and stabbed another piece of chicken. Alan smiled, allowing the others—long used to the tensions between the two—to chuckle cautiously.

These had only worsened with Alan's release. Part of a king's credibility, as Buddy saw it, lay beyond his prowess on the water, and was reflected in his family. There were allowances, of course. Misfortune and error were forgiven, within reason—a stretch in the big house and a criminal record for drug dealing were harder stains to overlook. And Buddy was not of a generous nature.

"I'm sure Alan has better prospects than that," his mother proposed from her end, adding, "Don't you, dear?"

"A couple," he said agreeably.

It was Sunday dinner—a Budney family tradition. The one time every week when the entire clan gathered to share a meal. Back in the day, this was when Buddy laid out the week's marching orders. Nowadays, it had a less formal function, largely traditional, mostly as a way to assuage Buddy, whose hurt feelings, when anyone missed the event, were subtly made known within a day.

It amazed Alan that they all still practiced it, and thereby honored their father, even though most of them had homes of their own. He looked around the table, Buddy being distracted with dismembering his chicken leg, and pondered—not for the first time—how this family had taken the turn it had. They had been a part of Blackmore Harbor for so long that their fabric and the village's had finally completely blended. Buddy had yielded to the rhythm and habits of his community to where this weekly dinner was now as rooted—and, to Alan, meaningless as a family affair—as Saturday night Bingo at the firehouse.

Except that this time, he was here on a mission.

His father finally looked up. "Your parole officer called me today. Asked if I'd let you back on the boat. I asked him what was in it for me. That had him stumped."

Alan doubted that. He'd told the poor bastard what to expect. He wasn't surprised he'd called anyway—the guy was almost as big a jerk as the Old Man.

"I bet," he said.

"Yeah. Is he really called Dudley? What a stupid name."

"Stupid guy, too," his son said mildly.

Buddy put his fork and knife down for emphasis as he spoke. "*He's* stupid? You're one to talk. He's got a job, bucko—he's not some loser with a college degree and a record to cancel it out. You coulda stayed on the boat and done that much, and still be profit sharing the load with Pete and me, rap sheet or no. Instead, you got nuthin'."

"You tell him you'd take me on?" Alan asked, mostly to shut him up.

He got the response he'd anticipated. His father's eyes grew in his head. "Take you on? Are you out of your fucking mind?"

"Buddy," his wife cautioned.

He stared at her. "What do you mean, 'Buddy'? Did you hear what he said? The man's a drug dealer, Jane. Did you miss something these last few years? He's a goddamn felon. He took everything we gave him and blew it out his ass—made front page news so everyone could see that a Budney had finally hit the big time." Buddy spread his stubby hands wide apart, as if hanging quotes around a banner headline. " 'Pharmaceutical Salesman Caught Selling Drugs.' "

He stared incredulously at the entire table. "You all read that in the paper, didn't you?" he asked. "Or were your heads too far up your butts to realize our favorite little boy had turned into a crook and disgraced his family?"

Jane Budney stood up abruptly, pretending to be reaching for a plate of corn, and stopped his diatribe cold. "Buddy," she said, "we get your point. Give it a rest."

"Yeah," he muttered, stabbing at his chicken again. "Well, that's good."

Everyone knew better than to thank her. She wasn't much happier than Buddy with Alan, since, unlike her husband, she'd pinned a lot of hope on her son's ascension to college—and was heartsick by how he'd turned out. But she had her pride, and a sense of propriety, and this house was her realm—even if the rest of the Budney estate might be deemed Buddy's.

Buddy had learned the hard way to respect that, if little else.

The rest of the meal was spent in anesthetized conversational recovery. Alan gave up on Helen, who'd fallen to staring at her untouched plate, and the rest of them uttered only occasional one-liners about sports, the upcoming weather, or requests to pass along some item of food. Buddy stayed silent.

There'd been a time when Alan would have been enraged by such an attack, and certainly would have stormed from the house in midmeal, much to his father's satisfaction. But not now. This time, he actually smiled, joining the aimless chitchat, knowing that what his father had just complained about didn't approach what he'd done since leaving prison—and which would pale in comparison to what he had planned.

They cleared the table as a family once the meal was over—all but Buddy, who silently left for the den to watch TV. Afterward, leaving his mother and sister in the kitchen to wash up, Alan quietly approached his brother, Pete, and suggested they take a walk.

Pete looked at him suspiciously, always uneasy around the youngest brother who forever had the biggest plans. "A walk? Where?"

"Jeez, Pete." Alan laughed at him. "You afraid I'll set you up for a mugging?"

"Wouldn't be the first time" was the response.

But he accompanied Alan outside to the cluttered porch, and from there into the cooler night air and the equally junk-festooned yard.

"Where we going?" Pete asked.

Alan pointed ahead with his chin, indicating the dock at the bottom of the slight incline. Buddy's holdings covered a couple of acres and consisted of a medley of sheds, garages, a few boat slips, and a dock fully equipped with two oversized block-and-tackle rigs and the usual stacks of lobster traps so typical of the Maine coast. The patriarch's three-hundred-fifty-thousand-dollar lobster boat floated just barely within sight, illuminated by a single bulb at the top of a pole at dock's end.

Given the sheer magnitude of all this accumulation—not to mention two trucks, a flatbed, multiple boats and cars, and several ATVs and motorcycles—it was blatantly obvious that the place was owned by somebody with a serious positive cash flow. The King was not shy about advertising his success.

They stepped onto the dock, the soles of their shoes resounding quietly on the oil-stained wooden planking, and slowly proceeded toward the big boat—the one piece of equipment most responsible for the family's upkeep.

It was a beautiful night—clear and calm and warm. The black sky's sharp, pulsing stars grew in strength the farther they walked beyond the house's wash of electric light. As if imitating what arched overhead, different, harsher pinholes of light dotted the shore, identifying the other houses and businesses that lined the small bay.

It was very quiet, the lapping of water against the dock's piers barely audible over the occasional rev of a distant car hot-rodding away from the town's most popular bar, or the gentle slapping of lines against the metal masts of the smaller sailboats, moored somewhere ahead of them, embraced by the inky gloom.

The air smelled of salt, oil, gas, and the lingering scent of old fish and stagnant tidal mud. Despite Alan's dislike of the fishing life, and his resentment of the years he'd spent crewing for his draconian father, he did feel at one with this environment, which forever had hold of his core, however he might struggle against it. In fact, as if speaking to the issue, Alan was dressed in slacks and an open-neck business shirt—a citified outfit rarely seen in these parts.

"How you been?" he asked his brother as they strolled farther into the night's embrace.

"How d'you think?" Pete answered. "You worked with him."

Alan nodded. So he had. Pete was the second youngest, older than Alan by only eleven months. Not the brightest kid around, but one of the hardest workers by far—an attribute that Alan had repeatedly warned him their father would exploit. Not that Pete was in denial; he was aware of the Old Man's game, despite the latter's assertions that the boat would be Pete's in the long run. In fact, Pete had come to Alan first, complaining about how Buddy planned to see him in his grave before the title was ever transferred. But where Alan had always been the rebel of the family—partially protected by his mother and by his success in high school—Pete tended to sulk, nursing his resentments with booze and drugs.

That last part was knowledge their father didn't share. Had Buddy known what Alan did—that Pete was more often than not high when he served as the old man's sternman—he might well have thrashed the boy half to death.

"So, it's not getting any better."

Pete snorted. "Guess not. People're talking that the bonanza's about to bust—that we'll never see the prices of a couple of seasons ago. Dad's talkin' hard times already, that we better get used to buckling down . . . All that shit."

"Code for, 'Sorry, son, but there's been a change in plans'?" Alan asked, sounding sympathetic.

Pete pulled a pack of cigarettes from his pocket, in direct violation of one of his father's rules when around the boat. "Whatever," he said, holding the flame from a cheap lighter against the tip of a cigarette and inhaling deeply. In the flame's quick flare Alan saw the tired face of a far older man.

Which, of course, only encouraged him. "Then maybe you need a Plan B," he said softly.

Pete had started walking again toward the end of the long dock. He paused and looked over his shoulder, the cigarette in midair.

"What's that mean?"

Alan shrugged. "What d'you do when the boss says he's lookin' to lay people off? You check out other jobs."

Pete laughed derisively. "Right. Like I'm gonna find another boat after I tell the Old Man to pound sand. Not on this coast, I'm not. And I ain't lookin' for a job at the processing plant. No, thank you. It's bad enough fucking with those damn things out there." He gestured toward the inky sea beyond them.

"I wasn't talking about another boat," Alan told him. "I was talking about a second source of income. Something quiet that'll give you the freedom to go out on your own—even buy yourself a boat and give the old bastard a run for his money."

He expected Pete to laugh at him again, or just tell him he was full of shit. Pete had been down for so many years Alan wasn't sure he could ever get up.

So, he was surprised when his brother kept staring into space and murmured, "I used to dream about that."

Alan smiled in the darkness. In truth, what he was about to suggest was but a fragment of his overall game plan, most of which was now already in place. He couldn't have cared less about Pete's welfare. He'd never much cared for the guy. As a kid, he'd been a pretty dull blade, and occasionally cruel to boot. But perhaps for those very reasons, Pete had always been their father's favorite, which is truly what lay at the heart of this conversation.

Alan Budney, despite his teenage ambitions and the encouragements he'd received, had always been resentful of those closest to him. He remembered every slight, bore grudges for every embarrassment, and held everyone accountable for each of his misfortunes. In the end, he'd come to despise even those like his mother and his teachers, whom he'd seen as getting their kicks vicariously by living their dreams through him.

To Alan, the world was always out to mess with him, one way or the other.

Well, no longer.

He was about to turn the tables on all of them—to prove his mettle and his brains and his independence, in one fell swoop.

And at the top of that list was Buddy. Alan was going to give that man the education of a lifetime—and humiliate him in the process.

And he was going to use his dull-witted brother to tumble the king off his perch.

He laid his hand lightly on Pete's shoulder and suggested, "I may have a way to turn everything around."

And he wasn't kidding.

CHAPTER ELEVEN

Joe stared out the window with increasing curiosity, wondering if he'd ever seen a bird and a squirrel occupying the same tree branch at the same time before. He'd walked in the woods a good deal, had done so as a boy with his mother time and again—she being keen on taking both her sons for regular instructive day trips. There'd been specific topics for these outings—trees, mushrooms, birds, animal tracks—and she'd always brought the appropriate teaching aids to help.

But he couldn't remember ever seeing a squirrel and a bird sharing a branch. Damndest thing. Probably happened all the time.

There was a momentary stillness around him. He took his gaze off the scenery outside his boss's conference room and raised his eyebrows at the Department of Public Safety's press secretary.

"So, you're on board with this?" the latter asked.

Joe pushed his lips out thoughtfully, piecing together the few fragments that had actually worked their way into his brain over the past few minutes despite his complete lack of interest.

"Totally," he said.

The press secretary—a young man named Jeff—still looked uncertain. "I don't mind working something out where I fly rough drafts by you first."

But Joe was shaking his head. "Nope. No need. You can coordinate with Bill or your boss. If they have questions, they can check with me. Otherwise, I'm more than happy to let you handle everything. I'd just as soon focus entirely on the case."

Jeff nodded slowly, as if allowing Joe to change his mind. Clearly, he couldn't comprehend why anyone in his right mind wouldn't want to control how and what information got to the media.

In fact, Joe couldn't have cared less. He'd been at this kind of thing long enough to know that all the bells and whistles in the world wouldn't stop the press from doing whatever it pleased, regardless of what it was given.

Bill Allard, the actual head of VBI, glanced down at the meeting agenda before him and cleared his throat quietly. "Okay," he said. "That takes care of the information flowing out. What about news we might have to share among ourselves?"

Joe looked around the room. The two of them and Jeff were joined by the Commissioner of Public Safety, Dave Stanton; the colonel of the state police, Neal Kirkland; the Addison County sheriff, Arvid Knowlton; and Harry Seeger, the state's attorney general. It was a high power group, reflecting both how seriously Sleuter's death was being considered, and how thoroughly the news people were beginning to address it. Already, there'd been calls that Joe had ducked, coming from New York and Boston TV stations, among others, inquiring about the investigation's progress.

The conference room was on the top floor of the Department of

Public Safety's building in Waterbury, geographically the most convenient for Allard, Kirkland, and Stanton, the last two of whom had offices just downstairs.

Jeff's boss caught the meaning of Joe's hesitation and nodded to his press secretary. "Actually, Jeff, that probably does it for the time being. None of the rest of this will be for release right now."

Jeff rose a little too hastily and smiled awkwardly, the acknowledged outsider. "Of course. Right. Need-to-know and everything. Got it." He collected his papers and stepped over to the door. "Well, just let me know as things develop."

Stanton smiled and nodded. "Thanks, Jeff. We'll talk later."

A lingering silence lasted thirty seconds after the door closed. Kirkland—a muscular, gray-haired man, dressed in full uniform—broke it with, "I'd be happier if we could just flush the media down the crapper."

Allard, always the diplomat, merely said, "Better with us than not." He turned to Joe, adding, "What've you got?"

Joe paused before answering, mentally reviewing the previous two days. "After the shooting on Dot Ave," he then said, "I think Lenny Chapman was embarrassed or pissed off or maybe just needed something to do, so he took Sam and me to jack up a CI of his named Flaco. Flaco knows Grega, did some smuggling across the Canadian border for him, and had a vague idea of what was being brought over, but he didn't know names, and didn't know anything about the setup."

"A dead end?" Stanton asked.

"Not as it turned out," Joe countered. "He told us that the whole organization had been shaken up by a recent killing. We thought he meant Sleuter, but that wasn't it. He was talking about a double homicide in Maine—Rockland, specifically."

Harry Seeger looked up from the legal pad he'd been covering with notes. "Maine? What's that got to do with anything?"

"We had no idea," Joe explained. "Which is why Chapman put a little fear into Flaco before cutting him loose with a tail, just to see where he'd head and who he'd talk to."

"Which was where?" Stanton again.

"That caught us by surprise," Joe admitted. "He got into a car and drove to Portsmouth, New Hampshire. Not what we were expecting. He made a beeline to a low-end housing development on the edge of town. We were half hoping we'd find Luis Grega, but the apartment belonged to someone named Daniel Wilson. Nothing had come up yet in Grega's Dot Ave apartment, and forensics was still going over the cell phone we'd found there. So we had nothing to lose by driving up to Portsmouth and checking it out in the meantime."

"I take it you got nothing," the colonel suggested.

Joe didn't react to the negative undertone. Kirkland was old school and saw the advent of VBI as a slap in the face of his own detective branch.

But Gunther actually enjoyed the occasionally contrary viewpoint and valued the man's opinion.

"I'm not sure what we got, yet," Joe admitted. "As soon as we reached Portsmouth, I called a friend of mine on the PD there, and she got her people onto Wilson's background. He ended up having a pretty healthy rap sheet, the most interesting part to me being that he originally came from Maine."

"Rockland?" Allard asked.

Joe smiled. "Bingo."

Kirkland was unimpressed. "Which still gives us nothing. Where's Grega in all this?"

"That's where this got interesting," Joe told them. "While we were trying to figure out what to do with this, we heard back from forensics on that cell unit from Grega's apartment. It was the usual deal—a throwaway phone, good for a few calls only—but it did have Wilson's number on it, which we used as probable cause to toss him after Flaco took off."

"Were there any other numbers retrieved?" Allard asked.

"Two," Joe said. "As far as I know, they haven't been pinned to anyone yet—they were probably other disposables."

"What did Wilson give you?" Stanton wanted to know.

"The connection between Grega and Maine," Joe answered. "We grabbed Flaco again, too, to use as a control for anything Wilson might tell us. Of course, we didn't tell Wilson that, but he was pretty straight about what passed between Flaco and him, which adds credibility to what he gave us on Grega."

"Why *did* Flaco go up there?" Seeger asked.

"We'd told him in Boston that Grega was on the run and Marano had been shot," Joe explained. "We didn't go into details. Chapman just recommended that he better watch his back 'cause something was obviously stirring. The hope was that Flaco would go to the most dependable person he could think of who'd know what was going on."

"And did Wilson know?"

Joe nodded. "The double killing Flaco thought we were talking about was a Maine drug dealer named Matthew Mroz and his bodyguard. Mroz was the one Grega—and sometimes Flaco—worked for."

Knowlton, the sheriff, a taciturn man and the dead deputy's erstwhile boss, finally broke his silence. "And Grega was doing that when he killed Brian?"

"We know Grega was a main man," Joe answered him. "Maybe a lieutenant, certainly one of the regulars for the Canada–Boston run. Course, that's just the part we figured out. Flaco described Grega as a 'bad man, on the move.' We have no idea what else he and Mroz might have had cooking between them."

"Is anyone saying Grega whacked his boss?" Allard asked.

"No," Joe said. "Again, according to Flaco, he was in Boston at the time."

"Mroz had a network?" Kirkland inquired, his interest at last stirring.

"So says Wilson. Although," Joe added, "as soon as we were fed Mroz's name, we ran it through the computer and watched it light up. I've just started looking into him, but he may have either cornered or had a hand in almost fifty percent of the drug business in the state."

Kirkland leaned forward slightly. "Who *did* knock him off?"

"Good question. Nobody has a clue."

"How reliable is Flaco about it not being Grega?" Harry Seeger asked, hoping for a slightly tidier legal case. Joe didn't doubt that the AG was formulating how to piece together a capital crime whose reach in the last few minutes was already stretching across four states.

Joe couldn't help him out. "I have to bow to Chapman here—he says Flaco's been solid for three years, so I guess that would mean pretty reliable."

"Could Grega be dead?"

That came from quiet Arvid Knowlton and surprised Joe a little. "I have no reason to think so," he answered.

"But you are thinking he might be in Maine," Allard suggested leadingly, presumably considering—like Seeger—the growing geo-graphical aspects before them.

Joe answered carefully, "I'm thinking Maine deserves some scrutiny."

"Why did Flaco go to Wilson?" Seeger pressed him, changing tacks. "How's Wilson inside this loop? You said Grega or Marano might've called him on a cell."

"He's been around a long time," Joe reported. "Used to work for Mroz. Quit a couple of years ago to take care of his dying mother in Portsmouth. There were no hard feelings, so he kept in touch with the old crowd. He said Marano called him, asking about Roz, but that he had nothing to tell him. That tallies with Flaco telling us that Wilson was the only man in the business he really trusted— that being half in and half out made him everyone's friend and no-body's enemy."

"But he doesn't know enough to put you directly on the scent?" Kirkland asked, his voice incredulous. "Grega's a cop killer, for Christ's sake. Wilson must know dozens of people who might know where he is. How's playing coy with us going to win him any favors?"

"I don't think he cares," Joe admitted. "We don't have anything on him, we didn't get him for anything when we tossed him, and he doesn't want to burn any bridges."

Kirkland considered that before saying more calmly, "Techni-cally, it's an ICE case; not our call. What do they want to do?"

"Chapman's hot to trot," Joe told him. "Of course, that's easy for him. They've got offices in Maine, and I would bet he's dying to get out of the office for some fieldwork."

"You pretty sure going there will take you to Grega?" Allard asked, ever mindful of his tight budget. The VBI had been created by the governor and was funded by the legislature, both of whom liked big headlines and small headaches. Sending the state's elite investigative unit abroad on a whim—even if for a good cause—was potentially tricky territory.

"I'm not sure of anything," Joe answered honestly. "I was struck by the fact that Flaco headed north when he felt the heat. If I were Grega and I heard about a violent change in management, I'd either run for the hills if I felt I was next, or run back to the mansion to find out whose ass I should kiss."

"And you're choosing the second option, why?" Stanton asked.

Joe lifted one shoulder slightly. "Because it's the one that makes the most sense at the moment. Grega's described as upwardly mobile, and we know he's a killer—therefore not a guy to run."

Kirkland was shaking his head. "You're guessing. The old boss is dead; you don't know who killed him or why; you don't know who might've replaced him; and Wilson's a dead end, so you don't know what to do next."

Joe conceded the point with a smile but then tilted his chin toward the closed door. "All true. But if we're going to help young Jeff out there with the media, we better feed him something, even if it's that we're chasing down a lead. And you have to admit that the Maine connection reaches that level, if nothing else."

Mike Bradley looked up at the sound of his office door opening and saw a man and a woman standing before him, the man with his left hand awkwardly stuffed into his trousers pocket.

The woman he recognized—Sammie Martens. He'd coordinated

with her on a case years ago, when he was still with the Burlington police and she with the Brattleboro PD.

Bradley knew the man with her only by reputation, which was enough to make him think he might now be in for trouble.

He rose with a smile, circled his desk, and stuck his hand out in greeting, his defenses on high alert.

"Hey, there. Mike Bradley. Nice to have you on board. Good drive?"

Sam was all smiles as well, returning the handshake and making pleasantries. Kunkle ignored their host, turned on his heel slightly, and began studying the hangings on Bradley's walls—a younger man's version of what Sam had seen in the Boston ICE SAC's office two days previously.

"You guys do all right up here, close to the money," Willy cracked, shifting his gaze to the larger outer office, visible through Mike's interior window. Burlington was but a half-hour drive from the capital, and the VBI office here, the largest in the state, had six agents and a three-room complex on the top floor of a modern downtown building. Bradley was the unit supervisor, one of four who worked directly under Gunther. As such, he knew of the Brattleboro facility, having visited it once while Willy was absent. It had struck him as a claustrophobic dump.

"Yeah," Mike said, his hackles nevertheless raised. "But you've got the boss."

Willy let out a sharp, derisive laugh. "Yeah. There's a plus."

"He keeps *you* employed, Willy," Sammie cracked to thaw the air slightly.

Mike had heard that the two had become a couple. Involuntarily, he shook his head slightly, startled at the thought. She was attractive, too—if undoubtedly dysfunctional somehow.

He waved a hand at the two guest chairs he had opposite his desk. "Sit, sit. You want any coffee?"

Willy remained standing while Sam took a chair. "How 'bout a grande café espresso with a shot of hot milk?" he said.

"Stuff it," his companion cautioned him, smiling at Mike before adding, "It's his colon—full of shit."

Mike nodded and sat behind his desk, too startled to comment, but assuming the coffee question could sort itself out.

"So," he segued, determined to keep up appearances, for her, at least. "What sends you up here? News from the front? Joe's still in Massachusetts, right?"

"Nope," Sammie told him. "He is hooked up with ICE, but he's back in Vermont for a day or two, meeting with the big bosses. You read about what happened down there?"

"The shoot-out on Dot Ave?" Bradley answered, tapping a sheaf of papers before him on the desk. "Just got the report. Sounded like a cluster fuck."

"Would've been fun to be there, though," Willy said, finally sitting.

Ah, thought Bradley, remembering that Sam had accompanied Gunther. Maybe that was the problem—the guy was feeling left out.

"We're here," Sam returned to Mike's question, "purely as support troops—setting up or manning a command center, or just doing go-fer jobs that your guys are too busy to handle. We are not about looking over your shoulder or doing any second guessing."

Mike immediately considered sending Kunkle to Siberia for doughnuts. Instead, knowing both of Sam's closeness to Joe and—thankfully—of her general competence, he answered instead,

"No, no. That's fine. We could use the help, to be honest. The press is all over this and constantly getting in the way."

"What've you got going so far?" Sam asked.

Mike relaxed slightly, feeling himself on more familiar ground. Kunkle and Martens would in fact be useful, even if, as he suspected, they were here with more on their minds than they'd just admitted.

"We do have a command post in place—or the start of one. I have reps from the sheriff's office and the state police and the AG's and even one liaison from the Vergennes PD, just to be totally PC. We have a hot line set up for anyone who may have witnessed Sleuter's traffic stop; a direct link to the Mounties for what they can find on Marano and Grega; and several guys going through every record we can locate where either name might crop up, on both sides of the border. I've also got a man doing the normal follow-up on Sleuter, making sure he was aboveboard."

"How's that going?" Kunkle asked lazily.

"Good. Haven't found anything yet. He was obnoxious and ambitious—he didn't hide the fact that he saw the sheriff's job as a springboard, but so far—going over his past cases—he's clean. Of course, that's just gotten started, and the man was busy. Anyhow, we won't have any problem finding you things to do."

He rose and gestured toward the outer office. "All right. Then let me introduce you around and get you settled in. You'll probably know half my crew anyhow, so I bet in a day or two, it'll be like you were here from the start."

Not that he actually believed a word of it. A small but potent headache was already telling him that much.

CHAPTER TWELVE

Cathy Lawless added a stick of gum to the one in her mouth. Dave Beaubien glanced up from the radio receiver he was fine-tuning in his lap and took note. She was winding herself up, getting into role. Cathy was the most high-strung person he'd ever known—thin as a piano wire and just as tense—and one of the fastest nonstop talkers, too, which, given his own general stillness, made them quite the team.

But a good one. She'd made the comment that they were like Fred and Ginger—she could do everything he did, backward and in heels. Old joke, and he'd never seen her in anything but sneakers or boots, but there was truth to it, too. For all their contrasts—he was actually the one with the softer contours of a Ginger Rogers—they seemed to instinctively know what the other was thinking, or about to do.

And so he knew now that she was steeling herself for the encounter just ahead.

Of course, gum chewing wasn't her only outlet. She was talking, as well, while staring out the passenger side window at the fishing boats at anchor, barely visible in the ambient light from the homes and businesses ringing the harbor. They were in a tiny port near Machias, some twenty-five miles shy of the Canadian border. She was preparing to meet one of her regular contacts, named Bob, who knew her only as Suzy, thought she was a doper transplant from Boston with lots of ready cash, and, least fortunately, also had a crush on her, despite her best efforts to redirect him.

"I mean, for Christ's sake, what doesn't he get? Not once have I led the son of a bitch on—no flirting, no boob-flashing, no batting my eyes. I make my buy, I get my intel, and I leave. It's gonna blow him away when we finally decide he's not worth the trouble and we shut him down. Can you imagine the look on his face? I half bet he'll give me one of those 'after all we meant to each other' lines. You know what I mean?"

Dave knew better than to answer.

"The only saving grace is that he likes to meet outdoors, 'cause I tell you, if these things were held in some trailer in the woods, I wouldn't do it, not even armed to the teeth and with ten of you as backup. Life's too short to get what we get paid and be stared at by some creep who can barely keep his dick in his pants."

She abruptly held up her hand, as if Dave had just given her grief. "I know, I know—totally against department policy. Don't rub it in. I shouldn't have opened that door. But what else was I gonna do? If I hadn't let him search me that first time, he woulda made me as a cop. It was a rock and hard place kinda thing."

She took her eyes off the scenery to look at him. "Jesus, Dave. You rebuilding that thing? It is gonna work, right?" She tapped the top of her head, where the tiny microphone was hidden in her hair.

Dave nodded, not looking up, and said, "Don't."

Cathy sighed and returned to her vigil. "I know this thing's the cutting edge, but I miss the old-fashioned wires. This feels weird, like wearing nothing at all. Plus, I only have your word that it'll work. How the hell do we know Bob won't suddenly change the rules? He could take me into a basement and you'd be screwed, and I'd be up shit creek without a paddle."

This time, Dave did react. "You wouldn't go, and it'll work."

She turned on him and punched his shoulder. "I know that, Dave. It's the principle of the thing. It just makes me feel naked."

Dave flipped the device over in his hand, turned it on, ran a quick diagnostic, and nodded. "You aren't. It'll be fine—and we'll all come running if something screws up," he told her.

She frowned, the shoe suddenly on the other foot. "Hey, don't go crazy, all right? Just listen to the conversation. If it sounds okay but then the sound drops off for some reason, don't go ape on me. I can handle Bob, for God's sake. He just wears me out, is all. It's not like I couldn't take him out with one kick in the balls. You all set?"

Dave opened his door. "Yup." He quickly radioed the backup team parked a couple of blocks away, announced that he and Cathy were out of the vehicle and going active and that they should begin monitoring her mike.

Cathy stepped out of the van and breathed in the night air, cool and tinged with salt and oil and the faint smell of decay. She actually hailed from the Moosehead Lake region, far from the Maine coast, and hadn't even seen salt water until she was in her teens. She'd never gotten used to the coast as a result, always feeling like a tourist. That was one of the reasons she told dealers that she was from Boston—to fill in the part of her that felt out of place.

She gave one last glance at her partner, who was patiently lingering by the rear of the van, waiting for her to move. They'd parked in the shadowy lot of the town church, with a narrow view of the harbor across the road. As she was meeting with Bob, Dave would stalk her from the darkness, listening in on her at all times, recording everything that was said.

"Good to go?" she reiterated.

He nodded.

She stepped free of the darkness and into the feeble glow of an overhead streetlight, and checked both ways before crossing the road. She needn't have bothered. It was past midnight, and in a lobstering village whose business required people to get up at three A.M. to be on the water at dawn, there wasn't much movement beyond the silent scurrying of a couple of cats.

The opposite side of the road bordered the water's edge, with a broad, built-up swath of concrete and wooden wharves, docks, storage sheds, and equipment yards. All were cluttered with equipment arcane and familiar, prominent among them the ubiquitous stacks of lobster traps, lately made less photogenic through the widespread replacement of the wood-slatted traps of yore by the more practical, durable, but less appealing wire models.

Cathy walked with a haphazard, slovenly gait, contrary to her nature, in the hopes of presenting a vague, possibly strung-out demeanor. She and Bob had met initially through the conventions of the business—she the user, and he the slightly larger fish up the food chain, introduced by a dealer who could no longer supply her needs. The name of this game wasn't busts so much as follow the prey upstream until a big enough specimen popped up.

Bob wasn't that player. They'd now met three times, each time with Cathy increasing her demand; it was clear he was running shy of resources. He'd been hedging on the dates they could meet, and trying to get her to split her orders over time.

She also didn't like him, which made his growing unimportance a relief. The first time they'd met—before she could stop him—he'd run his hands over her breasts, supposedly in search of a wire. She'd slapped his hands away and yelled at him—an inauspicious start she'd reluctantly worked to repair. As she'd said to Dave, she wasn't paid enough to be felt up by losers like him.

She reached a dock stretching out from the end of a weather-beaten building the size of a large garage and swung out onto its time-darkened boards, her sneakers slapping against their surface. As she approached a small shed on the dock's far end, the water's black, slightly oily surface around her barely undulated in the lights from the retreating shore. Bob preferred this place for his meets because he said it made him feel safe—he could see in all directions.

She glanced around. In fact, you couldn't see a goddamn thing, including the lurking Dave Beaubien. Walking out toward the middle of the blackened bay felt like a one-way excursion down a gangplank.

"If you can hear me, Dave," she said in a normal tone, still some distance from the shed, "make a noise."

The single solid thump of a boot stomp sounded far behind her.

"Gotcha," she answered. "Everything looks normal up ahead."

The shed had no real function that she'd discerned from her two previous visits. It was big for its location, though, made of two rooms and an overhead loft. She'd only made it into the first room, however—what Bob had laughingly called his office—the first time.

As she drew nearer, she saw his shadow move across the tattered yellow cloth hanging before the one window she could see.

"Got movement inside," she announced to Dave's mike, having long overcome any awkwardness about feeling like she was talking to herself. Indeed, by now, she'd lost count of how many times she'd made similar drug buys, always invisibly escorted by her backup.

Crossing the last few yards warily, mentally switching over to her stage persona, she placed a hand on the battered brass doorknob only to have the door swing open before her.

"*Whoa,*" she said, startled, taking a step backward.

A man stood before her, bearded, heavy, and nervous. " 'Bout time you got here."

Cathy gave him a wilting look. "What? You got a dentist's appointment? I said tonight. It's tonight."

Bob stepped out onto the dock and looked past her into the darkness. "You said midnight. You're late."

She touched his shoulder calmingly, maintaining a hint of scorn in her voice. "Fine. Relax, Bob. I didn't know you cared."

"I don't," he said shortly, but he, too, reached out, took her elbow, and drew her into the shed before closing the door again.

Cathy looked around at the wooden walls, covered with fishing gear and a few tattered pinups of naked women.

"You fixed the place up. You shouldn't have."

Bob stood in the middle of the room, looking uncomfortable. Cathy sensed that something was off kilter. She glanced at the door separating the two rooms and noticed it was slightly ajar. In the past, it had been wide open.

"You okay?" she asked him, as much for Dave's sake as out of any real concern. "You look a little tense."

He frowned. "You bring money?"

She decided to go along, for the moment. "Depends. What d'you got? If it's like the last batch, we might have to haggle. You ought to consider switching suppliers."

But he shook his head. "Uh-uh. First things first. Stick your arms out."

Her mouth dropped open. "Oh, for crying out loud, Bob. We're *not* doing this. You really want me to smack you again?"

He moved in, and for the first time in their few interactions, Cathy saw a dangerous look in his eyes.

"You do that," he said, "and you won't like what happens."

"Jesus H. Christ," she said wearily, but she held both arms out, as instructed, privately tensing against whatever might be coming.

She was surprised. Bob quickly and efficiently checked her over, without comment or lingering where he shouldn't.

She smiled at him as he stepped back, risking opening the Pandora's box she hated in order to keep in character. "You don't like me anymore?" she asked.

He pressed his lips together in distaste. "You're a crazy bitch."

She laughed. "Maybe. That's never been a problem before. You wanna do business?"

"Yeah. How much you want?"

"Two hundred," she said.

That stopped him, as she'd hoped it would. "That's a lot," he said.

"You asked what I wanted."

He chewed the inside of his mouth thoughtfully.

Cathy impatiently glanced at the cabin's front door. "Fine. Bob, either bump me up the ladder or sell me the goods. You can do this or you can't." She paused and then added, "Who gives you your stuff? Maybe I should deal with him direct. I heard there'd been a shake-up anyhow. You drying up on me?"

Bob's jaw muscles tightened under the abuse. "I'm not doing nothin'. I can get you the stuff. Just not right now."

She looked down at the floor and shook her head. "Shit. That's not how it works, Bob. Kmart doesn't have it, Wal-Mart gets next shot—that's the way it works. This is a capitalist country. Tell me who to go to, or take me to him now, or do something that'll stop me from walking out that door."

"How 'bout I sell you what I got, and we get together later?"

"Bullshit. I don't like you that much. Figure it out. Pull a rabbit out of your hat."

Her words worked like a stage direction in a play: The door between the two rooms swung open, causing Bob to stiffen and Cathy to recoil against the wall in alarm.

"What the fuck's going on, Bob? Who you got in there?"

A man appeared in the opening—short, of trim but muscular build, with black hair, a goatee, dark features, and the tattoo of a snake peering over the top of his T-shirt.

"It's okay," he said. "I'm with him." He pointed at Bob.

Bob plainly wished this wasn't so. "Yeah," he said without conviction. "It's okay. This is Luis. He's cool."

"Luis who?" Cathy asked, her features set but her mind in a turmoil. She was sure she'd seen this face before, if only a printed version. "I like to know who I'm dealing with. This your supplier?"

The newcomer smiled slightly, his eyes very watchful. "I think you're right," he said suggestively. "You like to know a lot. That makes me suspicious."

"What?" Cathy protested, still mentally racing through a catalog of mug shots and police bulletins, groping for an answer. "I just got here. You don't know shit about me." She narrowed her eyes, as if struck by a sudden thought. "Hold it. Are you a cop?" She shifted to Bob. "You son of a bitch. You set me up?"

Bob held up both his hands, but Luis cut him off before he could utter a word.

"I don't think he's the one setting people up," Luis said. "He's not that smart. You are, though."

He took three steps toward her, so that they were now only inches apart. "Aren't you?" he finished.

Cathy held her arms out to her sides again and smiled at him. "I get it. You want a feel, too. Fine. Knock your socks off." She spoke to Bob over Luis's shoulder. "Pretty lame, Bob—getting your faggy friends free feel-ups. I don't think we'll be doing business anymore."

Now that Luis was standing virtually face-to-face with her, Cathy was all but certain that she knew who he was, finally prodded by his threatening demeanor. He'd surfaced recently in a Be-On-the-Lookout as the suspected shooter in a Vermont police killing.

"You're sweating," Luis Grega commented quietly, still not touching her.

"Wouldn't you be?" she countered. "Slimy little guy pops out of nowhere. What the fuck do you want, anyhow?"

Grega's right hand reached behind him and reappeared holding a small semiautomatic.

Cathy didn't let him get any farther. Whatever he was planning, her chances of surviving it were about to vanish. As he began to speak, she struck upward with her fist, striking the gun and sending it, still in his hand, against his mouth. He shouted in pain as she then threw him off balance by shouldering him in the chest, before bolting for the exit, screaming, "*Gun, Dave. Gun.*"

Outside, Dave had already placed the receiver on top of a nearby lobster trap and was reaching for his own gun when he heard his partner's shout.

Ripping his earpiece away and throwing it wide, Dave took a shooter's stance in the middle of the dock and aimed at the small building's door. Behind him, in the distance, he heard the backup's van squealing to reach them quickly, along with several bursts from their siren.

Cathy was the first to appear, running fast and low, heading directly toward him with her eyes wide and her mouth open. Not moving a muscle, Dave stayed as he was.

Behind Cathy, another shape appeared in the doorway, staggering slightly, lighted only from behind. He brought the gun in his hand to bear on Cathy's retreating back.

Dave shot once, apparently missing.

The man's shadow shifted. There was a flash from his gun, an explosion, and a piece of wood went flying from the crate to Dave's left.

As Dave fired back, Cathy dove headlong into the water beside her, vanishing into the darkness.

With Cathy now out of the line of fire, Dave ducked behind the same crate for protection and tried to take better aim.

But the man by the shed merely stepped back inside.

"Dave—you okay?"

He quickly glanced down and to his side, into the black water. Cathy's pale face floated there like an expressive lily.

"Yeah," he answered. "You?"

"Fine. Where is he?"

"Back in the shed. Who was that?"

"The cop killer from Vermont."

"Luis Grega?" Dave asked immediately.

She should have guessed he'd know that. "I'm freezing down here."

Keeping his gun aimed at the shed, he reached down with his other hand and helped her up onto the dock behind the crate, just as the others came pounding up to join them. They all heard an outboard engine come alive in the distance.

"Damn," Dave said.

It was eloquent enough. With two men known in the building, and possibly more, there was no way the cops could safely break cover, charge to the end of the dock, and hope to stop whoever it was from leaving.

"Hey," Cathy said hopefully, her teeth already chattering. "Maybe he left Bob behind."

"Right," her terse partner said doubtfully, which, as usual, was all he really needed to say.

CHAPTER THIRTEEN

Joe watched Lyn as she sat before the mirror in her bedroom, deftly applying a touch of mascara to her right eyelashes. She was naked, as was he, and the lamp beside her—the only light in the room—caught the contours of her body just right.

"Maine?" she asked, leaning forward to better focus. "When do you leave?"

He admired her arched back as the shadows played across her shoulder blades.

"Soon," he told her. "We're putting the last details together with ICE in Boston, formalizing the task force."

She shifted to the other eye. She was getting ready for work. It was her night to run the bar, and they'd spent half the afternoon making love, "in preparation," as she put it. He hadn't asked what she'd meant, in deference to the very dirty laugh she'd used to accompany it.

"Seems a shame," she said, "to go there for that reason. I have such nice memories of Maine."

Joe thought back to when he'd first visited this apartment, on the second floor of a Victorian showpiece on Oak Street. Lyn hadn't fully moved in yet—there were boxes still piled around, along with a sense that even the items on display hadn't yet found their final niches. But he had discovered some family pictures lining the baseboard of the living room and from those—and her subsequent explanations—had learned a bit of her history.

The keystone there, not surprisingly, had been the loss of her father and brother at sea. Her life, as he'd come to see it through her eyes, had essentially fallen to both sides of that watershed, split like a thin piece of wood across the knee.

The allusion to Maine was a nod to the earlier times, when her lobsterman father, Abílo Silva, would take a little time off, usually around late May—when lobsters lie low to shed their outer carapaces and grow larger ones—and escort the family for trips along the Maine coast. None of them had been deceived by the choice of destination—Lyn's father was thinking competitively as he'd toured the harbors, fleets, lobster pounds, and markets—but they'd still made vacations of these jaunts, and her tales of kinship and humor and familial love had made the subsequent loss and sorrow all the harder. The abrupt and simple vanishing of both Abílo and José Silva, following a standard Atlantic storm, had been as traumatic for its impact as it had been for its lack of closure. As Lyn had once explained it to Joe, "One day the boat was there, the next it wasn't, and our life was over."

Subsequent to this upheaval, slowly but inexorably, Lyn's other brother, Steve, had slipped into drug abuse, dealing, and prison—from which he'd just recently been released, while her mother had become a virtual recluse, living in a tiny apartment in Gloucester.

Lyn herself had taken a more traditional route, marrying briefly and unsuccessfully, while producing a daughter named Coryn, who was now in her early twenties and working happily in Boston.

Not an end-of-the-world saga, as Joe knew from his own eventful life. Nevertheless, the very familiarity of Lyn's intimacy with grief heightened its poignancy for him. Perhaps, he thought, all joy had to be laced with darkness, simply to have a contrasting validity.

A cliché, he realized. But one he couldn't avoid, knowing how happy this woman had made him feel.

He rose from the bed and crossed over to her, carefully kissing the nape of her neck so that she wouldn't miss her target with the mascara. Nevertheless, she twisted her head and caught his lips with her own. He reached up with one hand and cradled one of her breasts with his palm.

"God," she murmured through the kiss, "I wish I didn't have to go to work tonight."

"Me, too," he agreed, breaking away slightly. "But, then, I have to head off, too, so I guess we'd still be in the same boat."

She looked up at him, surprised. "That's what you meant by 'soon'? I thought Maine was a day or so away."

He laughed. "It is. But I have to get with my crew in an hour—figure out who's doing what while I'm off gallivanting around Down East."

She returned to studying herself in the mirror. "Where are you headed? We used to go way up there in the old days—Machias, Jonesport, Lubec. Boy, there was a dump. Even Dad thought so, and he liked most disaster areas."

Joe nodded. "Machias came up earlier today—or at least right next door to it. Last night, one of the Maine drug cops accidentally ran into the guy we're after. He got away, so I'm thinking our first stop'll probably be Rockland. A drug bigwig got himself killed there a while back, which apparently shook up the marketplace. We're wondering if there's any connection to our case."

Lyn put the mascara brush down carefully and looked up at him, her expression serious. "What was the bigwig's name?"

Joe raised his eyebrows slightly, caught off guard. "Matthew Mroz, nicknamed 'Roz,' of course. Why?"

She dropped her gaze to the floor and muttered, "I just wondered."

Joe crouched down so he could better see her face. "What's up?" he asked, although he now suspected the source of her mood change. "Is it about Steve?" he guessed.

Lyn let out a small puff of air. "Yeah. That sure came out of nowhere. I never thought I'd hear that name again."

Joe was astonished at this development, even though each intervening step between this woman and a major dealer in Maine not only made sense in itself, but reflected how small a world northern New England still could be. He got up and sat on the edge of the nearby bed, his elbows on his knees.

"You never told me how Steve got into trouble in the first place," he prompted, wondering how far this coincidence might take him.

"Well," she confessed, immediately addressing Joe's unstated question, "it wasn't Roz. Steve was already years down that road before his name came up, and I don't think he ever actually met the man. Roz was where Steve hoped to be headed before he got busted."

"They were going to go into business together?"

She quickly checked the bedside clock to make sure she had time enough to continue. "Hardly," she answered, satisfied. "Steve wasn't in that league. He just wanted to be a runner—get some steady income, along with enough junk to put up his nose. It wouldn't have worked out. It never does. But that was the plan."

"And Roz appeared in that plan how?" Joe asked.

"As the ideal," she told him. "We were living in Gloucester. Boston to the south, Maine to the north—or more properly, Canada. The southern opportunities, as Steve saw them, were scary, even to him—people who would cut your heart out for no reason. Cape Verdians, Jamaicans, Asians of all stripes, you name it. Steve did some business with them, especially when he got desperate, but he knew it would end badly someday. When he heard about the operation Roz had in Maine, bringing stuff in from Canada, he got all excited. Told me that he'd finally found his ticket, whatever that was supposed to mean."

Joe listened to her tone as much as to what she was telling him, hearing the hardness there. He had met her when she was tending bar in one of the worst dives in Gloucester, surrounded by more people with aliases than the average U.S. Marshal. She'd had a psychological armor then—for when the odd customer would misbehave—that he was witnessing now concerning her one remaining brother, whose long-gone cheerful company she mourned. He already knew that they hadn't spoken in a long time.

"Did he and Mroz ever make contact?" he asked her.

She got up from her chair and crossed over to the bureau, where she quickly extracted a clean pair of jeans and a tight-fitting T-shirt which she tossed onto the bed.

"No," she answered him, her manner back to normal, her mind on what she was doing. "He made a sale to an undercover Gloucester cop right after. As far as I know, he never went beyond just hearing about the guy. Not that he confided in me. I heard most of this from some of his friends."

Joe had shifted on the bed to face her as she dressed, both to make eye contact but also to simply watch. "That must've been tough," he commented.

She paused in midmotion to look at him, her expression sad. "You have no idea. Well, you probably do," she added with a small smile. "Steve was such a great kid—a wonderful companion when we were growing up. José was serious, like Dad, and anyhow he was older. But Steve . . ." She left the sentence unfinished as she went back to dressing.

"He's out of jail now, right?" Joe asked.

"Out of jail, maybe," she conceded, pulling her jeans up over her hips. "Out of trouble, who knows?"

Joe turned away from the passing countryside to glance at his companion. Lester Spinney drove a car with the steadiness Joe had noticed in all troopers, past or present. It was as if they, more than other cops, had been specifically instructed on how to look both relaxed and alert at the wheel.

"This trip go down all right with the family?" he asked.

Spinney smiled gently. "Oh, sure. Sue and I have been pulling weird shifts for a pretty long time. And the kids'll barely notice."

Sue, Joe knew, was a nurse, and thus susceptible to working nights for weeks on end. "How's David doing?"

Lester faced Joe directly, his smile broadening. David, Les's oldest, had flirted with drugs a few years back. They both knew how close it had come to costing Les his job.

"Fine, Joe. Thanks for asking."

Joe nodded without comment and went back to studying the scenery. It had been raining earlier, but the sun was now out, shafting through the high clouds at irregular intervals, creating oases of dazzling light. They were in Maine, having opted to avoid the faster southern route, east through Keene, Manchester, and Portsmouth, New Hampshire, in exchange for the famed Kancamagus Highway, twisting among the White Mountains like a string of shining mercury. That leg of the trip had been predictably spectacular, running for thirty miles by the tallest peaks on the eastern seacoast, some with their heads in the mist, and all offering ghostly glimpses along dark, damp mountainous passes.

This southwestern section of Maine, however, was proving less of a treat. Hilly still, and blanketed with trees, it allowed few vistas, a lot of meandering traffic, and was turning into the literal slow road to Augusta, the state capital and their destination.

"Sue did ask," Spinney said, "how long we might be in Maine."

Joe laughed at the roundabout question. "Damned if I know, Les. We're not going on much—rumors of a drug war, a single sighting of Grega near Machias, a few one-liners from dubious sources. If Bill Allard hadn't been feeling generous—or maybe showing off to Colonel Kirkland—we'd probably still be at home."

Spinney hesitated before reasonably asking, "So, why are we going, instead of letting the locals dig up something solid? I mean, Grega took a boat when he skipped, right? He could be back in Boston by now."

Joe had considered the same possibility. In the past, when he'd worked for the Brattleboro police department, there wouldn't have been an option. This trip was easily categorized as a wild goose chase—as Kirkland would have called it had his department caught the case.

But that was one of the beauties of the VBI. Its charter was purposely less rigid, and its architecture less hidebound by any command structure's checks and balances. Joe suspected that Allard had signed off on the trip as much to once more set an example as with any hopes of success.

"Just a hunch," Joe therefore said.

He could tell that's all Spinney needed to hear.

CHAPTER FOURTEEN

Willy Kunkle got out of his car quietly, as was his habit. He didn't slam the door, and he'd long ago disabled his car's dome light. He'd also parked slightly down the road, to avoid being noticed. These were habits born more years ago than he could recall, when he'd been a night patrol officer and had valued being inconspicuous.

It was also eerily quiet where he was right now, unlike in the urban streets he normally frequented. He was in the countryside, between Burlington and Middlebury, in the midst of Addison County's farm country, surrounded by the night's vast emptiness. All around was where Brian Sleuter had once aggressively patrolled, looking for a ramp up to the big time.

Willy was at the address of Sleuter's ex-mother-in-law, a woman named Shirley Sherman, whose daughter Brian had divorced years before. Sherman was therefore a peripheral member of Sleuter's family tree, certainly in terms of Mike Bradley's check into Brian's past, and as such she hadn't yet been interviewed. But Willy was intrigued by what he'd interpreted from Shirley's raw data in the state's computer files. There seemed to be an independent streak to the woman that Willy hoped to exploit.

He paused at the foot of the driveway, studying the house before him. Beige, single-storied, wrapped in vinyl siding and topped with an asphalt roof, it was the epitome of suburban architecture, planted in the middle of nowhere. Glancing around, Willy could see only one set of lights from a far distant neighbor.

That and the single quavering light of an approaching motorcycle, its beam reflecting every dip and wrinkle in the road. Instinctively, Willy stepped over to the edge of the driveway.

Sure enough, the motorcycle pulled into the drive with a flourish, scattering a few loose stones toward Willy's shoes, before grinding to a halt just beyond him. On board was a tiny, squarely built figure, dressed all in black, wearing a full face helmet with its tinted visor down.

One gloved hand reached up, lifted the hinged front of the helmet up and away, and revealed the round, ruddy face of an older woman, her gray hair appearing in loose strands around her forehead.

"You looking to buy the place or just rip me off?" she asked.

Willy smiled and opened his jacket to reveal the badge clipped to his belt. "Neither. I'm guessing you're Shirley Sherman."

"That much I know," she answered him, a pair of steady blue eyes studying him carefully.

"Willy Kunkle," he introduced himself. "Vermont Bureau of Investigation."

Her eyes widened a bit. "No shit? I heard about you guys. Major crimes, razzle-dazzle, best and the brightest and all that crap?"

"Mostly crap," he conceded. "The best and the brightest in a state with twelve people doesn't mean much."

"You look smart enough," she commented. "What's with the arm?"

He admired her directness. Most people either didn't look at the limp left arm at all, as if it were hanging in the next room, or stared at it every time they thought he was looking away. Nobody simply asked.

"Rifle bullet, years ago."

"And they let you stay on?"

He made a face. "Like I said."

She pushed out her lower lip, seemed to consider something for a moment, and then gestured ahead, farther down the driveway. "Well, come on in. Let me ditch this in the garage."

She revved the bike, spat out a few extra stones from under her rear wheel, and made one last quick jaunt up to the slowly opening garage door. Inside, another motorcycle was already parked—a fluorescent dirt bike with knobby tires. This was what Willy had read about the woman—several speeding violations, registrations for two bikes and a four-wheeler, and hunting and fishing licenses dating back decades. She'd been listed as a widow.

He walked to the front door of the house and waited for her to join him, the helmet now off and the jacket unzipped to reveal a T-shirt hugging a well-formed, if matronly, chest. Willy, in a split second's double take, visualized Shirley Sherman as a small, up-ended steamer trunk—solid, tough, and sturdy, if a lot more attractive. For, truth be told, he imagined she could more than hold her own with men ten years her junior, and he wouldn't have been surprised to hear that she had a proudly held neighborhood reputation.

She preceded him into the house, which he immediately appreciated for its cleanliness and order.

"You want coffee?" she asked.

"Sure. Black."

The living room was conventionally rigged out, its assortment of impersonal, pleasant accoutrements looking like a movie set about middle-class life. The only exception was on the mantelpiece over the gas fireplace. Willy recognized there several shots of a woman he knew to be Brian Sleuter's ex—Kathleen Jabri, nowadays—holding a small child in various poses.

"My daughter and grandson," she commented, watching him from beyond the small counter between the kitchen and the living room. "Although I figure you already know that."

He wandered over to the counter and sat on one of two stools tucked under its edge. He didn't answer.

Sherman had removed her jacket and was efficiently preparing the coffee, moving across the kitchen like a well-practiced short-order cook. Willy knew that she'd owned a café for thirty years. He suspected that whenever her small family came by, they left well fed.

"You know why I'm here?" he asked her.

She looked at him with a pitying expression. "Don't you?"

"Cute."

He let a long silence fall between them, forcing her to finally concede. "Well, it's got to be Brian, right? I don't know why else I'd rate."

"When did you last see him?"

She kept at her task. "Oh, hell. I don't know. He'd come by now and then, always around suppertime, of course. Maybe a week before he died."

"You two stayed friends?"

She still didn't look at him. "We were never that. He was my grandson's father. I owed him that much."

"But not a nice guy?"

This time, she cast him a glance, if only quickly. "You're not a nice guy, either. So what?"

He didn't bite. "What happened between him and Kathleen?"

She pulled two mugs from a cabinet above her. "What happens between three-quarters of the people who get married? Most of them divorce, the rest make each other miserable. They got divorced."

"He was an ambitious man," Willy commented. "Putting in the overtime, fighting to be top dog."

He left it at that, but she didn't cooperate.

"So?"

"Some cops don't leave that at the office," he suggested.

"You asking or telling?"

He capitulated. "Asking."

She poured two mugs and brought them over to the counter, settling onto a stool he hadn't seen, opposite his.

She shoved one of the mugs directly before him. "Why're you doing this? He was shot by drug runners. Least, that's what they told me."

Willy gave a dismissive half wave before grabbing hold of the mug's handle. "Yeah, that's true, but we still gotta cover our butts. You know, stuff like, 'Was he in cahoots with whoever killed him?' It's all fill-in-the-blanks to make the bosses happy."

They both sipped their coffee in silence for a moment. Shirley spoke first. "Like I'm supposed to believe that."

Willy placed his mug carefully on the countertop. "You want to tell me something different?"

"Such as?" she asked.

"He piss off anyone enough to make them come after him?"

She paused before answering, "He pissed people off, probably just like you do."

"Your daughter?"

Her back straightened and she fixed him with a glare. "If Brian Sleuter was killed by drug runners, then that's none of my business."

"That doesn't answer the question."

"Too bad. I think this conversation just ended."

Willy didn't stir. "Meaning I leave with the wrong impression."

Shirley stared at him, motionless. He could virtually hear her working out the angles of the box he'd put her in.

"He hit her," she finally said.

"A lot?"

"A couple of times. That's all it took."

"Took for what?"

She pressed her lips together. "They were a bad match," she finally said.

"What happened after he hit her, Shirley?"

Her shoulders slumped. "I talked to him."

"He wouldn't listen to you. What happened?"

Her right hand closed into a fist. "I persuaded him to listen."

Willy thought back over what he knew of this woman. "I'm guessing it involved a gun."

She gave half a nod. "He was sleeping on the couch when I shoved a .45 under his nose and I told him he could kiss his career good-bye if he ever so much as raised his voice to my daughter again."

Willy found that utterly believable, in all its simplicity. "How long before the divorce?" he asked.

She smiled bitterly. "You know your creeps well."

And how, he thought, having been, at one point in his life, a lot worse than Brian Sleuter.

"He didn't last the rest of the week," she finished. "He didn't give a damn about either one of them. It was always that stupid job."

Willy took another sip of coffee, thinking back.

"And yet," he said, "he'd drop by here for dinner now and then. What was that all about—beyond the father-of-my-grandson thing?"

She shrugged slightly. "That matters to me."

Willy again let silence be his lever.

"I don't know," she finally yielded. "Maybe we connected like him and Kathleen never could. We understood each other." She sighed before adding, "I was a little tough on him before, with that not giving a damn crack. He treated my grandson fine, and to be straight, there were more than a few times when I could've smacked Kathleen myself. She has a real mouth on her."

"Did she know about his visits here?"

"She lives in Florida," Shirley said simply.

He knew that from Mike Bradley. Bradley's crew had gotten a local Florida cop to interview her down there, in part to find out if she had an alibi for the night Brian was shot. She had.

Which, of course, suggested the obvious. Willy tilted his chin at Shirley and asked, "Where were you when Brian died?"

She actually laughed, shaking her head at him. "What about the drug runners?"

He smiled back. "Still on the table."

When he didn't add anything, she was forced to address his question, floating like a balloon between them.

"I was here," she said, and then added, "Alone."

He nodded, took one last sip of his coffee, and stood up.

"Thanks," he said, and left her in her kitchen, lost in her own thoughts.

CHAPTER FIFTEEN

Joe stepped through the doorway, moved aside to let Lester enter after him, and stopped, nodding briefly to the small assemblage before them. There were only four people—three men and a woman—sitting around an undersized conference table littered with coffee cups, pads, a couple of cell phones, and a portable computer. The latter sat open before a square-set man, the only one among them wearing a tie.

The two Vermonters were in Augusta at long last, four miles northwest of downtown, in a tiny section of a sparkling, three-hundred-thousand-square-foot office building, also housing Maine's Department of Public Safety, along with a host of other operations—a complex that made the Vermont counterpart in Waterbury look straight out of Dickens by comparison.

The receptionist with them announced, "Here they are, Mike," and vanished.

Everyone rose. The man in the tie circled the table, hand outstretched, and introduced himself. "Joe? I'm Mike Coven, director of MDEA. I'm really glad to meet you at long last. You have quite the reputation."

Joe laughed and introduced Lester, adding, "You say that too loudly, they might mail me to you in a box, just to get rid of me."

Coven smiled and waved his hand over his colleagues. "This is Kevin Delaney, the outfit's northern commander, and two of his folks, Cathy Lawless and Dave Beaubien."

Joe commented to Cathy, "You were the one who took a swim, if I heard right."

Lawless gave him a wide smile and a firm handshake. "That's me—the MDEA Swim Team."

Chairs were shifted around and spaces cleared at the table to make room for the newcomers. Noticeably, two extra slots were left open.

"Lenny Chapman from ICE and one of his guys are still due," Coven explained, settling back behind the laptop. "You want some coffee, by the way?"

Both men had just used the bathroom in the lobby after their unexpectedly long drive and were happy to leave their bladders be.

Coven nodded and cleared his throat. "Okay. Actually, it's probably just as well that ICE isn't here yet—lets me fill you in on what we do here and how we do it. You know anything about MDEA?" he asked Joe.

The latter shook his head, although he wasn't in fact quite that ignorant. He just liked to take his time with people, and a small lecture from the director seemed as good a starting place as any.

"This organization," Coven began, "was started back in 'eighty-six, but we're actually a task force, and not a full-blown agency, meaning that each of us is still employed by some other state or municipal police agency. That basically makes MDEA a temporary assignment, although, to be honest, a lot of us seem to have made it a career."

He sat back in his chair and propped the sole of one shoe against the edge of the conference table. "The rules of engagement are that if anyone in Maine law enforcement gets a drug case during the course of business, we're supposed to be given a call. This excludes a few of the larger city departments, of course, like Portland, Lewiston, and Bangor, but you get the idea."

He shifted his weight. Joe noticed that the man's colleagues were exhibiting none of the restlessness he would have anticipated among a bunch of cops attending a leader they didn't respect.

"Anyhow," Coven continued, "that's the quick organizational snapshot. We work with other cops all the time, 'cause that's who we are; we also work with the feds a lot, specifically ICE, who have yet to screw us the way the old DEA used to and the FBI still does; and last but not least, we're pretty lean and efficient, and although there aren't enough of us to cover the ground or the caseload, we're pretty well funded and respected by all the players who count, from the politicians on down."

"What're your biggest problems here?" Joe asked.

"The usual stuff," Coven answered. "With the heaviest hitter being prescription drugs. That's taken us by storm. Oxy's the current favorite, and most of it's coming from Canada, because of the price differential."

"Where specifically?" Lester asked.

Coven caught his meaning. "No clue," he answered. "At least, not really. I mean, we catch people crossing all the time, and we know about a lot of activity involving the usual hodgepodge of retirement home rip-offs, crooked docs and pharmacists, and drugstore thefts. But that's not the mother ship. Someone, somewhere, is making a huge killing here, but we don't know who. The Mounties have been consulted, of course, but they're as much in the dark as we are."

"At least they say they are," Cathy Lawless added.

"The Mounties can be closemouthed at times," Kevin Delaney said, speaking for the first time. "I'm not as suspicious as Cathy, but we do have some history of being left in the dark. My personal feeling is that one of the Canadian manufacturers or warehouses has a serious leak, to answer your question, but, as Mike was saying, no one really knows."

"If you don't know its source," Lester asked, "then how do you know it's from Canada?"

Cathy laughed. "It's labeled, believe it or not. At least, the Oxys are. If the pill's marked 'CDN,' it's a product of Canada. 'OC' means the United States, and 'X' stands for Mexico."

There was a sound at the door, and the receptionist reappeared with Lenny Chapman, accompanied by a young, hard-faced woman, quickly introduced as one of the Maine-based ICE agents, named Dede Miller.

Once more, chairs were shifted and coffee offered—and accepted this time—before everyone was back to circling the table.

"So," Chapman asked, "you guys figure out a plan of attack?"

"Les and I were getting a history lesson," Joe told him. "Things are a lot different from back home."

"You folks have the Atlantic Ocean, for one thing," Lester said.

There was a pause, as everyone, his boss included, gave him a questioning look.

Les smiled apologetically. "I meant as a border issue. In Vermont, we just have a line in the sand between Canada and us, except for the lakes."

Still, no one seemed to grasp his point.

He forged ahead. "Luis Grega was last seen at a port, right? And escaped by boat? And for all intents and purposes, he's a smuggler. Made me think of your three thousand miles—plus—of coastline, a lot of it near Canada, and most of it unpatrolled, from what I've read."

"He has a point," Dede Miller said softly.

Again, there was a moment's silence, which Chapman filled with, "Dede's from our Washington County office—we've got about five people covering Washington and Hancock Counties. You've been working here for how long, Dede?"

"Five years," she told him. "And I think . . . Les, was it?"

Lester nodded silently.

". . . I think Les might have something," she continued. "We've been catching people on the dry border, as best we can, but what about the wet border? That was sure as hell the hot spot back in the seventies."

Coven, the most experienced of the group, if just barely ahead of Kevin Delaney, weighed in: "That was also marijuana from South America and elsewhere—not pills stamped from Canada."

"Lobstermen have been smuggling booze and cigarettes for generations," Cathy chimed in.

"Not to mention short lobsters," Delaney added.

"What?" Joe asked.

"Lobsters that're too short to be legal," Delaney explained. "Some guys bring them home instead of tossing them back like they're supposed to, sometimes hidden under the decking of their boats. Old tradition. Lobstermen are kind of like cowboys that way—do what they want because they wander the wet version of the open prairie, I guess."

Joe returned to their primary topic by addressing Miller directly. "Dede, if nobody's been caught importing pills by sea, what makes you think that might be happening now? Isn't something like Fish and Game out there on the job?"

"The Marine Patrol," she corrected him. "Fish and Game is inland. Marine Patrol *is* out there, but not looking for drugs—not specifically. There aren't enough of them. Their focus is the clam diggers, the lobster business . . . They're mostly conservationists, out to protect a cash crop. No disrespect, but they pretty much have to fall over any drugs to notice them."

Joe asked Cathy Lawless, "Did you get any notion that Grega might be working that angle?"

Lawless frowned. "I didn't even know he was there before he poked a gun in my nose."

"Yeah," Joe persisted, "but he was with somebody you knew, right? What about him?"

"Bob?" Cathy exclaimed. "Jesus. I don't know . . . I never thought of him that way." She paused before saying, "No, I don't see it. We met where we did 'cause he thought it was secure, not because he had any ties to the water. Far as I know, he doesn't own a boat and has nothing to do with fishing. Dave?" she asked her partner.

Dave, typically, merely shook his head.

"What happened to Bob, anyhow?" Chapman asked.

"Skipped with Grega," Lawless said, her voice toneless.

"That was hardly your fault," Delaney told her.

"But it is why we're all here, more or less," Joe contributed, adding,

"Somehow, Bob and Grega are connected. We may not have either one available right now, but we must have something on Bob—a way to maybe chase him down."

"Oh, yeah," Cathy acknowledged, ambition overcoming embarrassment. "We can definitely shake that tree, especially with a posse like this."

CHAPTER SIXTEEN

Alan watched Luis Grega carefully, as if looking for something to emerge from his head, which Alan could then use for guidance.

"You worked for Roz how many years?"

Grega parked his feet on the low coffee table facing him. He was sitting on a couch in the back of a restaurant in Jonesport—the sort of place where you ordered your coffee and sandwich from a counter and then took it to either a table or a cluster of easy chairs. The window overlooking the parking lot advertised free Wi-Fi and the speakers played soft pop tunes from the sixties—treacly crap Alan normally couldn't stand. It was a place where no one he knew was likely to visit, full of people wearing fleece and drinking herbal tea.

"I started out as a mule, a few years ago," Grega told him. "Roz liked how I did my job and moved me up."

Alan already knew that. When he was first considering this business for real, back when he was skimming from the pharmaceutical company, he'd applied his college education, if solely for the organizational techniques it had instilled. Having heard about Mroz, he'd quietly interviewed some of the man's people, done the homework without tipping his hand, and finally crunched the numbers. It had cost him a lot of money, wasted a lot of time, exposed him to a lot of losers and liars, and paid off enormously—even if he had ended up doing most of his strategizing in jail.

Along the way, the name of Luis Grega had surfaced as a rising star.

"So, you got to know how the business ran?"

Grega was watching him with his own careful scrutiny. "I did pretty good."

"You know about me, right?" Alan asked him.

"Bernie told me you were the new boss" was the neutral response.

"How's that sit with you?" Bernie had been Mroz's bookkeeper, and was already slated to stay on as Alan's. Still, Alan was interested that Bernie and Grega had been talking, since Bernie was notoriously—even pathologically—self-effacing, to the point of being a hermit.

Grega hesitated, unsure of the question's intent. "Fine," he finally said.

Alan smiled. "Fine? Upwardly mobile guy like you? Some newbie pops up out of nowhere and steals your action, and you're okay with that?"

Grega played along, also pretending to be affable. "I don't see you stealing my action. I'm doin' okay."

"You weren't aiming for the top spot?"

To Alan's satisfaction, Grega looked genuinely surprised. "Roz's?" he asked. "What the fuck I want with that? Bunch of headaches."

"What *are* your ambitions, then, now that there's been a change of leadership?"

Grega looked thoughtful.

"Depends on the leader," he said.

Alan found that acceptable. In fact, what he'd discovered about Luis Grega was that the man had a kind of old-fashioned work ethic. As far as Alan could determine—ironically by also consulting Bernie, among others—Grega was in the game for the money, the adrenaline, and the chance to tell society to screw itself. No tales of betrayal or double dealing dogged his heels, no reports of violence that hadn't seemed appropriate and properly surgical, no troubles with women that might come back to haunt him. As societal fringe operators went, Grega had appeared to be a good soldier.

Which was precisely what Alan was looking for.

Budney pursed his lips. This was a turning point—a final stage in his plan. Matt Mroz had taken the conventional route to his moment in the sunshine. He'd used violence and coercion, a modicum of brains, and the rudiments of leadership to hammer together a loosely knit, porous amalgam of illegal products, import routes, and marginally capable people—the likes of Bernie and Grega notwithstanding—all to create an operation as substantial as a spec house built on sand. It had been a recipe for short-term profits and long-term disaster, at best. Under his aegis, this wobbly, inefficient, careless operation had grabbed for everything, let a lot slip through its fingers, and had largely trusted to luck for its success. Bernie had admitted as much in a frustrated outburst days earlier. Had it been run in a less rural state, according to Bernie, where there was more law enforcement and a hotter sense of moral outrage, it would have collapsed long ago. That had explained why the bookkeeper had stayed out of the limelight.

But Mroz had been lucky—he'd lasted for quite a while. Until Alan had taken him on.

Now, things were ripe for an overhaul, where the product line would be streamlined for maximum profits, diminished loss, and minimal exposure to assault from the police.

It was in this last category that Alan saw a role for Luis Grega.

"Well," he told him, "this leader's big on recognizing hard work and loyalty. I'd like to talk to you about a role you may not have thought about before."

Grega nodded silently, not really understanding what this man was babbling about, but not much caring, either. In the short term, it meant more money—so much was becoming clear. Beyond that, it didn't matter, since Luis had his own big plans.

"Hey, there," Joe said into the phone, shoving the motel's thin pillow more comfortably behind his neck.

"Hey, yourself," Lyn answered him, her voice low and soft. "How's my favorite cop?"

"Not bad. It took us forever to get here. I always forget how big this state is."

She laughed. "I remember. We used to bug Dad about that every time he took us on those so-called vacations, asking him to pull over so we could eat, or stretch our legs, or have a pee—or do *anything*.

He always held on to the wheel like Ahab at the tiller. What is it about you men that you can't mix fun with business?"

"I don't know," Joe told her honestly. "The hunter/gatherer instinct?"

"Right," she came back. "Blame the caveman. Any progress?"

"Some," he said. "We met the Maine team—good bunch. There's a woman who reminds me a bit of Sammie, except she talks a lot more. Mostly, we just kicked around our options."

"You better have a better spiel before you come back to Vermont," she warned him. "That's not gonna wow 'em."

"Wow who?"

"The press. They're grumbling about an informational black hole. Who's Stan Katz, by the way?"

Joe's eyebrows shot up. Opposite him, across the room, the muted TV tried informing him about the vagaries of dandruff.

"He's the editor of the *Reformer*. Why?"

"He called me," she said.

"At your home?" he exclaimed, impressed by both his old nemesis's lack of decorum and the accuracy of his information. Joe's relationship with Lyn was not a secret, but he, like all cops, liked to keep his personal life private. "What did he want?"

"He was looking for you. He was really nice."

Joe struggled to remember if he'd ever heard that adjective applied to Stan before. When Joe worked for the Brattleboro police, Katz was a constant source of irritation, his integrity and accuracy barely compensating for his holier-than-thou, voice-of-the-people arrogance. He was a reporter back then, of course, always hot on the scent. They'd eventually moved him up to editor, and the paper changed hands to become a corporate pawn of some midwestern be-hemoth. Finally, even Stanley had aged and slowed down a little. But, become nice?

"He didn't just hang up when you told him I wasn't there, did he?" Joe asked, anticipating the answer.

"Oh, no," she answered cheerfully. "We had a great talk."

Joe rolled his eyes.

"He got a little worked up toward the end, trying to get me to agree that the cops should be less closemouthed, and that paranoia was a poor substitute for the—what did he call it? Oh, right—the re-sponsible management of information."

"That sounds like him," Joe murmured.

"I didn't disagree," she added, "but I also told him squat. He ended up telling me that he thought we made a perfect couple."

Joe now understood what she'd meant by having had a great chat. Katz must have been ready to reach through the phone and kill her.

"How *is* the news about the case?" he asked. "Have you gotten a sense of that?"

"I'd have to be deaf and blind. It's all over the place. Katz, I just told you about, and some guy named McDonald is on the local ra-dio every day griping about it. TV has it on every night. It's a big deal, a cop getting shot in the head."

Joe closed his eyes briefly. "Yeah—that it is."

When she spoke next, her voice was softer—more concerned. "You sound a little down. It's not going well, is it?"

"Not particularly. Everybody's on board and helping, but we don't have much to go on. Grega's the proverbial needle in a haystack; the guy he was last seen with has vanished; we can't seem to get a break, despite beating the bushes."

After a brief silence, Lyn softly asked, in part to herself, "I wonder if Steve might know anything."

Joe frowned at the phone. "Your brother? I thought you weren't talking."

It came out too bluntly, and he regretted it immediately. "I'm sorry."

"No, no," she answered. "You're totally right. We haven't talked since he got out. But it wasn't because we were mad at each other. Disappointed . . ." Her voice trailed off.

"Anyhow," she continued after a moment, "he used to know people up there. I suppose that kind of information changes all the time . . ." She added a small, ineffectual laugh. "God knows, it did for him. I certainly don't mind asking."

"Wouldn't that be a little awkward?" Joe asked.

"Not like you'd think," she told him. "Steve and I were always pretty straight with each other. That's one of the reasons all this hurt so much. But the more I think about it, this may be exactly what I need to open things up again, or at least try . . . I'm not so sure what he's like anymore."

Joe considered what she was offering. "Lyn, I really appreciate it, but think about this, and only do it if you believe it might help you get back together, okay? It's a long shot—like you said—so it's certainly not worth breaking your heart all over again."

"I love you, Joe Gunther" was all she said before hanging up.

CHAPTER SEVENTEEN

Lester slapped his face several times in succession. "Christ almighty. How can a place *have* so many bugs? I thought we were bad, but this is ridiculous. Aren't they driving you nuts?"

Joe glanced at him sympathetically, reached into his pocket, and handed over a small bottle of high-test repellent. "May shorten your life, but do you care?"

"No," his colleague said forcefully, reaching out. "Give me that."

He began lathering it onto his neck and into his ears.

"Watch your eyes," Joe cautioned. "It'll sting like hell."

"Who's this guy supposed to be?" Lester asked, keeping his voice low and daubing his cheeks and forehead. He'd just returned from an emergency trip back home, where his daughter had broken an ankle in a soccer game. They were lying side by side under a huge blue sky, the prickly, heatherlike undergrowth poking at them through their clothing, and the black flies forming clouds around their heads. They and several others—some of whom were wearing head nets—were positioned just shy of the crest of a low hill, overlooking a house that sat in the field before them like a toy left on a rough wool blanket by a giant child.

"It's a woman. Remember Bob? The dealer Cathy Lawless was trying to hustle when Grega popped up and started shooting? It's his common-law wife."

"What's her name?"

"Jill Zachary, according to Dave Beaubien."

Lester stared at him. "You got him to talk?"

Joe smiled and shook his head. "Hardly—that's all he said."

He cupped his chin in his hand, the stink of fly dope strong in his nostrils, and went back to studying the house. There was nothing extraordinary about it, aside from its setting. It was two-storied, with an attached garage, slowly losing its coat of pale blue paint. Its foundation was still girthed in plastic and hay bales against the winter chill, although such weather had long gone. But that detail, and the cheery color, had already struck Joe as a distinctly Maine attribute. Winters were long here, and bleak, especially in those parts without either mountains or seascape to relieve the eye. The need for warmth spoke for itself, but the thirst for color was important. And while both may have seemed unnecessary during the summer months, they spoke to the inevitable forthcoming cold, along with this state's admission that, like it or not, it would always be a grandchild of glaciers.

But the condition of the building's paint was as evocative as its isolation. Maine was a vast piece of real estate, some of it remote and difficult to reach, not to mention ill-suited to sustaining a living. Most Mainers admitted that the two southernmost counties, York and Cumberland, carried the financial load for the rest. These others tended to be thinly populated, economically depressed, and politically undermuscled.

Jill Zachary's home, peeling, worn, and looking as if it could be wiped from the earth with a sweep of the hand, was testimony of both grit and fragile impermanence.

Joe took a moment to scan the bare horizon, realizing that some of his conclusions were being influenced by the starkness around him. Of course, this wasn't typical—Maine encompassed almost every geographical trait natural to the continent. There were entire sections of swamps, fields, mountains, and forestland—areas where you would swear that all the land around you had to be exemplary of the whole.

But none of it was. Maine evolved as it spread across the map, changing at an almost leisurely pace from one topography to the next. Vermont, by contrast, was known for being lumpy—big lumps for the Green Mountains; smaller ones for the rolling farmland edging Lake Champlain. Each of Maine's characteristics, however, was distinct and placed far apart—the coastline was at odds with the peaks around Katahdin; the forests of the north country out of synch with the bracken fields farther south; the rushing white rapids inland belied the broad, lazy, watery boulevards pouring into the ocean.

It was as if Maine had been created when both a lot of spare parts and the leisure to spread them out had been available.

This very house, for example, was surrounded for as far as the eye could see by blueberry fields—low, curvilinear, painted rust red and ochre and dull green. It was too early for the berry harvest, so the scene merely looked wild, although it was a highly prized and much tended environment. But to Joe, it seemed like it would all make more sense located in Greenland, or near the Hudson Bay. Huge, extended, and billowy—a near-barren landscape better suited to the Wessex of Thomas Hardy seemed odd in a state whose symbol was a lobster.

"We sure Bob's in residence?" Lester asked, breaking into Joe's reverie.

"One of Cathy's CIs told her he was here two days ago," he said.

Lenny Chapman, sporting his dark blue windbreaker with "ICE" stenciled across the back, sidled up to where they were lying, making sure not to show himself beyond the top of the rise. He carried a pair of binoculars and also smelled strongly of repellent.

"Hey, G-man," Lester greeted him, "got any skin left?"

Chapman laughed. "Amazing, ain't it? Worst bugs in New England. Everybody's in place around the perimeter," he told them both. "We got vehicles hidden and ready to block the road in case someone makes a run for it, and one of the MDEA people just got a movement sighting from inside the building."

"That movement attached to anyone like Bob or Zachary?" Joe asked.

Chapman gave the hint of a shrug, still intent on the house. "One step at a time, Joe. At least we know the place is occupied."

It was certainly that, as was proven two seconds later when the front door banged open far below them and a young boy, ten or twelve, stepped out into the yard, a large plastic trash bag in his hand.

The three men on the back side of the knoll instinctively hunkered down. Chapman muttered into his radio, "We have someone at the front door—pre-teen male in sneakers, jeans, and white T-shirt, holding a black garbage bag. Everyone hold their positions."

Instinctively, Lester twisted his dark baseball cap around so the bill faced the nape of his neck before he raised his head just enough to take a peek.

"What do you see?" Joe asked him.

Les ducked back down. "It ain't good."

Chapman finished for him by saying over the radio, "Subject is heading uphill, toward the east, still carrying the bag."

"That's us, right?" Joe asked softly.

"Straight as an arrow," Lester confirmed.

"Shit," Chapman muttered, sliding down and looking around quickly. He pointed at a pile of small plastic bags and debris, barely visible in a ditch far behind them. "I bet the little bastard is dumping the garbage. I shoulda caught that detail."

He addressed the radio again, "All units. We are assuming subject is on a garbage run. We will apprehend as he reaches our position. Stand by."

In the meantime, Lester had snatched another fast glance, only to look back at them, his eyes wide, to report, "You got three seconds. He's at a dead run."

No sooner had he said this when the boy topped the low hill and came to an abrupt stop, the bag still swinging in his hand.

"Who're you guys?" he asked.

Chapman didn't bother answering. He lunged at the kid instead, hoping to gain control first, before any long-winded explanations.

He missed. Exhibiting surprising grace, the boy nimbly leaped backward and smacked Chapman across the head with his bag, blinding him with a sudden shower of strewn garbage. Joe and Lester looked like geriatric gymnasts as they stumbled to their feet and tried to give chase.

"Subject's on the run, back to the house," Chapman shouted into his mike, adding, "Hold your positions," as the boy screamed, sprinting away at full tilt, *"Mom. Cops."*

Instinctively in pursuit, but trailing by several yards, Joe looked beyond the retreating boy to see the front door open and reveal a tall, skinny woman with long black hair. No doubt trained by past experience, she instantly assessed the scene, shouted something over her shoulder, and slammed the door against all comers, her son included. Even at a full run, Joe could appreciate her street smarts, if not her maternal instincts—the boy was in safer hands among cops than he might be inside that house.

Behind them, Les and Joe heard Chapman yelling, *"Hold it, hold it.* Go to cover. They could have guns in there."

It was a good point—which Joe was embarrassed he hadn't heeded. Abandoning the chase, he cut right and slid to a stop behind one of the boulders that dotted the landscape like oversized marbles.

Les skidded in right behind him. "That would've been awkward."

"Yeah," Joe growled, quoting the possible headline, "Idiot Vermonters Caught in Cross Fire; Local Police Baffled by Stupidity."

Lester laughed between panting. "Hey, you might've caught the brat."

But Joe was not to be comforted. "Did you see the distance he was putting between us? He deserves a track medal."

They peered out from behind their rock to see what had happened to the subject of their conversation. The boy was pounding fruitlessly on the door with both fists, screaming for entry.

"Ouch," Les said, "that's not going to go down well at family counseling."

Lenny Chapman had come to rest behind a boulder some twenty

feet away from them. Picking shreds of garbage off his jacket with a disgusted expression, he shouted across, "You two all right?"

Les answered for them both, "Yeah—sorry 'bout that. Thought we could catch him."

Chapman waved his hand dismissively. "No sweat. Might've worked." They saw him raise the mike to his mouth again to utter more commands they could no longer hear.

But the day's surprises had just begun. Lester pointed to the closed double doors of the slightly sagging attached garage and asked, "Hear that?"

Before Joe could answer, there was a large cracking sound, and the doors blew apart under the weight of an oversized, much-battered pickup truck. A man was at the wheel; the dark-haired woman sitting beside him.

"Jesus," Les let out. "It's Bonnie and Clyde."

Joe wasn't watching them as the truck fishtailed out of the garage and tore down the dirt driveway. His eyes were on the boy, who, with equal disbelief, watched, rooted in place, as his mother chose her companion over him. Whatever family counseling there'd be would be taking place in jail—and only if everyone was lucky.

Over the roar of the truck's engine, Joe heard Chapman ordering up the roadblock. The ICE agent was running toward them as he spoke.

"The house empty?" Joe asked.

"We got people checking," Chapman told him, pointing. "Better head for our car in the meantime."

They began jogging back over the hill that had once shielded them from the house, just as the truck abandoned the driveway and went lurching 'cross country, rendering moot the roadblock around the corner. They could see several people breaking cover over the open landscape—a cross section of ICE and MDEA agents, along with a couple of uniformed locals, perhaps ten people in all not counting the few on the roadblock. Joe saw Cathy Lawless heading their way at top speed, ludicrously tearing off a netted hat.

"Smart boy, old Bob," Lester gasped, picking up speed to keep up with Chapman, who was running at full tilt.

The three of them, now joined by Cathy, piled into Chapman's black Suburban, its interior alive with radio chatter, and, with Chapman driving, tore away, tires spinning, hoping to catch up to the pickup before it was swallowed whole by the Maine countryside. Fortunately, there were few if any trees for miles around, and the hilly terrain—as on a storm-tossed sea—afforded them occasional sweeping views of their surroundings.

There was also the radio. Chapman passed it to Joe as he concentrated on his driving.

"This is Gunther," the latter announced. "We're mobile in Chapman's car. Any sightings or coordinates?"

"They're headed southwest," said a voice. "Toward where the road loops back around."

Lawless glanced up at the electronic compass mounted to the Suburban's roof. "Should be ahead of us somewhere."

Chapman powered up a hill, all four wheels tearing into the delicate ground cover, before bursting upon a sweeping view of the terrain to the southwest, to startling effect.

"Bingo," he said unnecessarily, as they were already staring at the pickup, careening over the rough ground ahead of them by about two hills, its skittery motion adding to the setting's tempestuous maritime feeling.

Chapman accelerated. Joe flattened the palm of his hand against the roof to steady himself.

"They're not gonna make it," said a different voice over the radio.

"Why not?" Gunther asked.

"There's a seasonal riverbed ahead of them, and it's still got water."

Chapman roared downhill, hit the bottom of the swale ahead with a bone-jarring thud, and flew up the opposing slope, as before. Joe began thinking that his final ocean-related metaphor might end up being seasickness.

"There they are," Cathy called out, pointing between them from the backseat.

Not far in front, at the bottom of the hill they'd just topped, the pickup had reached the edge of a thin, sharp-edged stream, unbreachable at right angles. The truck driver, realizing the same thing, but too late and traveling too fast, cut to his left, either to find another way or hoping to flatten the angle. In any case, the height of the truck and his own momentum betrayed him, as his rear wheels slithered sideways, caught the downward edge of the embankment, and dragged the rest of the vehicle over.

Chapman finally slowed somewhat as they saw the truck first teeter—still driving fast with a forty-five-degree list—and then tumble onto its side and into the shallow water in an explosion of mud and debris.

"Jesus," Spinney half whispered at the sight.

The Suburban skidded to a halt some fifty feet from the wreck, and all four occupants quickly got out, their eyes glued to whatever movement might emerge from the partially submerged truck.

"Slow, slow," Chapman cautioned, his gun out, keeping near the hood in case he needed cover. "We don't know if they're armed."

"We also don't know if they're drowning," Cathy reasonably pointed out, nevertheless staying put.

But Joe knew Chapman was right. Officer safety came first, and Joe had acted precipitately once already.

There was movement from the truck at last. A head with long black hair appeared from under the water on the submerged passenger side.

"*Federal agents,*" Chapman shouted. "*Move away from the truck and keep your hands where I can see them.*"

On the wreck's far side, something flashed, like the wave of an arm, and then another head appeared briefly, before ducking back down.

Chapman repeated his command.

Instinctively, Joe, Lester, and Cathy spread out along the riverbank, doubled over and guns drawn, taking advantage of whatever obstacles they could find for cover.

Jill Zachary stayed on her knees, perhaps partially pinned, her face now visibly looking in their direction. But her companion once more began moving on the far side of the truck, suddenly holding up something over his head.

A distant shot rang out and the arm vanished before any of them could figure out what the object had been.

Over the radio, a voice announced, "Suspect down, suspect down."

Chapman and Joe exchanged glances from their respective places, before seeing—on top of the rise across the stream—a man in a state police uniform slowly stand up, a scope-equipped rifle in his hands.

"Shit," Joe heard Lenny Chapman growl, before he broke cover and began moving cautiously toward the truck, his gun still pointed in its direction.

Joe and the others joined him as Jill Zachary began yelling, *"What've you done? What've you bastards done to him?"*

"Do not move, lady," Chapman repeated, getting closer. "Or you will be shot."

Joe stepped into the cold, rushing water and, with Cathy close behind him, peered carefully around the edge of the upturned truck's rear bumper.

Splayed out in the stream, his face down and submerged, his arms outstretched and with a rifle in one hand, lay the driver of the truck.

Joe and Cathy picked their way slowly toward him, noting the bloodred ribbon of water emanating from the body's head, bright at its source, but a pale pink some ten feet farther down.

"I get him?"

They both glanced at the young trooper, now standing on the bank, impressed by the comment's inanity. The man's expression told them nothing.

Lawless couldn't resist. "Gee—what d'ya think?"

Joe, shielded from Jill Zachary's protests by the bulk of the truck and the sound of running water, stooped by the body's head and gingerly reached out for the rifle. He retrieved it without resistance, wedged it against the truck, and then felt for a carotid pulse. There was nothing.

"He's dead," he told Cathy, who passed along the news over her radio.

Joe then took up the rifle again—a bolt action, iron sights, .223 Remington—and checked the chamber. There was nothing there.

"I don't dare ask," Cathy said.

He looked over his shoulder. Lester was standing beside her.

"Empty" was all he said.

"Could you see what he was trying to do, just before he went down?" Lester asked.

They looked at each other, knowing the implications. Joe took in the trooper, out of earshot but still staring at the body, his face as pale and blank as before.

"I'd only be guessing," Joe answered.

Cathy didn't respond. Lester merely said, "Me, too."

On the truck's far side, though, they could hear Zachary's voice even better, now that she'd been pulled from the wreckage, accusing them all of murdering her husband.

Joe leaned over and twisted the body's head to one side, allowing Cathy to see its face. Black flies were already hovering close by. "That Bob?"

She nodded once, undeterred by the blood still leaking from the hole in his temple. "What's left of him."

Joe sighed. "Great."

CHAPTER EIGHTEEN

Lenny Chapman, Cathy Lawless, and Joe Gunther stood side by side, looking through the one-way mirror into the interrogation room containing a bedraggled Jill Zachary. Her long, matted, mud-streaked black hair contrasted starkly with the yellow blanket wrapped around her shoulders.

"Technically," Lawless was saying to Joe, "you're the reason we're all here." She jerked her chin at the woman in the other room and added, "Including her."

"You sure?" Joe asked. "This is a federal case, on your turf. Seems a stretch to give me first shot."

Chapman laughed softly. "Jesus, you *are* the diplomat. Both those agencies are standing right here, Joe, telling you to take a crack at her. Go for it."

Joe conceded with a smile. "You just don't want to keep hearing how we murdered Bob in cold blood."

"Right," Cathy agreed with a smile.

In fact, none of them was particularly worried about that. They

were all veterans; they couldn't swear what Bob had intended—
suicide by cop was common enough; and they knew the trooper was
likely to be found innocent by Internal Affairs, if overly enthusiastic.
Plus, in the final analysis, they also shared the belief that Bob had
made his own choices.

"We've got nothing so far, right?" he asked them. "From the
house or the kid?"

"Not so far," Cathy acknowledged.

He nodded finally. "All right, I'll see what I can get."

Zachary started violently at his entrance, as if she'd been dozing
off, which she might have been, given her recent adrenaline rush.

"Ms. Zachary," he said. "My name's Gunther."

"When am I getting out of here?" she demanded, twisting in her
chair and glaring up at him.

He crossed to the other metal chair in the stark room and sat
down.

"I have a child to take care of," she persisted.

He didn't show how that struck him, and didn't plan to until he
got a better handle on how to deal with her.

"I understand that," he answered instead. "But you have to know
we've got a couple of questions for you. Your son is with Child Serv-
ices for the moment, and being well taken care of. He seems like a
nice guy."

"You saw him?" she asked, which he should have expected.

He hedged his answer, since he hadn't seen the boy since the car
chase. "Yeah. He's doing fine."

Her face hardened, as if he'd just delivered an insult. "He can be
a jackass."

He didn't rise to the bait. "Can't they all?"

She shook her head and added, "Just like his goddamn father."

"He was a handful, too?" Joe asked.

Again, she flared up, fixing him with a baleful stare. "He didn't deserve what you people did to him. Fucking cops."

"That was bad," Joe conceded.

Her brow furrowed in confusion.

"People do the craziest things when they get in a jam," he went on. "Turn a relatively small thing into a huge deal, all because they didn't stop and think for a second."

She tilted her head to one side slightly. "What're you talking about?"

He smiled, sensing she knew all too well. "Grabbing that rifle; taking off, when all we wanted to do was ask him a few questions."

Her eyes widened. "Are you shitting me? You were after him for shooting at that cop."

Joe dropped his jaw in theatrical surprise, although he was embarrassed to have been taken off guard. *Of course* the Bobs of the world would tell a lie like that to look good. "He told you that?"

"You saying it's not true?" she challenged.

"Absolutely," he said. "Bob was just trying to score a deal. The guy he was with fired those shots."

She seemed stunned by the news, staring off into some middle space, as if in consultation. "That asshole."

"Like I said," Joe resumed conversationally. "People do the craziest things."

She focused back on him, struck by a sudden thought. "Then why were you all around the house? I saw you people when we drove out of there. You were everywhere."

Joe looked back at her with an appealing expression. "Think of the company we last saw him keeping. We didn't know if that other guy was still around. We were a lot less happy about running into *him* unprepared."

"Such a creep," she muttered.

"You met him?"

Her face darkened. "Yeah, I met him. Bob brought him to the house, the stupid jerk. A real cocky bastard, bragging about how tough he was, and all his prospects."

"He offer to make Bob a partner?" Joe asked. "Maybe that explains why Bob invited him home."

She pressed her lips together tightly before answering, "I don't know. They didn't talk much in front of us. It was all secret, secret shit, like they were boys in a special club or something. I figured it was more drug business, anyhow. I kept telling him that would get him screwed someday."

"I heard you two had your troubles," Joe commented sympathetically. "That must've been tough."

"It was a pain in the butt," she said angrily.

"What was he doing with that guy, anyway?" Joe asked. "What was his name?"

"Grega," she said bitterly. "Luis." She pronounced it "Lu-eece," with a mocking flair, adding, "He thought he was a real lady's man. Typical."

Joe let the ethnic implication slide. "You think he was pitching a big deal to Bob?"

"All I know is that Bob was real hyper, talking about getting us out of the rut. That's what he called it, as if what we had was so terrible." She looked up at him accusingly, her eyes narrowed with anger.

"What is it with guys? Always so worked up about hitting the big time. What the hell's wrong with life the way it is?"

Joe shrugged, struck by a vaguely similar remark he'd heard from Lyn. "The culture, I guess. The American Dream."

"Fuck the American Dream. That's what I say."

Joe returned to the reason they were here, "Still, you got into that truck with him when Bob ran for it."

She looked away, thoughtful and a little lost. When she returned to him, there were tears in her eyes. "He was such a kid, you know? Our son was more grown-up than him."

Joe let a moment's silence elapse before asking, "What happened to Luis?"

Her voice was distracted. "Who cares?"

He leaned forward, his elbows on his knees, as if sharing a confidence. "You might ought to," he suggested quietly.

Zachary wiped her eyes with the palms of both hands. "What do you mean?"

He dropped his voice even lower. "I'm not one of the local cops. I was brought in from outside, but I know what they're saying. With Bob dead and Luis missing, you're about all they got."

She looked stunned. "What're you saying? I didn't do anything."

He held his finger to his lips, cautioning a lower tone. "You and I know that, but they better have something to show. Like you said, it was a big operation, cost a lot of money."

Her face darkened as she hissed, "They killed my fucking husband. That cost me, too."

"And who do you have left?" he asked her, all sympathy. "You don't want to risk losing him, too."

It was an old gag—a cynical manipulation. In fact, Joe had his doubts that mother and child would ever share a roof again, given what had happened. Of course, the flip side of his implication also failed the grade—Jill Zachary hadn't even been charged with an offense. She was free to go whenever she chose.

Thankfully, she grasped neither reality. Instead, her eyes widened in alarm. "Risk losing him? What the hell are you talking about?"

Joe chanced reaching out and touching her damp, blue-jeaned knee, establishing friendly contact. "About throwing them a bone. Show them you're the innocent bystander here. You've got a life to lead, Jill—you and your son, both. Hasn't all this cost you enough already?"

She was looking genuinely perplexed. "I told you: I don't know nuthin'. They didn't talk in front of me, and I didn't listen anyhow."

"You knew about Luis. You knew his name."

She straightened, surprised. "That's what you're talking about?"

He nodded. "Everything and anything. Names of people Bob brought by; descriptions of their cars; any dates you can remember; pieces of conversation you might've overheard. All of it."

She rubbed her forehead. "Jesus H. Christ. Who gives a shit?"

"You hope they will," he suggested.

She sat back and stared at the ceiling, visibly casting about for a solution. Finally, she fixed him with an intense look.

"Bernie," she said. "They talked about Bernie."

"Who's Bernie?"

"How the hell do I know?" she exclaimed. "You wanted a name. There's a name."

"You ever see him?"

"No. They just mentioned him. I walked in to ask if they wanted dinner, once, and I heard Bob talking. He yelled at me because of it."

"Did you get any feeling for who he *might* be?" Joe asked, keeping his tone just shy of bored, adding, "A dealer, maybe, or a big customer?"

But Jill was adamant, shaking her head. "No. That's why Bob got pissed at me later. He asked me what I'd heard, and I told him. Same as you—it was just a name. Stupid part was, I only knew it was important 'cause he got all worked up. It still never meant anything to me."

Joe absorbed that for a moment, and then got to his feet. "And you never heard Bernie mentioned again?"

"No."

He went to move, as if he was done, and then stopped, pretending that he'd just remembered something—in fact, the biggest reason he was here at all.

"Jill," he said, "when Luis was bragging and putting on a show for you, did he ever talk about having been to Vermont?"

"Vermont? No."

"How 'bout something that might've happened there? A shooting?"

Her eyes widened slightly. "He shot somebody?"

Joe leaned toward her, sharing a secret. "It was a cop, Jill. That's what I was talking about earlier, when I was telling you how important it is to play ball. These guys are serious—this is literally a federal case. They can throw away the key."

He had her attention.

"Luis Grega mentioned nothing about shooting a cop in Vermont?" he repeated.

Her face turned sullen. "I told you."

He crossed the small room and put his hand on the doorknob. "I'll have somebody come in with a recorder, Jill. You'll like her—she's not one of the boys, in more ways than one. Tell her what you told me, with as many details as you can remember. I guarantee you it'll help."

He left the room, closed the door, and raised his eyebrows at Cathy Lawless. "You ready to sweet talk her out of some memories? I figured I'd use you since you'd probably know any names she might mention."

The MDEA agent smiled broadly at him. "You are an evil man, Joe Gunther. I hope they know that in Vermont."

He shook his head. "They think I'm a saint. Did Bernie ring any bells with you, by the way?"

But Cathy shook her head. "Not offhand—and definitely not as a major leaguer."

Later that night, Joe was again on the phone with Lyn. As usual, he was lying flat on his back in the motel room, his head propped against a bunched-up pillow, the TV on but muted. Balanced on his chest was an open can of Vienna sausages and a Cheez Whiz dispenser. Dinner was consisting of a careful line of the latter being applied periodically along the abbreviated length of one of the former, all washed down with occasional swigs of Coke. A small bag of barbecue-flavored chips was by his side, ostensibly for roughage. The phone was cradled, hands free, against his ear. Lyn had called him in the middle of his meal. As was his habit when on the road—and whenever possible—he'd been watching a western.

"Not at the bar tonight?" he asked her.

"It's Penny's turn. I'm on tomorrow. You don't want to know how we came up with this schedule. Very much a girl thing—lots of compromise and sacrifice and hidden resentment."

His laughter made the can shake on its perch.

"How did things go today?" she asked.

"Not great," he admitted, thinking of how best to describe the unintended shooting of a prime suspect, followed by several hours of gathering near useless information from the man's widow. "We had a lead that didn't pan out."

"Still no Grega?"

"Still no Grega," he conceded.

"I spoke to Steve today," she said, her voice neutral.

Joe had been absentmindedly gazing at the screen across the room. At that, he reached out for the remote by the bag of chips, hit the Off button, and responded, "How did that go?"

"He was very sweet," she said. "It had been a long time, like I said, and he felt badly about that. We talked about the family, or what's left of it, and how we both played a role in letting things slide. He was really interested in trying to pick up some of the pieces."

"Great," Joe murmured, adding support while not wanting to interrupt. He was dearly hoping this was heading somewhere he wanted to go.

"Anyhow," she continued, "he asked how I was, and if I was seeing anyone. One thing led to another, and I told him how you were working on a drug case in Maine, and how I'd mentioned his past involvement with Matt Mroz, or how he'd *wanted* to be involved, at least."

"That go over all right?" Joe asked.

"Better than I thought," she reported, still obviously relieved. "He laughed about it, and was very open. It made it easier to ask him if he might help."

"Did he think he could?"

"He said he'd be happy to try, Joe. He stressed, like we thought he would, that a lot of water's gone under the bridge, but he was willing to give you what little he had, in his words."

"That's great," Joe told her, although considering what they'd extracted from Jill Zachary, he wasn't overly hopeful.

"One condition, though," Lyn added. "He's a little insecure about meeting you one-on-one, and asked if I could be there."

"Sure," Joe agreed readily. "What's he have in mind?"

She hesitated. "What do you mean?"

"Would he like me to travel to wherever he is?"

"Oh," her voice lightened. "No, no. He saw this as a trip to Maine. He'd be like a guide—show you places he'd been, describe people he knew. He said that otherwise he wouldn't be much use, since most everyone in the business uses either first names, street names, or fake ones."

Joe frowned at this, caught off guard. "I didn't know he did much business in Maine."

"I didn't, either," she admitted. "I thought it was something he was planning to do, but it turns out that's how he heard about Mroz in the first place. He'd been up there a bunch of times and was learning who some of the players were."

Given Joe's other options, this didn't strike him as a stretch. "I think he's got a deal, Lyn," he said. "I really appreciate it. Let me fly it by my handlers up here, so I don't step on any toes, and I'll let you know. But in any case, thank Steve a lot for me. It's a generous offer, and much appreciated."

They hung up after sharing a few more exchanges on other topics, Joe enjoying the growing familiarity that was developing between them. As he stared afterward at the now blank TV set, his food all but forgotten, he mused over the serendipity that he could deepen his knowledge of her background, while maybe also advancing the case. If Chapman and Cathy Lawless were agreeable, this might be a way to shake things up from an unexpected angle.

God knows, they were due for a break.

CHAPTER NINETEEN

Willy raised his eyebrows. "You saying I can't talk to him without pissing him off?"

Sammie cupped her cheek in her hand, her elbow resting on the arm of her chair, and smiled at him. "Maybe if you're asking him about the weather."

Willy scowled. "You are so full of shit."

"Takes one to know one," she answered him. "That's my point. He's got a reputation like yours, although, God knows, I doubt he's in the same ballpark."

"I never heard of him before now."

"And you know for sure he's heard of you?" she asked.

"We're both cops."

She remained silent, allowing the absurdity of his comeback to float in the air. They were sharing a motel room in South Burlington, their home-away-from-home while assigned to Mike Bradley's office. Not that Bradley or his people necessarily knew of their relationship. It wasn't something they hid—especially in a state that functioned like a small village—but they'd found it easier not to have to explain it to everyone. Besides, given Willy's high profile among social dysfunctionals, all Sammie usually got for telling people about the two of them was a look of incredulity.

"What I'm saying," she continued, "is that I might fly under the radar better than you—avoid the whole testosterone thing you guys get going."

To her surprise, he suddenly capitulated, reaching for the TV remote and hitting the On switch. "Whatever," he said sullenly.

She watched him for a moment, sitting on the bed in his T-shirt and shorts. He was a head case—she knew that. Or, at least she understood what other people meant when they described him as such. But she also knew more—about his combat-born PTSD in the military, his struggles with alcohol, a painful divorce, and a difficult childhood in New York City. He had teetered on the edge all of his life—even losing his job with the Brattleboro police after being crippled early on, until Joe got him rehired under the Americans with Disabilities Act.

Willy Kunkle was no prince, but he kept coming back, and despite a personality about as cuddly as a guard dog's, he always stayed on the side of the righteous, not just regarding the job, but with her, as well. For that last attribute alone he was a rarity in her life, she who'd previously made a habit of only associating with men who kicked her in the teeth. Willy might have been a mess in many ways, but he was more loyal to her than anyone she'd ever known, which made her about the only person who understood why Gunther always went to bat for Willy, whenever his ways jeopardized his job.

"So, we're good?" she asked, risking his ire to make sure.

He surprised her again, as he often did, by hitting the Mute button on the remote and smiling instead of lashing out. "Yeah, we're good. No point putting two assholes in the same room. All we'd do is get in a pissing match. Tell me what you find out."

Doug Boyer lived in a trailer park somewhere between Addison and Vergennes—a sprawling, scraped-together collection of modest but maintained homes haphazardly aligned along both sides of a dirt horseshoe that backed up against a copse of second-growth trees, reminding Sammie of a pile of piglets, all lumped against their mother's belly. Around them, the rolling hills of this part of agricultural Vermont looked exposed and faintly vulnerable—a sensation enhanced by the ominous twin mountain ranges to the distant east and west.

Sam drove slowly past the trailers, scanning what numbers she could locate, until One Forty-eight finally drew abreast. She pulled off onto the grass and got out.

Almost immediately, she saw a man standing by the corner of the trailer, watching her, his body half hidden, as if he expected her to open fire. She recognized him from the personnel file that she'd read at the sheriff's office.

"Deputy Boyer?" she asked officially.

"You the one who called?" was his answer. He had apparently seen her approaching through the window and had come out to meet her. His manner was guarded, bordering on hostile.

"Yeah," she replied, holding out a hand in greeting. He shook it without enthusiasm, obviously wishing he didn't have to.

"What do you want?" he asked bluntly, skipping the amenities.

"We're looking into Brian's death, like I told you on the phone," she said. "I was hoping you might be able to help nail whoever did it."

He straightened slightly, as if struck by an offensive odor. "You got a tape of whoever did it."

Sam gave him a half smile, looking straight into his eyes. "We got a tape, but we don't have the man on it, and we don't know much about him."

"You saying Brian did?"

She shook her head. "I am not. Right now, it just looks like Brian was in the wrong place at the wrong time. But you worked with him, spent time with him, sure knew him better than I did. I'm trying to get a sense of the man, pure and simple. For all we know, that car got itself stopped on purpose, just so those guys could whack him for some reason we know nothing about."

Doug Boyer raised his eyebrows. "That how you VBI guys think?"

She kept the smile in place. "Apparently. Will you help me out?"

"I got a choice?"

"You don't want to?" she shot back.

Her meaning spoke for itself. Boyer dropped his gaze to the grass between them and snorted once. "Jesus. Our tax dollars at work." He turned on his heel and walked around the corner of the trailer, speaking as he went. "Might as well be comfortable, if we're gonna do this."

Sam followed along the length of the home to a flimsy aluminum set of stairs leading up to a narrow front door. Boyer preceded her, letting the screen door swing back and almost hit her in the head. When she got inside, she found herself in a gloomy living room/kitchen combination, lived in but not a mess, with every visible item looking purchased from a ten-year-old Kmart clearance sale. The TV was on quietly, showing a college football game.

Boyer sat wearily on the worn couch facing the set, reached for a can of beer he'd previously abandoned on the nearby coffee table, and took a swig. He wiped his mouth with the back of the same hand and stared at her after a quick glance at the screen to check out the score. He didn't offer her a seat or anything to drink.

"Fire away," he said instead.

Sam chose a high stool at the counter that acted as a partial room divider, thinking that in retrospect, she should have let Willy handle this guy, regardless of any fireworks.

"How well did you know Brian?" she started out.

"I worked with him."

Great, she thought. "Were you friends?"

"No."

"Did you dislike each other?"

"No."

"When you worked together, was it ever in the same car, or did you keep your distance from each other?"

"Sometimes one, sometimes the other."

"When you did ride together, did he ever open up and share personal details?"

"Sometimes."

She paused to look at him carefully. He matched her scrutiny, his eyes boring into hers, daring her to take issue with his mulishness.

She kept up her end. "What was the nature of those details?"

"Like all cops—he'd bitch about the bitch."

She let that ride—too obvious a taunt. "Who was that?"

"Kathleen Jabri. Lives in Florida now."

"You ever meet her?"

"Yeah."

Still with the aggressive stare. Sam pondered shutting this down but realized that's exactly what he was after.

"What were the circumstances there?"

"She came by the office with the kid. Something to do with child support. Good-looking woman. Nice tits."

"How would you rate the level of their animosity?"

He smiled. "Ooh. Big word. They complained. They weren't out to kill each other. It was a standard cop breakup—she hated the hours, the pay, and the company he kept; he hated her whining. They split. End of story. She ended up getting laid in the sun, and he probably ended up screwing her mother."

"Shirley Sherman?" she asked neutrally.

That stopped him. He dropped the stare, glanced at the rug, pursed his lips, and then admitted, "Nah. Shirley's good people. He just went over there to shoot the bull."

Sam enjoyed that. The first crack in his armor. "Brian regretted the marriage breaking up?"

"Yeah, but he deserved it. He could've made it work. He just fucked it up."

She wondered if, in fact, Doug Boyer hadn't been a little envious of his colleague for the latter's choice of wives.

"Too much the cop?" she suggested.

He shook his head. "Stupid. This job is for people who don't have a life. A woman like that . . ." he paused. When he looked up again, the anger was scaled back. "Even the kid was okay, and I hate kids. But she made him polite and quiet. He was smart, too, unlike the Old Man."

Boyer put the beer can back on the coffee table and wiped his palm against his jeans to dry it off.

"But Brian was all ambition, all the time. Wore me out, listening to him."

"I heard he was angling to get out of the sheriff's department," Sam said.

Boyer chuckled humorlessly. "He should've lived at the police academy for all the courses he took. He learned how to do stuff we'll never get near in a hundred years, like rappelling out of helicopters. Jesus. Spare me."

"How 'bout his police work?" she asked. "Did he push the envelope there, too?"

Boyer sat back in his couch and appraised her, the TV totally forgotten by now. His smile was wry when he asked, "So, we're back full circle, huh?"

She didn't respond.

He thought before answering. "I think so. The sheriff was comfortable with it—I heard him bragging once that Bri was a real go-getter, like he was a Labrador. But I wondered about some of the stuff he poked into."

"Like what?" she prompted.

He shrugged. "Drugs. What else? He was obsessed that a big drug bust would put him on the fast track." He spread his hands. "I mean, shit. Look around. I been a deputy for fifteen years. No wife, no kids, no overhead. This is still the best I can do. The Eliot Nesses of our world don't come from sheriff's departments. We're the butt of every-one's jokes—Deputy Dawg, you know? We stand around court-houses or transport prisoners or look like cartoon characters in uniform." He pointed a finger at her. "Not like you guys—The VBI. The Holy of Holies—fancy badges, major crimes only, roaming the state like wannabe Feds. Guys like Brian grow an ulcer just looking at you."

She met this outpouring with a poker face. "What kind of drug work was he doing?" she asked.

Boyer was comfortable matching her stride, apparently happy enough to simply vent now and then. "He didn't tell me," he conceded. "I was one of the enemy when it came to that stuff— somebody who'd steal the credit at the last second, as if I gave a shit."

He crossed his legs before adding, "No, he'd work off the clock, on his own. That was one of Kathleen's biggest complaints—that when he did have time off, he still didn't spend it with them."

"You have no idea what he was doing or who he was seeing? Was he developing snitches maybe?"

"Partly," Boyer conceded. "He did have a pretty good network. But he went to Burlington a lot, and to Montreal at least a couple of times. He wasn't secretive about that, but he sure didn't share what he was up to."

"But you think it was drug work."

"That much, he couldn't resist talking about. I never gave it much thought, though. Brian was a jerk—you gotta keep that in mind. Yeah, he went to school a lot, and yeah, he had a wife like a centerfold, but none of it mattered. He was still a loser. He bitched too much, bragged too much, swaggered around, stepped on toes. It never surprised me that he could never bust out of this department. He was the only one who couldn't see what was staring him in the mirror."

"Did other people see him that way, or is this all you?" she asked, risking Boyer's irritation now that the interview was nearing an end.

But the deputy was past his earlier defensiveness. His eyes widened as he told her, "Ask around. I know I'm an asshole, so you don't have to believe me, but I don't know anybody who could stand the guy. Even the people he pulled over for a ticket thought he was a pain. We got complaints all the time. An 'arrogant bully,' was how one woman put it." He smiled suddenly and added, "Of course, not that I'm complaining—he made me look good in comparison. Not too many do that."

Boyer paused and then asked, "Why *did* you come see me, anyway? It sure wasn't my nice-guy reputation."

"You're the department's straight shooter, according to who we asked," Sam told him. "A jerk," she added, "but honest."

He burst out laughing. "Yeah—I guess that's me."

She stood up to leave but asked one last question at the door. "You ever hear of a Vermont cop named Willy Kunkle?"

"Nope," he said. "Why?"

"Friend of mine," she admitted. "I was just wondering if you'd like each other, or kill each other."

He smiled and reached out for his beer again. "Who knows?"

She thought she might.

CHAPTER TWENTY

A lan leaned past his brother to peer through the wheelhouse's smeared front glass, shielding his eyes from the combined glow of the radar, the GPS, and the assortment of radio equipment clustered around the lobster boat's wheel. It was late at night, on a calm sea, with the closest lights coming from the Maine coast on their port side, most prominently Lubec's, identified by intermittent flashes from the West Quoddy Head light. To starboard, more distant, was the dimmer, twinkling evidence of Grand Manan Island, in Canada, the Yarmouth light on the tip of Nova Scotia beyond it having just slipped from sight. Finally, and oddest of all, twenty miles to their stern, in Cutler, there was the tight cluster of bright blinking lights—twenty-six of them, each suspended atop a one-thousand-foot antenna, all looking like a hovering flight of patiently waiting UFOs—that marked the location of the Navy's huge low frequency radio station, the most powerful in the world.

All of these combined served as time-honored navigational

landmarks, backing up the high-tech instrumentation that was becoming routine even on the smallest of boats nowadays.

"Better hold here," Alan cautioned Pete. "We don't want to wander into Canadian waters."

Pete was more than happy to comply, cutting back on the boat's power before taking another swig from the bottle he had nestled among the racked charts to his right. They were in a narrow jurisdictional cul-de-sac, with Canadian waters both a mile dead ahead and barely two miles to their southeast. The Canadian border police didn't spend all that much time out here, especially after dark, nor did the Maine Marine or the U.S. Border Patrols, especially since the old days of huge marijuana deliveries dropped from foreign freighters. Nevertheless, it remained nostalgic turf for law enforcement activity, as smugglers of liquor, cigarettes, and drugs had known for generations.

And despite the lack of a moon, the night sky was vibrant with stars, making Pete feel he might as well be standing in the open, under a sign reading, "Arrest this man—Drug Runner." He glanced at his little brother's profile as the latter continued scanning the horizon ahead. Pete had never known what to do with Alan. The kid was a troublemaker, as their dad had always insisted, but his enthusiasm was hard to resist. No matter how many times Buddy had whaled on the boy, or put him down, or worked to thwart his dreams, Alan had always bobbed back to the surface. Just like when he got out of prison—he didn't run and hide from family and old friends. He came straight home to Blackmore Harbor, as if to shove his survival and his pure will to live right up the Old Man's nose.

Pete's wife, Sophie, shared Buddy's distaste, which was saying something, since she also despised Buddy. In fact, Pete sometimes wondered if part of the reason he ended up listening to Alan all the time was to simply display that he had a mind of his own, and maybe a bit of the rebel in him, as well.

Only that rebel was feeling a little insecure at the moment. He reached out and took another swig from his bottle—something he had to be a whole lot more discreet about when he acted as Buddy's sternman during their daylight runs onto the water.

"There he is," Alan said softly.

Pete squinted into the gloom, seeing the tiniest of lights, barely visible above the black void of the water. "How the hell do you know that?" he wondered aloud.

Alan stooped to retrieve a small canvas bag he'd brought on board, unzipped it, and pulled out what looked like a cross between a sniper scope and a broken pair of binoculars. He snapped a switch on its side and held it up to his right eye.

"Yeah. Definitely them."

"What is that thing?" his brother asked.

Alan handed it over. "Night vision. I got it surplus. Probably better'n what the cops use."

Pete peered through the device and instantly saw the vessel ahead, sized like their own, magnified and bathed in a surreal green glow, its navigation lights burning as brightly as search lamps. He saw a couple of shadowy figures moving around its deck. He put his right hand out and rested it on the controls.

"Just stay put," Alan cautioned him.

"We're not gonna meet up with 'em?" Pete asked.

"Nope. We're not even here. I just wanted to check 'em out. Make sure they were solid."

Pete stared at him, thinking back at the risks and hassles he'd gone through to be here—catching hell from Sophie and borrowing the boat while the Old Man was at an Elks convention in Augusta. "We're not here?" he asked, his voice rising. "You told me we were gonna pick up a package. That I'd make more money tonight than I make in three months."

Alan took back the night scope and returned to studying the other boat. "Relax," he said dismissively. "We *are*. They just think we'll be coming by to these coordinates later in the week. I wanted to see them in action, that's all. The whole point of the exercise is that we never meet—never even know when one or the other of us is either dropping stuff off or picking it up. It's the randomness of it that gives us security."

Pete lapsed into silence, thinking that over. Alan hadn't shared much with him, but Pete thought he'd gotten the gist of it. He'd better have, since that's what he was going to be passing along to a select couple of others in his small group of disaffected younger Blackmore lobstermen, most of whom felt squeezed between their elders, who ruled over them like stubborn lords, and their significant others, who—in Pete's instance, anyway—were less tolerant, less supportive, and a lot more expensive to maintain than the older harbor women. According to Buddy and his pals, this disintegrating dedication to both the fishing trade and a frugal lifestyle cut across the board—young men like Alan and Pete had become lazy and seduced by easy money, while women like Sophie had replaced support and sacrifice with impatience and greed. Buddy blamed moral turpitude, of course, but the fact was that the lobster trade's very success had played a part. Many fishermen and their families had come to expect over a hundred thousand dollars a year and vacation time to boot—a blatant absurdity to any old salt with even a little knowledge of the Great Depression.

Buddy, too, owned some of the blame, though. The claims of

turpitude he wielded like a bludgeon were the sore point that Alan was using to sway Pete and his friends. Drug and alcohol use on board had been on the increase, and while fishermen were traditionally famous for their onshore antics and barroom excesses, rarely had they been foolish enough to bring such behavior onto the water. No longer—or, at least, not as often. Nowadays, it was common to hear of drug use at sea. It was still far from the norm—fishing remained too complex and dangerous to tackle with a muddled brain. But the exceptions were growing. And those exceptions were precisely whom Alan was targeting through his alcohol-dependent brother.

Indeed, this trip was supposed to show Pete just how easy it would be to kickstart a stalled income—which insight he could then use to enlist a miniature navy of like-minded clandestine importers. As Alan had put it to Pete at the end of the pier, on the night of the family Sunday supper, lobster boats were as common as seagulls off the Maine coast—so taken for granted they were virtually invisible. And even when the Marine Patrol did board a boat, what were they looking for? Short lobsters, by and large, or other violations of the fishing rules. Using fishing boats for drug running was a virtual birthright, according to Alan—steeped in historical tradition, and a piece of cake, as well.

At least that was his pitch. In fact, Alan had no intention of making this operation a centerpiece of his grand plan. This was all personal, and all about payback. Once Pete was on the hook—using Buddy's boat—Alan would have them where he'd always wanted them—especially Buddy—and his revenge against the King of Blackmore Harbor would be his to take with a simple anonymous phone call to the cops.

"Okay," Alan said, breaking away from his meditation. "Our turn. Move ahead slowly."

Pete blinked, the effects of the alcohol playing tag with a growing adrenaline.

"What about the border?" he asked.

"We're barely going over and we're not even stopping. If they do have us on radar, they won't know what we're doing and they won't have enough time to react. Besides, it'll look like a simple mistake. I worked this out, Pete. I got a lot more riding on this than just this one run, trust me."

Pete pushed on the throttle, underwhelmed by Alan's argument. The boat's rumble deepened under their feet as the propeller began pushing more water. Alan had the night scope virtually glued to his eye now, as he scanned the horizon before them.

"See anyone?" Pete asked nervously. "Where'd they go?"

"They left. As planned."

Pete made a face but no comment and glanced at the bottle among the charts, longing for another pull. But he kept both hands on the wheel.

"Okay," Alan told him after five minutes. "Let her drift for a second." He reached back into his zippered bag and pulled out another device, slightly larger than a deck of cards. This, too, he turned on, illuminating a small screen. He hunched over, staring at the screen and entering commands. After a couple of minutes, with Pete staring at him, he moved to the more familiar onboard GPS and studied its larger display. Their own boat was featured as a small red arrow amid blotches of various shades of blue and a dense scattering of yellow numerals, denoting the depths of the water around them. In contrast to a standard road map, the two bordering land masses of Maine and Grand Manan were simply dark and featureless. This was the tool that Pete used most commonly when piloting on his own, so he was startled to suddenly see a tiny white blip pulsating very near the icon of their boat.

"What the hell's that? What did you do?"

Alan laughed, as much at his brother's comment as at his own success. "Like I said," he explained, "I'm testing the system here. They sank a buoy with our package, with a GPS and a wireless release attached to it. When I enter one code, the release lets go of the weight and the buoy takes the package to the top; a second code, and the GPS tells us where the goods are." He pointed ahead and slightly off the starboard bow. "Right there."

Pete followed the direction with his eyes to a small, sharp LED, blinking on the water's surface like a desperate, crash-landed firefly.

"No shit," Pete murmured wonderingly.

"No shit," his brother echoed, adding, "Grab a gaff and get ready to be a rich man."

Alan took over the wheel as Pete stepped back, between the snatch block and the bait barrel, and readied himself to snag the buoy's line. It only took one pass, given both men's familiarity with the maneuver, and Pete effortlessly swung the heavily wrapped package onto the deck.

Alan set their course back toward where they'd come from and locked the wheel before joining Pete, who was already slicing into the package.

"Carefully, bro," he cautioned. "Carefully. Don't cut too deep."

He helped Pete undress what became a waterproof canvas bag, which he then undid to reveal two dozen large plastic bottles. Alan unscrewed one and showed his brother its contents with the help of a flashlight.

"What do you think?"

"What are they?" Pete asked, extracting a single tablet and holding it daintily between his discolored, calloused fingertips.

"Oxys, Pete," Alan chided him. "Where have you been? This is what I been talking about."

Pete dropped it back into the bottle. "I guess I'm mostly a Scotch man."

Alan shook his head. "Look at it this way: What do you think it's all worth?"

Pete sat back on his haunches. "Shit. I don't know. Five hundred bucks?"

"Try about twenty thousand."

There was no need for a flashlight to see the whites of Pete's eyes. "*Twenty thou?* Holy Fucking Christ, Alan. For this little pissant package? You gotta be kidding."

Alan closed the bag back up, threw the wrapping overboard, and returned to the wheel. "That's my point, Pete. You gettin' it now?"

Pete ran his hands over his skull, as if recovering from a nightmare. "Jesus, Alan. Jesus."

Alan merely smiled and returned to the wheel, watching the GPS display and the radar beside it. This was not the time to get sloppy. Twenty minutes later, safely out of the Canadian cul-de-sac and abreast of the Cutler radar towers, he cut back the power again, ducked through the hatchway into the forward cabin, and reappeared almost immediately with a metal plate and some meshing attached to a large metal disk, twice the size of a hockey puck.

"What's that?" Pete asked.

"The crucial piece," Alan explained. He slipped the bag of drugs into the meshing, attached the disk—which turned out to be a powerful magnet—to the metal plate, and finally tied the plate with a short rope to one of the boat's mooring bits. He then threw the whole bundle into the water, where it instantly sank.

"Shit, Alan. What now?" Pete virtually whined.

Alan showed him a small plastic box, a single button mounted prominently to its faceplate.

"This," he explained, "controls the magnet connecting the mesh bag to the metal plate I just threw over. If the Coasties or the Marine Patrol or the goddamn Seventh Cavalry starts breathing down our necks, all we do is hit this one button, and every piece of incriminating evidence disappears into the deep." He snapped his fingers. "Just like that."

For one of the first times in his life, Alan saw his older brother stare at him in open admiration.

"You really got this figured out, don't you?"

Alan seized the moment. He laid a hand on Pete's muscular shoulder and looked him straight in the eyes. "All but the last part, where you get the others on board with this. If we're gonna make a killing, we need to do this a lot, and we need to do it with people we can trust with our lives. Your buddies think I'm a flake, or a turncoat, or whatever the fuck. But they respect you. You're the sternman of the King of Blackmore Harbor, and his son, to boot. You're also the one who puts up with his shit, just like they put up with the shit from their Old Men—the Keepers of Tradition who think you have nothing to offer except cheap labor."

"Yeah," murmured Pete, as if he were warming up for the "Amen" refrain at a revival meeting.

"I can't do this without you, Pete," Alan kept on, stoking the mood. "You seen what I can do—set up the action, line up the players, anticipate every possibility. But I need you to carry the ball across the line. I always saw this as a team thing, in my mind, when I was working this out in prison. But to have you—my family— actually helping to make the most crucial part happen . . . That, I only dreamed about."

Pete was nodding rhythmically, his gaze fixed on some middle distance, no doubt consisting of a misty future where he had his own boat and was free of their father.

Alan stopped long enough to cup his brother's cheeks in both his hands, holding his face so that their eyes were a foot apart.

"Will you help me, Pete? Will you help me make a life we never had?"

Pete reached out and mussed Alan's hair. He was laughing when he said, "You bet your ass I will."

Georges Tatien watched Alan Budney appreciatively. This time, the meeting was taking place in a motel room, again not far from the border. But Tatien had been the second one to arrive, if solely because Budney had booked the room. Now, Alan was sitting in the only armchair, by the curtained window, expounding on his progress in rebuilding Matt Mroz's empire. It was a well-organized speech, set out in logical steps. In a nutshell, Alan had opted to restrict the diversity of Roz's old holdings in exchange for increasing its most profitable and least risky aspects, most particularly Tatien's specialty, prescription drugs.

There was more to it, of course—a verbally descriptive flow chart of supply and distribution. But it was more Alan's style than his plan that caught Tatien's imagination. Alan was suffused with nervous confidence and high hopes, like a young athlete on the verge of his first major competition. He had the arrogance and strut that Georges had once seen in himself and that he suspected he still aspired to by staying in a business usually reserved for far younger men.

His soft spot for Alan had little to do with the latter's grand plan anyway, despite it being well designed. Georges had enough money already, and several other businesses, and knew that success depended as much on luck as on organizational savviness. This particular deal, in fact, was comparatively straightforward—shy of being mundane only because of its illegal nature.

Maybe it was that Georges was getting older and finally feeling it; maybe it was that, despite their different backgrounds, he felt a kinship with the younger man. But whatever the cause, Georges simply *liked* Alan, which was virtually a first for him.

"Did you enjoy your voyage on the water near Lubec the other night?" he finally asked at an appropriate interval.

"The transfer?" Alan asked, smiling broadly. "You should've seen my brother's expression. I might as well have put him on a rocket ship. He was blown away. It work okay from your end?"

Tatien nodded. In fact, he had been delighted with the arrangement. He'd often thought the water route had advantages the land-based border crossings lacked, but he'd never found an American importer so inclined.

"It was entirely satisfactory," he said.

"Cool," Alan responded. "Well, it was satisfactory for me, too, because it did the trick in pulling Pete in all the way. He can't wait to get started. I now have a fleet of boats available to us, and I know for a fact that it won't be restricted to Blackmore Harbor for long." He leaned forward in his seat, his eyes shining. "And the kicker is that Pete's carrying the ball. I told him how to break the group into cells, so that if anyone gets caught, he only knows about one or two other guys, and vice versa. For the cops to take this system apart, they'll have to nail everybody in it."

Tatien smiled back, less confident of his partner's accuracy here but also not really caring. Alan, after all, still didn't know Georges's real name, and had never seen him without some more or less subtle disguise. His whole operation could collapse without injury to Georges, and, soft spots notwithstanding, that part remained key. Georges knew how to be sentimental without being foolish.

Of course, he also didn't know of Alan's eventual fine tuning of this part of his operation—how he intended to sacrifice his brother and father while maintaining the integrity of the water route through the cell system. The irony that Pete would create the very system that would survive his own and Buddy's arrest for smuggling was a catch only Alan planned to enjoy.

"And the finances?" Georges asked, mostly to be politely conversational.

"Nailed down tight," Alan told him. "You know Bernie, right?"

"I do, yes."

"Well, that's about the only part of Roz's setup I'm keeping. Bernie's solid—solid and careful. So I'm keeping all that in place, which means you won't have anything new to learn there. How 'bout Luis Grega? You ever hear of him?"

Tatien merely shook his head.

"Maybe you will and maybe you won't," Alan explained. "We'll see. I'm bringing him in as my number two. He used to work for Roz, so he knows the ropes. I want as much distance from the street-level ops as I can get, and to restrict myself mostly to Bernie, you, and Grega, representing the three major branches of this setup. Roz was too high profile, got too easy to pick off. I'm gonna protect my-self more."

Tatien nodded with genuine fondness. "It is an excellent thought," he said, but only to be encouraging. In fact, he was think-ing that his attraction to this young man's energy and drive was largely because he was planning for it to be so short-lived.

CHAPTER TWENTY-ONE

The last time Joe had visited Gloucester he'd ended up investigating the death of a man he had been hoping to interview, mostly by hanging out at the Main Street bar the guy used to frequent. Not only had he picked up the lead that had finally led him to the killer, but the person providing it had been the barkeep, Lyn Silva.

Joe had fond memories of Gloucester.

This time, however, he was loitering along a different stretch of Main, west of where he'd been before, away from the fish packing plant and the grittier section of the harbor, surrounded by more genteel offerings—mostly brick-clad, upscale boutiques—without a workingman's rooming house within view. Lyn had selected the venue—a trendy bakery offering the usual dozen types of coffee—and he suspected it was because she'd be less likely to encounter any of her old customers here.

He sympathized with her need for a little control. Despite her being a single mother who now owned her own bar, had several employees, and dealt with difficult, drunken, sometime lecherous customers during every shift, she remained by her own admission surprisingly insecure. Who could blame her for being a little self protective? She'd been handed her fair share of emotional mishaps over the years, including the one she was bringing to meet him.

Joe thought back to a conversation with Lenny Chapman, Kevin Delaney, and Cathy Lawless about using Lyn's brother to dig into Mroz's old drug network. He'd been shy at first about broaching the subject, both because of his relationship with Lyn, and because of Steve's admittedly slim credentials. But he'd been as struck by their ready acceptance as by what it had revealed of their desperation for any kind of breakthrough.

He saw Lyn enter the place before she caught sight of him, which allowed him to study her companion unimpeded, if only for a few seconds. Steve Silva was taller than expected and looked more battered by life than the family photos had revealed. For good reason, of course—those dated back to happier times, and Steve had put the interim to hard use.

Joe rose and waved to Lyn, whose face broke into a broad smile. She took up her brother's hand and led him across the room, kissing Joe as she drew near.

"Joe, this is Steve," she said simply, looking from one of them to the other.

Steve appeared as if all his courage might drain away. He held out a limp, moist hand in greeting and muttered, "Hey."

"I really appreciate your coming, Steve," Joe immediately told him. "This must be tough."

"Sure," Steve said softly.

Joe gestured to the booth he'd been occupying. "Would you like to sit? My treat; they have coffee here I've never heard of before."

Steve didn't answer, but Lyn touched Joe on the elbow. "We were actually talking about that on the way over," she explained. "Thinking it might be easier to get right to it—get in the car and head north now."

Joe immediately shifted gears, envisioning how much cajoling, massaging, pleading, and maneuvering she'd practiced to get even this far. He laid a ten-dollar bill on the table and pointed toward the door.

"I'm parked right outside, unless you want to drive your own car."

Lyn smiled up at him gratefully. "That was the other thing—might make it easier for Steve to do the driving. We will use your car, though, if that's okay."

Joe handed Steve the keys and ushered them both outside.

On the road, the mood was careful and poised, all three of them acting as deliberately as eye surgeons. Steve drove slowly, staying to the right on the interstate through New Hampshire and into Maine, so that Joe was tempted to stretch out and stomp on the accelerator. The conversation, also, was stilted and cautious, each of them so watchful of what he or she said that silence finally became preferable.

Joe wasn't too worried, since he quickly recognized that he was no part of the problem. The two siblings were new to each other's company, and it was apparent that Lyn had gotten a little rusty with with the easy banter they'd once freely exchanged. Joe was less sure about Steve, of course, not knowing him well enough to guess if he was uncomfortable or just naturally closemouthed. He finally assumed the former, from what Lyn had told him earlier, and at last decided to act on it.

As the "Welcome to Maine—worth a visit, worth a lifetime"—sign slipped by—a greeting Joe had always considered at best a little awkward—he'd progressed far enough beyond social niceties to ask, "So, how many other people avoid asking what you been up to recently?"

Through the corner of his eye, he saw Lyn actually wince in the backseat. Steve, however, barked out a startled laugh.

"A lot," he answered. "Especially if they've never been inside themselves."

"Like your sister?"

Lyn groaned. Smiling, Steve glanced quickly over his shoulder. "Nah. She's trying her best. She was always the mom our mom couldn't be. I never made that easy. Sorry 'bout that, sis."

"It was worth it," she said cheerfully. "We had our fun times, too."

He nodded. "Yeah—that we did."

"Until you got the shit kicked out of you emotionally," Joe suggested, wanting to keep to the edgier side of any reminiscences.

"Yeah," Steve repeated more quietly.

"Why react the way you did, though?" Joe asked almost aggressively. "With drugs and drinking? Lots of people suffer loss without going there."

It was his tone of voice he was hoping Steve would hear rather than the criticism it implied. Not that he wasn't challenging him a bit. Joe needed information from this man, and needed it to be reliable. For that, he had to discover how much strength Steve had restored to his character. He also knew that most self-help programs in prison used soul searching and inner honesty as ladder rungs toward improvement. Steve should've been as habituated to such questions as Lyn was wary of them.

In fact, Steve was nodding thoughtfully.

"Self-esteem, I guess," he answered. "Our dad was a pretty strong guy, and so was José. That can be big in Hispanic families."

"Was José younger or older?" Joe asked.

"Older, meaning that when they died, I was both the only male left, and the one who'd never carried the ball, so to speak. Lyn was great, doing what she could," he added, again casting a look at her over his shoulder, "but I couldn't take the pressure, not with Mom falling apart like she did. She basically fell on me like a brick, like I was supposed to do it all, from the finances to the household repairs to being the Rock of Gibraltar like Dad."

"She was the one who introduced the liquor," Lyn said from the back.

That caught Joe by surprise, despite his years of experience.

"Really?" he asked stupidly.

Steve chuckled sadly. "Yeah. Figure that one. Well, she wanted company, and my gender helped, even if I was a kid. I was amazed, of course—still a teenager, all my friends getting in trouble for doing what I did with my mom every night. We even started sneaking around on Lyn, 'cause she was telling us to knock it off, which only made the bond tighter."

This time, Joe looked at Lyn, who merely shrugged.

"We'd go to bars," Steve went on, "where Mom would know the bartender, or she'd buy us stuff from the store and we'd go drink in the park or in the car or wherever. It was pretty pathetic."

"Meanwhile," Lyn said, "I'd be going all over town, looking for them, hoping to keep it quiet at the same time."

"Yeah," Steve chimed in. "And, of course, she was having her own problems at home, taking care of Coryn and trying to hold her marriage together. She basically had two households full of juvenile delinquents to handle. Doomed from the start. Come to think of it, Coryn was probably the most adult of the bunch."

"It wasn't *that* bad," Lyn said weakly.

For the first time, Steve showed a little emotion, swinging around and rebuking her, "*Sure* it was that bad, Lyn. Don't deny it."

She held up a hand and sat back. "Okay, okay."

"It was a fucking disaster," he reiterated. "I'm not blaming Mom. I milked it all the way, and when she got so bad that she didn't need or want my company, I went out on my own and started in on the drugs. I liked being zoned out, and I couldn't have cared less about keeping everything together. I didn't see the point, especially when I saw how bad things had gotten for Lyn, who was supposed to be the one with her shit together."

There was no comment from behind them.

"How's your mom doing now?" Joe asked.

"Still in the house," Steve said, "living with me. I'm trying to do now what I should've done all along."

"You were a kid," his sister remonstrated.

Steve jerked a thumb at Joe. "Like the man said, sis—lots of people got it rough. Doesn't mean they give up like I did."

Steve actually entered the passing lane to get around a slow-moving truck, his inhibitions apparently loosening at last.

"Mom's not doing well," he answered Joe. "She's a recluse, basically, and can't really take care of herself anymore. It was either I moved back in or she went into a home, and I think that would've been too tough on her, with her thing about other people. So, that's what I've done—just recently—meaning I don't really know if it's going to work. We're sort of circling each other right now, getting a routine worked out."

"I didn't know about all this," Lyn said. "Most of it happened over the past week or two. Up to then, Mrs. Garcia had been taking care of her, checking in and buying groceries and making sure she took her pills. But Mrs. G. was running out of patience, so Steve showing up's been a godsend."

"Jesus," Joe murmured. "I wish you well. Doesn't sound easy."

"It'll be okay," Steve said.

"You're not worried about sliding back?" Joe asked him.

He laughed again. "Every day. All the time. That's one of the reasons I finally told Lyn I'd agree to help you out."

"How so?"

Steve glanced at him and raised his eyebrows. "'Cause I need to confront my demons, keep pushing myself. Part of what's working for me is going back in time and shaking hands with what I did."

Joe thought about that for a moment, impressed by its eloquence— even if the language was reminiscent of therapy. His trust in their tour guide was improving.

"Lyn tells me you never actually met Matthew Mroz."

Steve shook his head. "No. He was Mr. Big—a 'Tony Montana,' as they used to call the heavies. I think that was old hat even then, but I kind of liked it. You see that movie?"

"*Scarface?*" Joe responded. "Yeah—hated it. Walked out."

Steve smiled. "Guess that figures. Anyhow, Roz wasn't available to the likes of me, but his organization was very appealing."

"Why?"

"Not as scary as what's in Boston, mostly. Plus, the people I was hanging out with were more connected to the Maine scene than the Boston one. You sort of go with who you know, right?"

"You ever know somebody named Luis Grega?"

"No—Lyn told me that's who you're after. Sounds like one of the types I was avoiding—the Dot Ave crowd."

"How 'bout James Marano?" Joe asked.

"Nope—him neither. That doesn't mean much, though. People change a lot, and names do, too, even if they're on the same faces, sometimes. That's why I hope you're not expecting much from this trip. Lyn did warn you, right?"

"She did."

"I want to show you what I can—where I went, give you names, stuff like that—but it may all be different by now. It doesn't take long, and from what I heard through the grapevine, it's all being dumped on its ass anyhow, what with Roz getting killed."

"What did you hear?"

"Just that. No names, no nothin'. In fact, that's one of the interesting things about it—real quiet. Course, my sources aren't what they used to be. I don't hang out with the old crowd—don't want anything to do with them. But you know how it is with day-to-day conversation. You hear things, even if you're not asking."

"How was it when you were interested in joining up?" Joe asked, as much to keep the conversation going as to gain actual knowledge. He wasn't here, after all, to cure Maine's drug trade. In fact, he'd been increasingly concerned that hunting Grega might slip to second rung status as the other task force members got more excited about Mroz. However, the linkage between the two interests remained clear for the moment, not to mention that the drug trade in upper New England had an internecine aspect to it. It was perfectly possible that what he learned over here might prove useful in Vermont.

"It was weird," Steve said, answering Joe's question. "In some ways, Maine was like a frat party. The Dorchester people, they were after your blood—there were turf battles, ethnic issues, real down-and-out gunfights. Up here, people were just trying to make a little money and have fun. At least that's how it seemed to me. That's why I wanted in. It sounded like Roz had created a never-ending party where you could make some money, too."

"But it didn't turn out that way?"

"Never found out," Steve admitted. "I got busted before I could get my feet wet. I mean," he added, "I *know* that was all bullshit now, but I didn't back then."

Joe was remembering what Lyn had told him earlier. "But you did go up there, to check it out?"

"Oh, yeah," he said cheerily. Joe noticed that they were pretty much constantly in the passing lane by now, comfortably keeping up with the flow of traffic.

"Actually," Steve continued, "I had it better than somebody just knocking on the door. I had a connection." Once more, he abruptly twisted around in his seat to make eye contact with his sister. "You're not gonna like this, but remember those trips to Maine we used to take with Dad?"

"Of course," she answered, her expression questioning and a little apprehensive, sensing one of those surprises that Joe knew she disliked.

"Well," her brother said lightly, "there was more than just lobster fishing we were researching, whether any of us knew it or not. A couple of the boat captains he introduced us to also did some smuggling on the side. I bet Dad didn't have a clue, since he was all lobster, all the time. But I found it out later, when I went back on my own. It was actually kind of funny, being older and meeting the same guy in a totally different context."

Lyn leaned forward and propped her elbows on their seatbacks. "What're you talking about? I don't remember any boat captains."

He waved one hand in the air. "All right, all right. It was one boat captain. You and Mom went shopping. We were in Jonesport, and me, Dad, and José went down to the harbor. That's when we met him."

"Who?" she persisted.

"Wellman Beale," Steve said. "How can you forget a name like that? He didn't talk to me—that was all for adults—but they let me check out his boat, which was state-of-the-art. Actually," he suddenly added, "I think that part helped me out—that he never got a good look at me then, 'cause when I met him later, he didn't know who I was, and I never told him." His mood darkened at that, as he admitted, "I was embarrassed he might connect me to Dad, if he heard my last name."

"But what were you all doing with him?" Lyn asked. "I mean, the first time."

"Nothing," he explained. "We bumped into him. We were walking down the dock and he was there fueling up. You know how José was with new boats, and like I said, this was a beaut. They just got to talking. I thought Beale was a big shot then—he said he owned an island, not far from Jonesport, fully equipped with a repair and maintenance shop. Of course, the boat spoke for itself. He was nice, too. Dad and he talked a lot."

Joe was wondering about a more recent connection. "And you're saying that Beale worked for Mroz?"

"Yeah . . . Well, no. Not exactly. The way I heard it, Beale didn't work for anybody, what with the island and all. But times had gotten tighter. The boat was history when I saw him the second time. I was told he knew Roz and, quote-unquote, did business with him now and then. That's why I was introduced to him by a mutual friend—another guy who's doing time right now. Anyhow, I asked Beale what Roz was like to work with—stuff like that. It didn't go farther than that."

"What did Beale say?" Joe asked.

"He was cool. Told me he'd be happy to introduce us when I was ready to make my move. He was cagey, though. It's not like he told me he was in cahoots with a drug dealer. All reference to Roz was roundabout, like he was an acquaintance."

Joe nodded thoughtfully. "You know," he suggested, "we probably ought to stop and see some of the people I'm working with before we hit your old haunts. Would that be okay? I bet they'd like to hear about Wellman."

"Sure," Steve said. "Glad to help."

CHAPTER TWENTY-TWO

Kevin Delaney—the only one actually in the MDEA office when Joe dropped by with Lyn and Steve—was happy to hear about Wellman Beale, but not because the name was new to him. Beale had been in their records for years as an interesting bit player; he just hadn't been heard from in a while. The fact that he might be active, therefore, was of more than passing interest. Delaney's real joy, however, was in pumping Steve for his other old memories, dated or not. For the other two in the room it was like listening to a couple of returning alumni, exchanging endless one-liners about what had happened to what's-his-name.

Later, as they were about to leave, Delaney asked Joe to linger for a short, private conversation.

"Vicious bastard," he said quietly as Joe shut the office door.

Joe settled back into the chair he'd been using earlier. "Steve?" he asked in surprise.

His host laughed. "Hardly. I like him—glad to see he's turning things around. I meant Beale."

"I thought you barely knew him."

Delaney frowned. "No. I was a little less than candid there—didn't want to say too much."

"Sure," Joe reassured him, well used to how cops tended toward discretion, as he often did himself. "Has he been acting up lately?"

"Not specifically, although rumors are his fortunes have improved—which tweaks my interest. Also, he pounded the snot out of one of my informants a couple of years back, he has a history of assault and battery, and—more to the point—we can confirm he knew Roz because he once tried to organize a weird kind of labor movement against him on the part of all the suppliers."

"You're kidding," Joe exclaimed. "Like a strike?"

"Beale said people like himself—mules, importers, shipment facilitators, or whatever you want to call them—were getting the shit end of the stick while running the biggest risks. He had a point, even if it wasn't late breaking news.

"He didn't get anywhere, surprise, surprise," Delaney went on. "Didn't stand a chance from the start, since the people he spoke for couldn't have cared less. I think he was basically pissed off and tried to legitimize it, at least in his own eyes. The point is that he threatened Roz in the process, got mauled by the bodyguard, Harold, and was frozen out of ever doing business with Roz again. I'd forgotten all about that, since it dates back."

Joe shook his head. "Steve made Beale sound like everyone's favorite uncle."

Delaney's eyes widened. "Oh, he can be a charmer. Don't get me wrong. That's one of the secrets of his success. I'm sure as many people think he loved Roz as know he hated him."

Joe furrowed his brows. "You think Beale might've killed him?"

Delaney shrugged. "It's worth looking into. I'll shoot a memo to the state police and tell them to check him for that. We probably ought to take a squint at him, too, now that everything's in an uproar. Be a perfect time for him to make a play." He paused and added, "I would say that Steve got lucky never dealing with him. Do me a favor, will you? Take note if Steve mentions anything else about the guy. Could be he remembers something he didn't tell me."

That didn't happen. Wellman Beale was never brought up again, except in passing as they revisited the Jonesport pier. Otherwise, they drove along the coast, hitting harbor after harbor—Deer Isle, Bar Harbor, South Addison, Machias, and more—finally reminiscing less about Steve's solo travels and more about their shared family outings. The trip, however, remained valuable, if for reasons unconnected to Joe's initial thinking. When they parted ways the following day, all three of them felt richer for the companionship, and certainly, Joe and Lyn had moved a little farther toward something deeper. Joe's failure, therefore, to gain much new information mattered little to him. Indeed, he could now admit that the entire scheme had probably been more about wanting some time with Lyn. That he'd gotten to know and appreciate her brother was a bonus he hadn't expected.

Things were different the following day, however, after Lyn and Steve had left, and Joe was back among the task force. Once more in Delaney's office, they were all told that the case had finally gotten a break.

"Bernie?" Cathy Lawless virtually crowed. "The man of mystery? Turns out he's named Ann DiBernardo."

"A woman?" someone reacted.

"Don't you love it?" she asked. "I give credit where it's due—our own Dave Beaubien came up with this one."

"Attaboy, Dave," said Michael Coven, the MDEA director, who happened to be in the area.

Dave, his back against the wall, merely nodded.

"Do we know about DiBernardo?" asked Dede Miller, of the ICE team.

"Portland PD does," Lawless answered. "They've had her under surveillance now and then, brought her in for questioning several times, and generally would love to have the taxpayers pay for her room and board. But they've never been able to pin anything on her."

"What's her angle?" Miller asked.

"Crooked finances," Lawless said. "Mostly drug-related. Dave discovered a minor rap sheet dating back to a misspent youth—well, misspent twenties, at least. She's mentioned in connection with a business fraud case, about ten years old; and she's a person-of-interest in an embezzlement, same vintage. After that, she's been all but invisible, except through inference and innuendo—the ultimate person-of-interest."

"And she lives in Portland?" Lester Spinney asked.

"Yup—a city girl."

"Why would Bob and Grega be talking about her?" he pressed, recalling what Jill Zachary had told him.

"No clue," Cathy said.

"Which is probably why we should sit on her around the clock for a while," Joe suggested. "She being the hottest lead we've got, for both my homicide and your drug case."

Delaney spoke what immediately leaped to every local cop's mind at that—he pointed at Chapman and asked, "Lenny? The federal government's writing the checks here. None of us is going to cover that kind of expense."

Chapman sighed slightly and asked rhetorically, "We've had no sightings of Grega anywhere, right?"

"Nope," Cathy confirmed.

"If it helps," Mike Coven said quietly, using his senior officer status to clinch the deal, "you might end up killing two birds with one stone, like Joe said. On top of that, since Bernie's news to us and seems involved in the drug business, you'd be doing MDEA a huge favor as well by funding an operation we could never justify on our own."

"And credit would be paid publicly where it was due," Joe added.

Lenny smiled and shook his head. "You guys sure know how to say all the right things, don't you? Okay. I'll run it by my handlers. I'll also run her through our computers and have a chat with the Portland PD. No promises, but keep your fingers crossed."

Luis Grega waited for a full hour before making his move. He'd mentally rehearsed how he wanted this to go, and now that the time had come, he wanted to make sure everything went perfectly. It was a game he played with himself, especially when the stakes were high—balancing the adrenaline of such situations with disciplined cold-bloodedness. He'd seen too many people lose control just when they shouldn't—whether they were responsible for what was about to happen or simply the victims.

He'd played both roles in his life—the latter only when he'd been weak and young. That was why he was always the aggressor now. He would never be on the short end again, no matter the cost.

He eased himself out of the guest bedroom closet, the hinges of which he'd oiled earlier in preparation, and stepped soundlessly across the room in his sneakered feet, acutely attuned to the house's every sound.

He stood in the hallway for a few minutes, enjoying the power of being the only one awake. He'd done this sometimes in prison, slipping out of his bunk and merely standing at the bars, comparing his wakeful vigilance to so much surrounding unconscious vulnerability.

He walked slowly, gracefully, remembering from his practice runs which boards creaked. He passed the bathroom, still smelling of her shower and the cheap perfumed soap she used, to the half open door of her bedroom.

This he pushed open gently, again confident of its silenced hinges, before slipping across the threshold like a ghost and positioning himself with his back against the wall.

Eight feet from him was the foot of the double bed—a beaten-up wooden monster, held together in two places with nailed-on lathing. The room, dimly glowing from the moon outside and the nightlight in the distant bathroom, was a depository of dropped clothes, discarded toys, strewn magazines, and unpaid bills. A mess, in other words, like its inhabitants—or what was left of them.

She lay on her side, facing him. One bare leg had already worked its way out from under the single sheet, and the T-shirt she wore as a nightgown had ridden partway up her stomach, revealing her under-wear. Her long dark hair partially covered her face.

He watched her breathing, studying the movement of her breasts under the thin cotton, enjoying this moment to the point of not want-ing it to end.

Except, of course, that it would have to.

Smoothly, conscious of how he'd look were he being filmed, Grega took several strides to the side of the bed, pulled the sheet back with a flourish, and laid the flat of his hand at the base of Jill Zachary's throat, effectively holding her down.

Her eyes popped open and he waited for her to scream, ready to shut off the noise with a violent squeeze. Not that it really mattered, of course. They were alone in the house, Bob being dead and their son a ward of the state. But it was the principle of the thing, and Grega didn't like loud noises.

But she didn't make a sound. She did straighten abruptly, how-ever, sliding up a few inches on the pillow, and pulled the hem of her T-shirt down as far as it would go.

Only then did she whisper in a voice shaking with terror, "What do you want?"

He sat on the edge of the bed, his hip pressed against hers, which she moved away ever so slightly, as if hoping he wouldn't notice.

He took the time to add to her discomfort by studying the length of her body, slowly cataloguing every detail. Her hands tightened on the bottom of her shirt as his gaze reached the top of her thighs. But he didn't stop there and made no gesture to heighten her fear.

At last, he returned to her face and smiled. "You don't like me, do you?" he asked softly.

A nervous twitch at the corner of her mouth suggested a failed attempt to smile politely. "I don't know you."

"That's my point. But I saw it on your face when I was here with Bob."

"All his friends make me nervous."

He laughed, reached up, and tapped her cheek with his open hand. She winced as if being struck.

"You are a liar, Jill."

"I'm sorry" was all she could say.

"I'm used to it," he admitted philosophically. "All of us spics learn the look you give us, even as little kids. It never changes. Except," he added, placing his hand where it had been, but a little lower, so that it rested between her breasts, "for times like these. You don't dislike me now, do you?"

"I fear you."

He raised his eyebrows, impressed. "Very good. Nice answer. You should."

She took advantage of his reaction to risk repeating, "What do you want?"

His hand slid farther down, to just above her navel. He could feel her trying to control her breathing. "For now?" he answered. "I just want to talk."

In the long silence that followed, she was forced to ask, "What about?"

"What you told the police, Jill."

"Nothing," she blurted out instinctively and then sucked in air as he suddenly pushed down with his palm, grinding into the pit of her stomach. In pain, she grabbed his wrist with both hands, writhing to get away.

He eased up slowly, cautioning, "Settle down, settle down."

She did so, resting her hands by her sides, as if at attention, and struggling to catch her breath.

"Good," he rewarded her. "Want to try that again?"

"I did talk to them," she admitted plaintively, tears now in her eyes. "They took my kid away, and killed Bob."

"What did you say about me?"

"They asked," she said, her eyes widening, as if presenting a gift to an ever-critical elder. "But what could I tell them? That you were there. That Bob brought you home. You didn't say anything in front of me, so I had nothing to tell them. That's what I meant."

Grega pushed out his lower lip thoughtfully and nodded slightly.

"But, here's the problem, Jill," he finally said. "I have a real good memory—places, people, faces."

He leaned toward her, simultaneously slipping his hand up under her shirt, which again made her start.

He ignored her reaction as he added, "And especially conversations. I'm like a tape recorder." He got even closer, almost face-to-face. "And I remember you walking in on us, asking if we wanted dinner. Does that ring a bell?"

She nodded silently, her head pushed back deeply into the pillow behind her.

"Tell me, Jill. Tell me what you remember, too."

"Bernie," she let out, almost in a gasp.

He smiled and straightened slightly. "Cool. What about Bernie?"

"Just the name, and that Bob got real mad at me after, for walking in when I did. I told the cop that's why it stuck in my head."

"And they found that interesting?"

"I don't know," she said with a touch of anger. "The cop didn't seem to know him, either, if that helps."

Grega's expression changed slightly. Jill noticed something a little like relief there, if only momentarily.

"He said 'him,' when he talked about Bernie?"

"Yeah. 'You ever see him?' 'You know who he might be?'—stuff like that. Why does that matter?"

He moved his hand off her bare stomach and worked it around to her side, sliding it up near her armpit, beside her breast. She began wondering if the dangerous part was over—if all that might be left was the sex she knew he'd force on her, and for which she began to brace herself.

"What else did he ask?"

"That was about it. He wasn't real pushy. He was nice—said he wasn't really with the others, whatever that meant."

Grega stopped stroking her rib cage and pinched her skin slightly. "Jill," he warned her, "I don't want to hear, 'That was about it,' and then nothing else. What was the rest?"

She shifted away from his hand and he let go of the fold of skin he'd been kneading. "It was nothing. He asked if you'd ever been in Vermont."

He was aware of the intensity in her eyes. She was fearful of what she was revealing. He slid closer to her on the bed and finally put his hand full on her breast, pressing it hard against her chest.

His voice was cold when he asked, "You know this is going to end one of two ways, right?"

She just stared at him.

"Answer me."

She nodded.

"You tell me what he really wanted to know, and all you'll have are nice memories, even if it's with a greaser—or whatever you call us."

Again, she didn't respond.

"But, you play dumb," he continued, "and I will cut you up."

He left it at that, letting her imagination do the rest.

"He said you shot a cop in Vermont—that it was a federal case, and that a lot of people were after you."

His reaction caught her totally off guard. He pulled his hand out from under her T-shirt and sat bolt upright, staring at her.

"*Those fucking assholes,*" he burst out, all snaky lasciviousness gone. "I didn't shoot the son of a bitch. Are they *still* stuck on that? That's what he said? Word for word?"

Once more, she pulled her shirt down as far as it would go. "Yeah. He made it really clear."

Luis Grega got to his feet and paced up and down a couple of times, kicking piles of clothes out of the way in the process.

"Jesus H. Christ," he said. "That is so fucking full of shit. Dumb bastards should've figured that out by now. Lazy pricks." He thumped his chest. "I thought *I* was the one who was gonna get it next."

He stopped abruptly and stared at her. "So the cop who grilled you was from Vermont?"

"I don't know. He didn't say."

He ran his hand through his hair and shook his head. "Fuck me," he muttered. "Why can't they get it straight?" He then bent forward at the waist and asked, "Did he say who he was, at least?"

She nodded, now totally unsure of what to expect. "Gunther," she said softly. "It was the same name as a doctor I used to have."

That seemed to satisfy him. He absorbed the name, muttered,

"Well, Mr. Gunther and I're going to have to meet, 'cause he's full of crap," and then he was gone.

Stunned, Jill listened to his footsteps retreating down the hall, heard him take the stairs two at a time and slam the front door on his way out.

For a moment, she continued lying there, still clutching the hem of her shirt, and then she curled up into a ball and began crying from the pit of her stomach.

CHAPTER TWENTY-THREE

Spinney and Gunther knocked on the door and waited. They were in the darkened hallway of an old apartment building in Portland, Maine, on Fore Street, in the town's historic port section. The place had probably once been a warehouse, but unlike most of the old, brick-clad, industrial-age buildings back in Brattleboro, this one and its brethren up and down the street had been carefully and expensively overhauled. Portland was benefiting from a renaissance of sorts, and monied interests had discovered it as they had never discovered Brattleboro.

The door opened to reveal silent Dave Beaubien, who simply nodded his greeting. Lester, the extrovert, was having none of that.

"Hey, Dave. How's it going?"

But Dave merely stared at him and shook his head sorrowfully.

"That's good, Dave," Lester laughed, conceding temporarily. "You're an eloquent man, in your way."

Joe had already proceeded farther into the borrowed apartment, which belonged to the absentee owner of one of the street's ubiquitous upscale restaurants. Beyond the foyer and down a dimly lit, short hallway lined with expensive black-and-white photographs, he came to a living room, only half visible by the streetlights outside, that was stuffed with antique furniture, thick Persian rugs, overly dramatic wall decorations, and a small clutter of cops, gathered around a tripod-mounted digital movie camera aimed out of the room's central window.

Cathy Lawless turned at his entrance and raised a cardboard coffee cup at him in greeting. "Hey there, Joe. Perfect timing for a fresh brew. Dede just made a run to Dunkin' Donuts."

Joe raised his hand and waved to both women, and to Michael Coven, who was the last person he expected to find there. Plainly, the MDEA director was a hands-on leader.

Coven was also seemingly good at reading minds. He rose from one of the ornate chairs by the tripod and shook Joe's hand. "Figured I'd keep the troops company. Gets boring just pushing paper around all day."

"I know the feeling," Joe said.

Cathy snorted "Don't believe a word of it. Mike has slave units to push his paperwork. He's out here bugging us all the time."

Coven laughed in turn. "I'm out strangling legislators all the time, Cathy, trying to justify your exorbitant pay."

"There he goes," Dede said suddenly, jutting her chin toward the street.

She turned to document the moment on the laptop hooked to the camera. Joe bypassed watching the screen and crossed to the window to glance around the curtain and see what was going on. It was very late, and there weren't many strollers out anymore. The skinny young man in a short leather jacket stood out, both for his hurried sense of purpose and his scrawny looks.

"Bernie's runner," Mike Coven told him. "Kid named Leon. Move over to the other window, and you'll see where he's going."

Curious, Joe followed the advice and saw Leon duck into a large drugstore at the end of the block. He looked inquiringly at Coven, but predictably it was the talkative Cathy Lawless who answered the implied question.

"A TracFone," she said, referring to a brand of disposable cell phone. "He buys them like other people buy M&Ms. In the half week we've been here, he's probably bought half a dozen of them."

"Five," Dede corrected—the keeper of the log.

"He always goes to the same store?" Joe asked.

"Yeah," Cathy said gleefully, "meaning that thanks to Leon's lazy butt, Bernie's sloppy supervision, and Lenny Chapman's federal legal magic, we were able to record the electronic serial number of every unit they have for sale in there. As soon as Bernie turns on whatever Leon brings home, we can follow her on our GPS."

Joe matched her smile and nodded appreciatively but had to ask, "And you're sure he's giving her the phones, how?"

"There are only the two of them in the apartment," Dede answered. "And any time we've seen her, she's using the same make and model that Leon's been buying. Plus, we've never seen him use the things. It's a calculated guess."

Joe shrugged. "Works for me."

He was still at the window and now saw Leon emerge back onto the street, a small bag in his hand. He returned to the building opposite theirs and vanished through the front door.

"Which apartment is hers?" he asked.

"Right across," Coven told him, pointing.

Moments later, Joe saw the door of the apartment opposite open and Leon enter with his bag. Behind him, he heard Dede typing.

There was no sign of any woman, though.

"She's got an office in the back," Cathy explained, seeing him studying the bank of windows. "To be honest, you don't really see much from here. Typical."

That much was true, as Joe knew from a small lifetime of watching other people's windows. Only in the movies did you catch more than the occasional glimpse of someone walking by. Surveillance was usually a frustrating, if time-honored, practice.

He stayed watching, with his back to the others, listening to their banter, and eventually saw Leon cross the room and go through a distant door, closing it behind him.

This small team had been in place since shortly after they'd learned of Ann DiBernardo—and after Lenny Chapman had received the go-ahead to finance it. Usually, there were just two people here, over twelve-hour shifts. Joe and Lester had taken advantage of the cycle to return to Vermont and—in Joe's case—get a briefing from Sam and Willy about the late Brian Sleuter.

They were all here now, however, because of the trap they'd recently set with the disposable phones.

The advantage of now having Bernie's own phone be part of the surveillance was clear, but the stimulus to make it happen had been born two days earlier, when she and Leon had gone for a drive and had displayed enough paranoia to make keeping a tail on them impossible. They hadn't used Bernie's own car, they'd kept switching from one transport mode to another, and the ICE team hadn't been well enough manned to cover all the angles.

That had been an embarrassment Lenny Chapman had vowed would not be repeated.

"Stupid question," Joe heard Lester ask in the darkness to his back.

"If you can live with a stupid answer," Cathy suggested.

"No sight or sound of Luis Grega so far?"

"Sorry" was the answer.

Joe pursed his lips, lost in thought. Maine was such a huge state, the cops so few and far between. None of them knew if Grega was within three thousand miles of here. He sighed slightly, seeing the fog of his exhaled breath briefly flare up against the windowpane. What he had learned back home, from Sam and Willy, and Bill Allard at their Waterbury headquarters, was that people were becoming impatient. The governor, too, had been leaning on Allard to deliver something for the press. Even Lyn had said that she was considering having dinner with Stan Katz of the *Reformer*, just so she could break the monotony of talking to him on the phone every day.

Joe reached up and wiped the remnants of his breath vapor with the side of his hand. So many people had so little idea of how tightly focused an investigation could get sometimes—all the way down to a handful of cops, hunched together in a darkened room. He finally moved away from the window to join them for a cup of coffee.

Three hours later, there were only three of them left—the regular shift of Lawless and Beaubien, and Joe Gunther, who had no reason to leave. Mike Coven departed first, to prepare for the next day's paperwork and arm twisting; Dede Miller and Lester went next—the one back to her family, and the other to a local motel to catch some sleep before he was scheduled to return in six hours.

Dave woke them up, the mere sound of his voice and the urgency it contained functioning as dual alarms.

"They're leaving."

Joe struggled up from a borrowed armchair while Cathy simply rolled off her couch onto the floor, where she immediately began pulling on her shoes.

"Talk to us, Dave," she ordered.

Dave was simultaneously glancing out the window and stuffing a few items into a canvas bag. "It's oh-four-hundred hours and they are not dressed for a trip to the corner store. And young Leon is packing heat."

It was the longest speech Joe had ever heard from the man.

At about the same time that the lights across the street went out, the three cops stepped into the hallway outside the borrowed apartment.

"Got the keys?" Cathy asked.

Dave merely patted his pocket.

"Got the GPS?"

Dave ignored her and began taking the stairs two at a time, the others in tow.

They paused at the door leading to the sidewalk, while Dave carefully checked the street. After a long pause, he raised his left hand and issued the go-ahead. They all three stepped out and quickly made their way toward a nearby alleyway, Dave activating a remote door lock as they went. Around the corner was an incon-spicuous SUV.

Dave manned the wheel, as Cathy climbed in beside him and Gunther slid into the backseat. Immediately upon fastening her seat belt, Cathy removed the laptop from her partner's canvas bag and fired it up. In the meantime, Dave started the engine, but stayed stationary.

"Okay—acquiring," Cathy reported, watching the screen. Look-ing over her shoulder, Joe saw a map of Portland on her screen, with a growing time-out bar blinking at its bottom. Suddenly a bright red dot appeared near the center of the map.

"Got ya," she said. "She's moving out, heading toward the Arterial—probably shooting for 295 after the obligatory diversions so she can see if we're on her tail."

Dave pulled into Fore Street unhurriedly. Joe sat back, admiring the ease of it all. Instead of struggling with Bernie's evasive maneu-vers, all they had to do now was follow that dot on the map, closing in only once they sensed journey's end. It wasn't a perfect solution, of course—glitches could and did occur—but it was a big improve-ment over earlier options.

"I was right," Cathy said soon enough. "Take the Arterial west."

Traffic was virtually nonexistent, making their ability to hang back all the more important. The Franklin Arterial soon led to the Back Cove, however, and the I-295 cloverleaf, where DiBernardo's car headed south. The number of vehicles picked up, if margin-ally.

Unlike the first time they were tailed, DiBernardo and Leon kept to their initial vehicle, their rearview mirror comforting them that they were in the clear with the cops.

Joe watched the city slide by the windows as Cathy continued chatting with—or at—Dave. The tidal flats of the cove soon yielded to parking lots and cheap housing on the right and the Deering Oaks tennis courts and playing fields to the left, which in turn were quickly replaced by the same monotonous landscape of a thousand other midsized cities. The sudden appearance of Casco Bay beneath them, and the futuristic, blinking lights of the airport's primary runway immediately to the west and seemingly aimed right at them, abruptly returned him to the here and now.

"What's your guess?" Cathy asked her partner.

Dave soundlessly shrugged in response.

"I say she's headed for a long haul—Portsmouth or maybe Boston. Perfect time of night for it. For that matter, if she really pours on the steam, maybe we can pull her over for . . . Whoa. Guess not. Get ready to exit."

Joe slid forward to look over her shoulder at the computer screen. She tapped its surface to show him where they were. "Route 9—Gorham Road. This is like the back door into the Maine Mall."

"That doesn't sound likely," he said. "What's beyond it?"

"Pucker brush beyond I-95." Again, she hesitated before saying, "Ah, that explains it. Dave? Take the next right, onto Westbrook." She turned back toward Joe, explaining, "It's a housing development—crackerbox houses, all in a row. For all intents and purposes a dead end, even with a ton of people living in it. Tucks right up against the side of the airport. I wonder who she knows here? It's a far cry from her ritzy neighborhood."

Dave was now driving very slowly, alongside a row of single-family homes, beyond which row after row of similar houses stretched off in concentric circles, deep into the streetlight-illuminated gloom.

"Stay right," Cathy ordered. "Looks like she's just skirting the whole complex." She held up her hand. "Hold it. Stop."

Dave did so, both hands on the wheel.

Cathy stared at the screen for a few more seconds before announcing, "I think this is it. Roll on by, just to make sure."

Dave got them going again, around a gentle curve, just in time for them to see a couple of distant figures walking from a car to a house just like the dozen they'd already passed. As soon as he caught sight of them, Dave gently turned left, onto a side street, and broke off visual contact, as if he were just another night crawler returning home.

"That's definitely it," Cathy confirmed. "She brought the cell with her, so now we have a reading from the center of the house." She copied the address from the screen and then switched programs, adding, "Time to get educated about who she's visiting."

Here again, Joe watched with appreciation, thinking back to his first days on patrol in Brattleboro, where Dispatch raised the beat cops by flashing a blue light attached to the side of a downtown building. Now, in a parked car down a darkened street, they were accessing encrypted files on a computer that they hoped would tell them who was entertaining the woman they'd just followed here via GPS.

As if completing his ruminations, Cathy murmured aloud, "Small world."

"What?" Joe asked.

"Darryl Mehlin. Not a name you'd know, but we sure do."

"Not from the trenches," Dave commented briefly.

Joe glanced at him, wondering at the significance of that. Whether it was true or not, Dave's trademark silences had Joe half believing that whenever the man opened his mouth, he offered only prized nuggets of wisdom.

But Cathy was also apparently a believer. "Yeah," she responded. "Good point. Darryl's a facilitator—a go-to man when you need someone with a special talent. I didn't know he lived here. He's a Down East boy."

"Probably needed to be near a hospital," Dave suggested.

Cathy explained. "He's a paraplegic. Used to work on a lobster boat a long time ago. Got injured and found a different career. He's on every creep's list of 'known associates,' but he's never been charged with anything, as far as I know."

"So," Joe wanted to know, "is Bernie consulting him?"

"My guess?" Cathy surmised. "We're seeing a reconstruction in progress." She held up one finger at a time as she went on. "Bear with me—a ton of this is super vague. One—Mroz gets whacked. Two—we tail his supposed Canadian supplier, calling himself Didry at the border, to a big powwow in Calais with somebody we don't know. Three—Dave and I get shot at by your guy, Grega, out of the blue and for no good reason. Four—Bob, who was there with Grega, then acts like a crazy man and gets himself killed, right after he and Grega were cooking something up involving Bernie. Five—what does Bernie do as a specialty? Finances. And, last—who is she meeting with right now? Mr. Go-between, Darryl Mehlin."

Cathy closed her fingers. "That all tells me a new organization is being built on the ruins of Roz's old one. A few of the key movers and shakers are missing, like whoever Didry is, and the person or persons he met with in Calais. But I bet it goes full circle—that the guy who met Didry that day is the one who killed Roz."

"Wellman Beale," Dave said, seemingly a propos of nothing.

"What?" Joe asked, surprised not only at the injection, but by the fact that he knew the name.

"That's what I been trying to remember," Dave explained, facing them both. "Darryl was on Beale's boat when he got hurt."

Cathy slapped her forehead and stared at Joe. "Shit—Kevin asked me to tell you what he'd found out about Beale. I totally forgot. Turns out he *is* on the rebound—new boat, flashing cash, struttin' his stuff. Which makes all this fit perfectly." She punched Dave's shoulder in her excitement. "Of course. What was I just saying? Why not? And Darryl wasn't only Beale's sternman back then; they're cousins. That makes the connections even tighter." She held up a succession of fingers again. "Roz ruins Beale; Roz gets whacked; the Canadian supplier pays a visit; Beale's cousin is now meeting a shady financier. Nice, close circle. I bet if we scratch hard enough, we'll find some tie between Bernie and Roz, since Beale would be an idiot not to make use of Roz's old outfit. That might even be where Grega fits in, since he also once worked for Roz."

They sat on Darryl Mehlin's house for over an hour and then followed Bernie and Leon back to downtown Portland. Periodically, Cathy would revisit her theory, sometimes working her computer to check one detail or another, her enthusiasm filling the inside of the SUV.

For the most part, Joe remained settled in his seat, unable to contribute. Two things did keep rattling around his head, however. One was the danger of leaping to conclusions not based on enough facts. The other was that he'd been the one to introduce Wellman Beale to the equation, almost by chance, albeit through Steve Silva's reminiscences.

Years earlier, he'd heard of the classic experiment of telling a subject to absolutely not think of a given topic—say, a pink elephant—with the result being that, of course, the poor bastard could think of nothing else.

He now began to wonder if Wellman Beale might not somehow be influencing Cathy's thinking the same way.

CHAPTER TWENTY-FOUR

W illy was sitting at the motel's desk when Sam stepped out of the bathroom, still toweling her hair. He was holding the phone in his hand.

"Calling someone?" she asked, glancing at the clock radio on the night table. It was after ten P.M.

"Someone called us," he said dourly. "The boss is in a funk so he had to share the pain."

"Joe? What happened?"

"Nothing," Willy said, dropping the phone back onto its cradle. "That's the problem. He says they're doing good work out there, but he's not so sure they're after the right guy anymore. I guess he's feeling like a second-class citizen. Welcome to the club. I told him to get his butt back to Vermont so he can be top of the dunghill again."

Sam knew he hadn't actually said that—even Willy had some limits. But she guessed he'd come close.

"So, he called you because you're such a good listener?" she asked.

He snorted. "Right. No, he was just micromanaging and bitching at the same time, wondering what the hell we've been doing, like we hadn't talked just a couple of days ago."

She finished drying her short hair and stood before the mirror to give it a few strokes with a brush. She knew from long experience that just as Joe Gunther had never bitched or micromanaged in his life, so had Willy never delivered a straightforward, simple message without adding his own dark-hearted twist. These were things she appreciated in both of them.

She returned to the topic that was driving them all. "I'm guessing still no sign of Grega?"

"Here and there, yeah," he told her, crossing the room, "but the task force is getting sidetracked by this whole drug dealer shake-up they got going. Course, Joe is all sympathy and understanding, saying he knows how they have to take care of their own patch first, but he's getting antsy."

"He give us any marching orders?" Sam asked.

Willy propped a pillow against the headboard, before sitting down to watch her. "Nope," he said. "But I came up with some. For tonight, in fact."

She turned toward him with a dubious expression and raised her eyebrows.

He, however, knew what a bird dog she was and that all he had to do was pick the right wording.

"I figured we might be able to help him out," he began. "Or at least give him something to chew on."

"What's that mean?"

"The way I see it," Willy continued, "both of us—that is, him in Maine and us over here—are getting nowhere fast. He's chasing all over hell's half acre, looking for one guy, being sidetracked by a bunch of people with other axes to grind. We're just interviewing people out in the open who're telling us that maybe Sleuter was a jerk and lousy family material but still a good cop."

Sam laughed and pointed her finger at him. "You said, 'out in the open.' What've you got cooking?"

He smiled. "Hey. What did the boss tell us? Find out what kind of cop he was, but keep that part under your hat. That's a direct quote. So far, we've been poking around without making a big deal out of it, but we've hardly been undercover."

"And now you want to go under?" she asked. "As what?"

He scowled. "Nothin'. I'm not talking literally. I just meant under the radar."

"Oh-oh." But her face told him otherwise.

He knew he had her. He swung his feet off the bed and began searching for his shoes. "Get your clothes on. We need to break into the sheriff's department."

Of course, that wasn't actually necessary. Getting into the Addison County Sheriff's Department in Middlebury amounted to opening the door and waving at the dispatcher. The staff had gotten used to them by now.

That was precisely what Willy was counting on.

After exchanging amenities with the night shift, who expressed no curiosity about the lateness of their visit, Sam and Willy eased themselves behind a carefully closed door, into a room complete with computers, filing cabinets, and nobody to watch them—a situation which, with the routine bustle of day-to-day business, they'd never experienced before.

"Okay," Sam said softly, looking around. "What's the plan?"

He gave her a rueful expression. "So maybe it's less about breaking-and-entering and more about snooping and not being seen. I just figured that if we really wanted to roll up our sleeves and get the dirt on this guy, we might be better off with all this available"— he waved his good arm around—"and nobody looking over our shoulders. You know how thin-skinned cops get about their own, even when they thought the guy was a jerk."

She saw his point and liked his thinking. She slipped her jacket off and sat facing one of the computers, to which they'd long ago been given passwords and entrance codes. "Let's get to it."

Several hours later, north on Route 7, the dawn slowly usurping their headlights, Sam and Willy shared a just purchased cardboard cup of iced coffee.

"Burlington?" she asked.

"Yeah. Get him early before he can start thinking."

She released the catch to lower the back of her passenger seat and wriggled down a bit to get comfortable. She closed her eyes and asked, "You good? I want to catch a nap."

He glanced over at her and smiled—a rare display of fondness, revealed only when he thought she wasn't watching. "Yeah. I'm good."

They were headed for St. Paul Street in Burlington, about an hour's drive away, to meet with Alfred Doyle, predictably called Al. From what they'd pieced together after poring over affidavits, interoffice memos, computer-mounted narratives, discovery forms, and person-of-interest references spanning hundreds of cases, Al

Doyle had been among the most reliable and often used of Brian Sleuter's snitches for his drug cases.

This conclusion was also supported by educated guesswork. Cops—especially those with ambitions like Sleuter—were loath to share their sources. Called Confidential Informants, or CIs, in the trade, these people were supposed to be on file somewhere and usually were. But not always. Also, a great many of them understandably came equipped with shady pasts that could challenge their credibility—another reason some cops kept such information private. It wasn't favored practice—some state's attorneys argued that it wasn't even legal—but Willy himself had been known to employ it. "What they don't know won't hurt them" was the usual logic.

Al Doyle appeared to have been Sleuter's CI more than anyone else, and Willy's sense of smell told him that Brian had probably used him as frequently off the books as on, making of Doyle a go-to guy to interview.

St. Paul is a quiet residential street leading off from Route 7 as one enters Burlington from the south. Like much of the city, which is by far Vermont's largest, it is paradoxically small town in feel. In fact, when Willy did pull over by the curb, there was little to indicate that the heart of downtown lay just a couple of blocks up and a couple to the right.

Being sensitive to their last conversation about an interview, Sammie asked Willy over the car's roof as they emerged, "How do you want to play this? You want me to talk to him or just scare him to death looking tough while you beat him?"

Willy laughed. "Nah—let's double-team him."

They crossed the road, followed the arrow appended to the bottom of a sign reading, "Doyle—out back," and walked the length of a short driveway to the rear of an old, bland, four-unit apartment building. There, beside a second sign, this one reading, "Doyle—upstairs," they found a flimsy screen door leading to a rickety porch running along the breadth of the structure.

At the back of the porch, they found an unlocked front door, which brought them to a miniature lobby and a narrow set of stairs leading up to the second floor. With a shrug Willy quietly led the way, coming to a stop at a hollow-core wooden door equipped only with a cheap, lockable doorknob.

He paused, his fingertips barely brushing the surface of the knob.

Sam could read his mind. "I know it's tempting, but knock this time, okay? We don't even know for sure who's in there."

Willy sighed and pounded on the door with his fist. "I hate to ruin the surprise."

"It's six A.M.," she told him. "We'll be okay."

They were. It took Willy three repeats to finally get a short, fat, tousle-haired man dressed only in his underwear to open the door.

"What the fuck do you . . . ?" he tried asking.

Willy already had his badge out and shoved it so close to the man's face the latter's eyes crossed and he took a step back. Willy took advantage of the move to get off the stairs and enter the apartment.

"Agents Kunkle and Martens, Vermont Bureau of Investigation. You Alfred Doyle?"

The man's back bumped against the wall behind him. "What? Who're you?"

"Police," Willy restated. "You Doyle?"

"Yeah," Doyle answered, scowling and blinking. "What the fuck do you want?"

"Where can we talk?" Sammie said, closing the door.

"About what?"

"Got any coffee?" Willy asked, brushing by and looking around the corner, down a short hallway to a small living room.

Doyle opened his mouth to protest, but Sam cut him off with, "You live alone?"

"What?" He shifted his gaze to her as Willy kept walking. "Yeah. What the fuck's going on?"

Sammie slapped him on his bare, hairy shoulder. "We need to talk. Got pants?"

Doyle stared down the length of his body and murmured, "Shit." He shambled off ahead of her to a bedroom door on the right. A pair of pants was lying on the floor next to a disheveled single bed covered with sheets Sam doubted had ever been washed.

She watched him pull on the pants and add a T-shirt, before gesturing in the direction Willy had taken down the hall. "After you," she said.

Meekly, still shaking his head and muttering to himself, Doyle complied. "What is it with you people? It's always kick down the door. Never just a phone call."

Willy's voice came through the living room from the tiny kitchen beyond it. "Come on, Al. Where's the coffee in this dump?"

Al, now the beleaguered host, told him, "It's instant—over the sink," and went to help him out, adding testily, "Here. Let me do it."

"I take mine black—she's cream and sugar."

"I don't have cream."

Sam was now leaning against the doorjamb, making the small kitchen feel like a crowded elevator. "What've you got?"

"Shit—I don't know. Some powdered stuff. You know—creamer."

"Flavored or un?"

Al closed both his fists in frustration. "Who *are* you people?"

"We told you," Willy said from behind him, standing close. "Cops. Flavored or un?"

"Assholes," Al growled and pawed through some packages and bottles toward the rear of a shelf.

He plunked down a small container. "Hazelnut," he declared. "Don't choke on it."

Sam stepped into the room and started running the water to put a kettle on. Willy steered Al over to the breakfast table, three feet away, just in the other room, and sat him down in the nearest chair, choosing another for himself.

"Brian Sleuter," Willy announced, once everyone was settled.

Doyle passed a hand across his face. "Oh, for Christ's sake."

"Talk to us, Al," Sammie said from the kitchen, turning on one of the stovetop burners.

"What's to talk about? The man's dead. No huge loss, if that's what you wanted to hear."

"Why would we want to hear that?" Willy asked.

Al shook his head. "I don't know. I just said it."

"But you said it for a reason. Was he dirty?"

"If you don't know, I ain't saying."

Willy leaned forward in his seat. "Al. Why do you think we're here?"

Doyle was obviously at odds, literally wringing his hands and staring at the floor. "The man's dead," he repeated.

"Meaning there's nothing to lose."

Al moved to stand up, but Willy reached out and placed his hand on his forearm. "Stay. Talk."

Doyle looked from one of them to the other, his nervousness climbing. "Look, I don't even know why you're here," he said. "I barely knew Sleuter. Helped him out a couple of times, maybe."

Sam pulled a printout from her back pocket, in fact a random document she'd forgotten she even had. She opened it up and pretended to consult it. "A couple? This page is full of times he used you, Al. You were his main man. You helped make him."

Doyle groaned.

Willy sat back and crossed his legs, smiling affably. "Hey, don't get all twisted up about this. Start with the general stuff. What was he like?"

Doyle stared at him. "*Like?* What do you mean? He was a shithead."

"You helped him out a lot."

"Sure I did," Al's voice rose. "What choice did I have? He caught me dirty, kept the goods, and used them against me from then on. It was either help him or go to jail."

"No prosecutor was involved?"

"No way—just him and me."

"And he paid you," Sam said.

He twisted in his chair to face her, still standing by the stove. "Sure he paid me—pissant amounts now and then."

"You could've bitched to his boss," Willy suggested. "This is Vermont. They hate dirty cops. The slightest hint of anything bad, and he would've been off your back."

"Right," Al said. "My word against his—the super cop. Spare me."

"How did you help him, Al?" Sam wanted to know.

Doyle shrugged. "Usual stuff. I told him what I heard. Lot of junk moves through this town, heading south right through his turf.

Dopers hate the interstates—too many troopers. Backroads're the latest rage. It was easy enough for me."

"You must've hated it, though," Willy commiserated with him. "And it must've been scary sometimes."

Al's eyes widened. "No shit. Do you know what would've happened to me? Not that Sleuter gave a fuck."

Sammie saw what might be next, so she momentarily ignored the slowly singing kettle to bend at the waist and virtually whisper in his ear, "Well, don't worry about that from us. This is completely off the record. Like you said, he's gone, and we will be soon."

"If you keep cooperating," Willy added.

"I *am*, aren't I?" he complained.

"Sure are," Willy agreed. "Duly noted."

Sam spoke as she spooned coffee into the cups. "Did it ever get hot enough that somebody threatened to shut him down? Keeping your ear to the ground, you must've heard that kind of stuff, too, especially since nobody knew you were working for him."

But Doyle shook his head. "It's not like New York here. People bitched, but they weren't looking to take him out. He was just known as someone to duck."

"It's getting more like New York than it used to be," Willy argued.

"Well, maybe," Al agreed. "But not that bad."

"Still," Willy persisted, "he did a number on you. How many others do you think he squeezed the same way?"

"He wasn't gonna tell me that."

Sammie placed a cup of coffee before him and smiled brightly. "Hey, Al, we all show off. He may not have mentioned names . . ."

Al consulted the floor again. "Maybe a couple. He did say he had others on the hook."

Sam pulled a chair around and sat down, after placing the other two cups on the table. "Great," she said. "Now we're cooking."

Later that morning, Willy pulled off the road, south of Shelburne, and rubbed his eyes with the heel of his right hand.

"Want me to drive?" Sam asked, knowing the answer.

"Yeah," he said, surprising her. She swung out of the car and switched places with him. He was either really tired or this was yet another minuscule crack that he'd allowed her through his armor.

She knew better than to ask. "What do you think?" she queried instead as she adjusted the seat and he settled into hers.

"Al killing Sleuter? Doesn't have the balls."

"I agree," Sammie said, "but I'm wondering generally."

"If somebody else might've?" Willy shook his head. "I'll tell you what: unless the boss gets a signed confession from Grega that he did the dirty deed, I'm open to any number of other people. Brian was a cowboy. He played fast and loose and he didn't protect his friends — makes me look like a goddamn saint. If anybody caught wind of what he was up to — blackmailing snitches and setting up busts like Al told us toward the end — running his own one-man, unofficial, antidrug task force — then I'd say he was lucky he lived as long as he did."

He looked out the side window as Sam picked up speed, getting back on the road, and added, "It was just a matter of time before somebody got him — us or the bad guys. I'm gonna take a nap."

Sam remained silent, and in moments, Willy's regular breathing told her he'd been as good as his word, as usual.

Of course, it wasn't as simple as he'd just said. The fact that

Sleuter's ambition had led him to customize the law only meant that the supposedly cut and dried story on the man's own cruiser tape was very possibly more complicated.

If so, the punch line then resided with Luis Grega. And therefore with Joe Gunther.

CHAPTER TWENTY-FIVE

Luis Grega waited quietly in his rental van on Lubec's Main Street in the predawn darkness, smoking a cigarette and watching the utter stillness before him. He'd never seen a street so devoid of life before, especially given his exposure to Boston. The double row of weather-beaten, two-story shingled buildings; the lumpy, uneven paving; the two parked cars, grand total, facing him at the end of the block. All of it seemed like a documentary about the Yukon. He couldn't believe he was on the threshold of making towns like this his new theater of operations.

But he wasn't going to deny good fortune when it stared him in the face. Matt Mroz had been a decent boss for starters, but the money should have been better, security tighter, and the hours less crazy. Good enough for when Luis was young and stupid, but no longer. Through Alan, he'd caught a glimpse of better things, which at first had seemed like an acceptable step up. But after hearing from Jill Zachary that the cops were still chasing the fantasy that he'd killed one of their own, everything had changed. He didn't have the time to stay in middle management, kissing ass, hoping for a break, and now waiting to be shot by some cowboy for the one crime he hadn't committed. He hadn't liked Alan's plan in any case—putting so much emphasis on prescription drugs. He hadn't seen anything wrong with Roz's operation. Plus, he was familiar with it; he had no idea what Alan was setting up, and the latter hadn't been overly forthcoming, which had made Luis pissed off.

So, he'd begun working behind the scenes, using his familiarity to quietly subvert Alan's plan, including forging alliances with key players like Tatien and DiBernardo.

He had two more crucial moves to enact. After that, he was hoping to earn a little peace and quiet. It had been a troublesome few weeks.

At the far end of the street, a pair of headlights turned the corner and began heading his way. He flashed his own lights once. The car ahead responded in kind. Luis waited.

The car pulled over, nose-to-nose with the van, its engine died, and the dome light came on as the driver's door opened.

Alan Budney walked over to Grega's passenger side and slid in beside him.

"Luis, how're you doing?" he asked.

Luis stuck his hand out for a shake. "I'm doin'. You okay?"

"Yeah. What you got at this time of the day? Better be a slam dunk. I am not a morning person."

"Me, neither," said Grega, starting the van, putting it into gear, and pulling out into the street. "But what I got to show you can only be seen now."

"What is it?"

Grega laughed. "That's the problem. I'm kinda embarrassed. If I tell you, you'll think I'm nuts, but it's still a great idea—a real money maker—and I'm betting you will, too, but only after you see it. It ties into your smuggling-by-sea idea, but with something extra."

Budney seemed content with that. He settled in and looked out the window at the flat countryside outside as they reached the outskirts of town in under a minute.

Upon leaving the neck of the small peninsula Lubec called home, Grega picked up speed and headed west down Route 189, the van's headlights the only signs of movement for as far as could be seen.

They chatted a little, but conversation was hard to maintain. They didn't have the skills, didn't share a background, and hadn't yet become familiar with each other.

Four miles down the road, Grega slowed slightly before turning left onto Dixie Road.

"Back toward the water?" Alan asked.

"Yeah—like I told you. What I got is at Hamilton Cove. You know that?"

Alan nodded. "Sure. I passed by there just a few nights ago, doing a test run. You got something anchored there?"

Grega pretended to be embarrassed again and waved it away with his hand. "Yeah—well, you're right. Still, I want it as a surprise. You really won't believe this."

Alan smiled and shook his head. "I didn't know you were into surprises."

"Oh," Grega told him, "you know us. We're a real sentimental bunch."

Two and a half miles down Dixie, he turned left again and bumped along for the final two on Boot Cove Road.

"This is really cool," he said, drawing near, hoping he wasn't over-playing his hand. "I'll be bummed if you don't like this."

Finally, he stopped the van and got out, letting his enthusiastic body language set the mood. He walked in front of the bumper and aimed toward the shore of the cove, a granite and evergreen-lined semicircle of water, barely visible in the gloom. He didn't look back, encouraging Budney to follow suit by example. He heard the van door open behind him.

"Hey Luis, hang on," Alan called out.

Grega didn't give him the chance to see the small open boat with the chain and concrete weights ready and waiting. He knew what Alan had done to Roz and Harold, and knew also that it would be seconds before Alan realized how stupid he'd been to come this far. That's where inexperience got you in trouble.

Grega shot him twice in the chest as he came into comfortable range. Alan went down without a sound.

Joe walked back and sat on the stern rail of the forty-foot Maine Marine Patrol boat that had been carrying him around for the past two hours. He was feeling a variety of emotions, most of them con-flicting, and none of them matching the general mood of his com-panions.

He stared up past the wheelhouse roof and took in the huge, fea-tureless void of the night sky. High, thick, invisible clouds utterly blocked its usual array of stars and made him feel as if he might sud-denly be sucked up into some black hole. It was perfectly calm—not the hint of a breeze, with a mere swell under the hull. There were lights here and there, marking a thin line between the indistinguishable water and the absent sky—along with, of course, the eerie cluster of Navy radio towers, fifteen miles away. Some lights were clumped together as on the mainland, especially around now distant Jonesport, while others were isolated and forlorn, as on the island nearest to them, the current source of their interest.

There, they were close enough that he could make out several buildings—a home, a boathouse, a large dock with a cabin at its end. A substantial lobster boat was moored at the dock. It all belonged to Wellman Beale.

Joe didn't need to be here. There was no known connection between Beale and Luis Grega, other than that they'd both worked for Matt Mroz at some point. Instead, Cathy Lawless's enthusiasm the night they'd tailed Bernie to that meeting with Beale's cousin had grown into a passion to give Beale a closer look—and resulted in both an ICE-sponsored warrant and a feeling inside Joe that he'd finally lost control of his case.

As he'd said to Sam on the phone, it was all good work against bad people. But how did it help solve Brian Sleuter's murder? The emotional weight attached to a cop killing had struck them all at first and made of Joe and Lester favored guests. But the assumption from the start was that since they all knew who'd shot Sleuter, time and luck would probably play bigger roles in catching him than any huge outlay of effort. Matt Mroz's enterprise coming under new management, on the other hand, was happening here and now, and begging for immediate action.

Joe could only hope that since Grega was apparently also involved, he might simply surface as a result of all the stirring. Also, given that Willy and Sam weren't faring any better in Addison County, Joe hadn't much to lose by sticking around Maine a little longer. For one thing, although ICE was still on board because of the continuing reference to transborder drug smuggling, it wasn't going to be long before Lenny Chapman pulled up stakes and returned to Boston, ending the task force entirely.

A shadow separated itself from the huddle inside the wheelhouse, and a tall, lanky form made its way toward Joe's perch.

"Taking in the night air?" Lester Spinney asked, sitting down beside him.

"More or less," Joe answered, before admitting, "probably less. I'm starting to think we may have outlived our usefulness here."

Lester laughed gently. "You could say that—I feel like I should be offering to hold people's hats and coats. Still, tonight should be interesting."

"The notorious Wellman Beale?" Joe asked.

"You don't think so?"

Joe shrugged. "Oh, sure. He's dirty as hell and has been for a long time. He hated Mroz, and now his fortunes have suddenly improved."

"But?" Lester asked leadingly.

Joe shifted his position. "Oh, hell. I don't know. I guess I just can't get worked up about it. I want Grega. Cynical as it sounds, Beale is Maine's problem."

Lester nodded quietly, and Joe felt suddenly embarrassed.

"That came out wrong," he said softly.

His companion patted his shoulder. "No. It actually came out okay. Gotta be realistic, Joe. None of us can do it all, and we all have our own fires to put out."

The door of the wheelhouse opened and Kevin Delaney stuck his head out. "Guys? We're about to rock and roll."

Beale's island was remote and far off the Maine coast, but it wasn't very large. Their flotilla of four boats proved big enough to hit it pretty much at the same time and from the only four available approaches. Joe's boat, carrying the brass, got to land at the dock.

It also tied off just a little after the others, since it also wasn't carrying the entry team types, armed to the teeth and fully protected with Kevlar. Joe's team, of course, landed with weapons drawn, but from the small amount of noise preceding their arrival, none of them expected any great violence.

In fact, once the entire island had been secured, their total human haul came to four: Wellman Beale, two women—one of whom was found sharing his bed—and an old man claiming to be the resident mechanic, and looking it.

Joe and Lester hung back for most of this, fulfilling their roles as guests, knowing how awkward out-of-towners could be during a coordinated action by people used to working together.

As a result, once the all-clear was given, but before they were invited into the main house, the two of them wandered around the complex for a while, admiring the self-sufficiency of Beale's tiny empire.

This brought them to the boathouse, already posted with a guard who let them enter with a proprietary smile—the temporary invader enjoying the rule of the roost.

It was a modest building in itself—one-story with two slips—but stoutly built to resist what had to be some occasionally horrific weather. Joe hit the lights—powered by a generator heard chugging in the distance—and was surprised to find that while one of the slips had an appropriately sized powerboat, the other berthed a full-fledged lobster boat, if smaller, older, and more battered than the fancy one docked outside.

"Jeez," Lester commented. "He's doing better than I thought."

"No kidding," Joe agreed distractedly, studying the contours of their discovery.

"What's up?" Lester asked him, noticing what appeared to be a growing level of concern.

Joe approached the vessel slowly, picking his way among a scattering of ropes and tools. "I don't know," he said cautiously. "There's something . . ."

Lester joined him. The lobster boat looked utterly mundane, indistinguishable to him from any of a hundred similar ones that he'd been seeing for days on end. The only two stand-out details were that its algae-green waterline showed it had been docked for a very long time, and that it had been heavily painted, if only in spots, making it look unattractively blotchy.

"It's like something my kids would do," Lester commented.

"Take a squint at this," Joe said, pointing to a white lump mounted just under the outside of the wheelhouse roof. "What's that look like to you?"

Both men left the berth and stepped into the boat so they could study the object just a foot above their heads.

"A rooster?" Lester suggested. "Looks weird, painted white."

Joe pulled out a pocketknife, exposed one of its blades, and reached up to the extravagant comb arching over the bird's head. He scratched away a small spot, revealing a patch of bright red.

"Jesus," he murmured.

Lester stared at him, concerned by his sudden pallor. "What?"

Instead of answering, Joe entered the open-backed wheelhouse and walked to a much-abused wooden cabinet in the opposite corner from the wheel. Once there, he lifted its lid, revealing a scattering of maps and navigational books.

But he wasn't interested in the contents. Lester saw him staring at the painted surface of the lid's underside.

"Come here," Joe requested and pointed across the cabin. "And bring that light."

Lester stepped up next to him with the flashlight.

Joe tapped on the lid's wooden surface. "Right here."

Both men bent at the waist, putting their faces inches from the fresh paint job.

"What do you see?"

Lester saw two distinct sections of writing, only visible under the thick slather of white because they'd originally been put there with a ballpoint pen, which had left a faint furrow.

"I don't understand the first line," he said, reading it clumsily. "But it looks like, '*Heróis do mar, nobre povo*,' whatever that means."

"'Heroes of the sea, noble people,'" Joe translated, his voice heavy with dread, explaining, "It's the opening line of the Portuguese national anthem, just like that rooster is a symbol of Portugal—the so-called Galo de Barcelos."

He then tapped his finger on the lower section.

Lester shifted his light to a sharper angle from the wooden surface and said, "Looks like names. I can figure out José, Evie or maybe Evelyn, Steve, something like Abe at the beginning, and a couple of others I can't read."

"Abílo," Joe said.

"What?"

"It's not Abe," Joe said dully. "It's Abílo. This boat belonged to Lyn's father. I recognized it from the pictures in her apartment. She told me about the rooster, the anthem, and how they all signed this lid, including her daughter and husband—so her dad would always feel them nearby when he fished."

Lester straightened and studied his boss's haggard expression. "I'm not sure I get it," he said carefully.

Joe explained: "Everyone thought this boat was lost at sea years ago, with both men on board."

CHAPTER TWENTY-SIX

W ellman Beale was a barrel-chested, red-faced, angry man of fifty, whose inclination to chat with the likes of Joe Gunther— if it had existed at all—had been atomized by several hours with Cathy Lawless and Lenny Chapman. He hadn't asked for a lawyer yet, but—according to them—that was mostly because he hadn't needed one. He knew how to handle cops just fine.

Originally, Joe hadn't even been scheduled to meet the man. Jurisdictional considerations and the fact that Grega didn't feature prominently in Beale's arrest had both played a role in denying Joe a one-on-one. The discovery of Abílo Silva's boat, however, had led to a fast gathering of minds, and Joe being given his chance.

They were still on the island, it was still night, although barely, and Joe was feeling the full weight of his dreary discovery.

He entered the small room they were using for Beale, rigged with recording equipment and bright lights, and sat at the table opposite him.

"Which one're you?" he demanded.

"Joe Gunther, Vermont Bureau of Investigation, officially attached to this ICE task force."

"Vermont? You guys don't have enough shit on me right here? I never even been to fucking Vermont."

"That's okay. You probably wouldn't like it. And I'm not here for anything you've been asked about."

Beale raised his eyebrows in expectation. "No shit? You from EPA or the ASPCA?"

"Nope," Joe answered him affably. "I already told you where I'm from. I want to talk to you about Abílo Silva."

The split-second hesitation before Beale answered gave the man away. "Who?"

Joe smiled. "Nice try. You see, the funny thing is that while you may have never been to Vermont, and I'm a minor player here, I'm the one who can cause you the most pain."

"Why's that?" Beale was forced to ask after Joe left his last comment dangling.

" 'Cause I'm the one pinning a murder rap on you."

Beale's eyes narrowed. "You're full of crap."

"The boat in your boathouse—where did you get that?"

"I found it."

"Where?"

"At sea. I was out fishing and found it floating empty, abandoned."

"So you stole it."

"Salvage of the sea."

"You have to be *awarded* salvage, Wellman," Joe told him, "by a court or the owner of the vessel. You stole it."

"I'll let a court decide that, since I was about to bring it in anyhow. I just found it a few days ago. My sternman will testify to that."

"Who painted over its name and identifying numbers?"

Beale smiled and shrugged. "Wish I could help you out, Mr. Vermont."

Joe studied him, all smug and comfortable. There were other topics to pursue. The whole subject of Luis Grega had yet to be broached. But he'd looked at Beale's criminal record earlier, and what he had facing him only confirmed his suspicions. Beale was a been-there-done-that kind of perpetrator—a hard case with a vested interest in staying just that way.

"You could help someone out here," he suggested, instead of following his planned line of questioning.

Beale laughed at him. "Meaning me, right? By trading the whole truth for the love of the prosecutor and my own self-respect? I heard that one before."

But Joe shook his head, yielding to a purely emotional impulse that he knew would be futile, but that he simply had to pursue. "Nobody's here to help you," he explained. "Least of all yourself. I was thinking of the family Abílo Silva left behind—a wife and two kids who have been twisting in the wind for years. They would love to know what really happened. Maybe you could give me that without screwing up either your legal case or your ego. You could tell me what a little bird told you, or that you found a letter floating on the water that later self-destructed. Anything so that they can know what to do with all that grief."

Beale tilted his round head to one side and considered Joe pitiably. "See? There's the catch," he finally said. "I've had a few wives and kids, too. But I don't give a fuck about any of them. Why should I care about this guy's? It's a hard world. And hard people are the best at running it."

Joe stood up, unsurprised but more depressed than ever, and frowned at the irony of what he'd just heard. "You better hope for your own sake you're wrong," he said.

Beale countered with a wide smile and offered Joe, in a sudden snapshot, what Steve Silva had witnessed all those years ago—a broad, welcoming, guileless friendliness, free of cant or subterfuge.

"Yeah. Well, the difference is," he said as Joe reached the door, "I don't give a rat's ass."

Joe didn't doubt him for a second.

What they'd all set in motion didn't end until midmorning the following day, after which, exhausted, they called it quits and retired to their various beds, in and around the Augusta MDEA headquarters, where Delaney had decided to process what they had.

They reassembled that evening, for only a couple of hours, mostly to make sure everything was where it needed to be, properly filed, logged, indexed, and accounted for.

And then, Lester and Joe found themselves back outside, in front of the huge office building on the outskirts of town.

"You want something to eat?" Lester asked.

"Not really," Joe admitted. "I'm tempted to go back to the motel, grab a candy bar from the machine, and call Lyn."

"You gonna tell her what we found?"

"Not on the phone. This is purely selfish. I just want to hear her voice. I'll wait on the other stuff until we get together—God knows, there's no rush and using a phone call is pretty harsh. How's your daughter doing on that broken ankle?"

"Fine," Lester said. "Says it itches. Won't be much longer now till she gets a walking cast. How do you think Lyn's gonna take it?"

"I really hate that I'm going to find out."

They were standing side by side by the curb, facing a parking lot built to accommodate some fifteen hundred cars. It was dark, but not terribly late, so there were a fair number of vehicles still scattered about. While a nice and modern setting, and certainly impressive to the underfunded Vermonters, it was nevertheless a little alienating and added to the two men's longing to return home.

"How 'bout you?" Joe asked. "Got any plans?"

Lester shrugged. "Maybe a movie."

They began walking in the general direction of their cars. "You know," Joe told his colleague, finally giving in to his exhaustion and low spirits, "I think we've done what we can out here. We had a thread to follow out of Boston, but with Bob's death and Beale finally lawyering up, that's pretty much run out. It's unlikely Grega's going to fall out of the sky and surrender just because we're here."

Spinney was walking with his head tucked down, listening carefully. "So, we go home?" he asked.

"Unless you can argue against it," Joe said.

Lester gave it honest consideration but finally shook his head. "I'm trying not to give in to just feeling homesick," he said. "But I can't say I disagree."

They reached the car Spinney had rented for use within the state, since he and Joe had often been forced to travel separately.

Joe placed his hand on the younger man's shoulder. "Okay. Why don't you get rid of this thing in the morning, and we'll hook up in the motel lobby at nine? We can come back here, pay our respects, and get a good jump on the day, heading back to Vermont. Sam and Willy have been hard at it from their end, but to be honest, we may just have to put this onto the back burner for a while—media hounds and politicians be damned."

Lester glanced up at the night sky, made milky by the reflected lights of the distant downtown. "Jesus—that's going to go over big."

Joe patted his shoulder and began moving toward his own car, several rows away. "It is what it is. People're just going to have to live with it. Have a good night, Les. See you in the morning."

He heard Spinney open up his car door and start the engine moments later. By then, he was no longer paying attention, searching instead for where he might have left his sedan only a few hours earlier. He hated huge parking lots.

"Do not move, Agent Gunther."

The voice was smooth, only slightly accented, and belonging to someone young—perhaps in his twenties, perhaps a little older.

Joe held his hands out slightly, to show they were empty and that he was considering no heroics. The voice had come from behind and slightly to his right.

"What's on your mind?" he asked, purposefully choosing a relaxed tone of voice, although his brain was working fast, considering his options.

"I want you to walk toward that delivery truck—the dark green one ahead of you."

"And if I don't?"

"You're after me for killing one cop already . . ." he didn't bother finishing.

Well, Joe thought, that cleared up one mystery, and pretty

ironically, too, given what he'd just said to Lester about ever locating this man.

"Meaning I'm supposed to make this easier for you?" he asked. "Shoot me now—here. I'd sooner take my chances that some cop'll hear you and take you out where you stand. You know this is Public Safety's home base, right?"

Grega's tone of voice grew testy. "Get in the fucking van, Gunther, or I'll shoot your damn kneecap off. You want to be a cripple for life just because you had to flash some attitude?"

Joe heard the implication—he was suggesting Joe would survive this encounter. "Okay," he said, walking to the van. "How did you find me, by the way?"

"You're a rock star, old man. I got your mug shot through Google, and then I waited around this big-ass parking lot, figuring you'd show up."

"Jesus. You could've been out here a long time. I'm going home tomorrow." Joe laughed suddenly. "We gave up on you—figured we'd wait for someone to rat you out, or for you to screw up."

"Could happen," Grega said philosophically from the darkness. "But I'm working real hard that it don't. Stop by the rear side door of the van, put your hands against it, and then step away till you're almost falling on your face."

Joe slowly complied, his self-confidence straining under an inevitable rising fear.

He heard Grega step up behind him, felt his hand as he searched for and located Joe's gun, and then heard him retreat a few paces.

"You got your cuffs," Grega told him. "I just felt 'em. Take them out and put them on."

"In front of me or behind?"

"In front."

Joe did as requested.

"Now slide open the door and get inside."

Once more, he followed orders. The van's interior was completely empty aside from two metal folding chairs facing each other.

"Comfy," he said. "Which one's mine?"

"Looking to the rear."

Joe awkwardly hefted himself inside and shifted around to get properly settled. While he was doing so, Grega quickly slammed the side door and reappeared at the back. He, too, then climbed aboard, closing the second door behind him.

They could only see each other by the filtered glow of an overhead parking lot light nearby.

"Okay," Joe said. "What's up? You ready to come in?"

Grega smiled and pressed the palm of his hand against his forehead—a gesture of utter amazement.

"That's really good. You're something else." He shook his head. "No, I'm not. In fact, I want you to disappear—you're my last piece of business before I get my life back."

"You an innocent bystander all of a sudden?"

He scowled. "Yeah, if you give a goddamn—probably easier not to, though. Fucking cops're always so lazy."

Joe considered Grega's sudden passion and the look of frustration in his eyes. A proud man, eager to take credit for what he did, and maybe one—unlike Bob, so quick to lie to his wife—who considered himself too honorable to claim other people's work as his own.

Joe sat back. "Okay. Tell me what happened."

"I didn't shoot him."

"That's it? We got you on videotape, ducked over and sneaking up to the cruiser."

Grega pounded his own knee. "I *knew* it. You assholes. I thought it was a smokescreen at first—that you were jacking my name in the papers 'cause you knew who it was and you were tryin' to flush him out. What bullshit. You guys are so lazy—course it has to be the druggie with the funny last name, right?"

He pointed meaningfully at Joe. "I didn't do it. Somebody else showed up—all of a sudden—and popped him." He held out his hand, his index and thumb out rigid, like a barrel and hammer, respectively. "Like that."

Joe scowled. "He was just there?"

"He showed up, like I said."

Joe shook his head sympathetically. "Luis, I was there, at the crime scene, a few hours later. There are no houses nearby. Did you see a car pull up?"

"No, but he was there."

"He? So you got a look at him?"

Grega hesitated and then stared at the floor. "No."

Joe leaned forward, for the first time feeling a twinge of empathy. "Look, take it from the top. Sleuter talks to you, collects your paperwork, and goes back to the cruiser to use the radio. What do you do?"

Grega pressed his lips together.

"For Christ's sake," Joe exclaimed. "You're already accused of killing the guy. You too embarrassed now to admit you had evil thoughts?"

"Fuck you."

Joe burst out laughing. "Fuck *me*? You *invited* me here."

Grega slapped his thighs angrily. "God *damn* it. Yeah, I wanted to whack him. The guy was an asshole and he was about to do me hurt." He grabbed his head in both hands, as if trying to hold it together. "Fuck," he said, resigned, and dropped his fists back into his lap.

"Okay," he tried again, calmer. "I don't know what I wanted to do. Maybe whack him, maybe mess him up a little. I just wanted to get back on the road. I was working on instinct."

Like an artist having a dry spell, thought Joe. "Then what?" he urged.

"I slid down in my seat, waiting for him to notice. After a minute, I popped open the door and kind of fell out, keeping low. He still didn't react. I got as far as his front bumper when I saw a flash of something moving—somebody, I thought, but I wasn't even super sure about that—and then, POW, a shot. I didn't know what to do. I felt like a cornered rat, all crunched up in front of his car like that. First, I thought he'd seen me, and he'd let me have it and I just hadn't felt it yet. I heard of that happening, you know? But that wasn't it. I was still alone, I was okay, but now there was this total silence."

"What happened to the shooter?" Joe asked.

"I don't know. There wasn't nobody. I still couldn't figure out how there coulda *been* a shooter. I kept crawling around to the driver's side, wondering what the fuck, you know? But I was alone, like I said. That's when I figured, what've I got to lose? And grabbed my paperwork and split."

"What about Marano?" Joe asked. "What did he see?"

"Nuthin'. I got back to the car, blood on my hand and on the license, and he just kept saying, 'What happened, what happened?' like I knew anything. He even thought I did it."

"Surprise, surprise," Joe couldn't suppress.

Grega flared up again, smacking Gunther's knee with his open hand. "Up yours, asshole. I'm telling you the truth. I want this shit settled. Why else would I grab you right in front of the fucking cop shop?"

"Half a dozen reasons, Luis, not least to make me *think* you didn't kill him." Joe then abruptly switched approaches, hoping the man's emotional state might make him more talkative. "And speaking of that," he said, "why do you give a damn what I think? Killing people should be a good rep for someone like you."

Grega made a face, still feeling sorry for himself. "I don't need the heat."

"That's right," Joe reacted conversationally, "you're in a new line of work now—upwardly mobile."

He had no idea what he was talking about, knowing only that Grega had been making plans with Bob.

But he'd hit a nerve. Grega looked at him carefully and asked, "What do you know about that?"

Joe thought fast as he opened his eyes in surprise. "About Bernie and the rest? More than you might think. We've been pretty busy."

Grega's face darkened and he glared ahead, recalculating his position.

Joe took a chance. "We've also been playing the usual 'what-if' game that you do when you're digging around, and we have more than one guy saying that it would've been smart for you to have whacked Matt Mroz."

That snapped Grega back to the here and now. "*What?*" he burst out. "I didn't do that. I wasn't even around. His murder was the whole fucking reason I came up to this stupid state. I was working for him when that peckerhead cop pulled us over. Holy shit, man—you got *everything* wrong. How the hell you make a living, being so stupid?"

"You have benefited, though," Joe argued, no more sure of that. "You can't blame us for connecting the dots."

Grega shook his head. But Joe thought he saw something besides outrage in his eyes when he spoke next. There was a hint of calculation, also. "Alan Budney did Roz. I had nuthin' to do with it."

Joe was briefly stumped. He'd never heard of Alan Budney, and a whole new name this late in the game was frankly startling. In most ways, the huge majority of police work in northern New England revolved around a small and finite—and generally well known—population base. To have something like this appear out of nowhere was unusual. His only comfort was thinking that Cathy or Kevin or one of the others would merely raise an eyebrow and say something like, "Oh, yeah—Alan. Didn't know he had it in him."

He therefore responded along similar lines.

"Budney," he said, nodding. "I was one of the Budney fans. Others thought that was a stretch. I'm not a local, so I bowed to their knowledge."

"Yeah, well—so much for the locals. They're usually assholes, if you ask me. Don't know their butts from a hole in the ground."

"They couldn't figure his motive," Joe ventured. "Why he'd stick his neck out so far."

Grega smiled knowingly. "Oh, that's real tough. What about the money?"

Joe smiled back. "What about the murder rap? That's got *you* all hot and bothered. Does that make Budney the bigger man?"

Grega frowned. "Fuck you. Budney had a crank against his old man. He was all screwed up—thought people owed him something. Wanted to show the world who was boss. Stupid. I'm lucky. I have no clue who my father was. Just another fast fuck. I got no hang-ups like that. Me? I just want the cash.

"Good luck finding Alan, though," he suddenly added, Gunther thought a little gratuitously. "The other thing that guy is, is super private. When he took over Roz's outfit, he said he was gonna tighten things up like never before, and was gonna make goddamn sure nobody could do to him what he did to Roz. He'll be like a rat in a hole to find."

Joe felt he was making headway, but he wondered how long he had before his host ran out of patience.

"You must like working with Beale—you two are birds of a feather."

It was either going to prove accurate or insulting. He didn't really care. He was just looking for a reaction.

But not what he got.

Grega stared at him blankly. "Beale? Who's that?"

Later, Joe knew his response should have been more creative. But his surprise was such that he simply blurted, "Wellman Beale."

Grega furrowed his brow, muttered, "Never heard of him," and half stood up to look out the van's front window.

When he sat back down, Joe knew his chance was over.

"Okay," Grega said brusquely, "enough of this shit. You get out the way you got in."

Joe held up his hands. "Cuffs?"

Grega cracked open the side door and peered outside. Satisfied, he threw it all the way open and gestured to Joe to leave, saying, "No way. You got a key somewhere, and if you don't, you got a hundred buddies over there that'll be happy to help you out." He smiled and added, "Right after they laugh their asses off. I'll keep your gun, too."

Joe did have a key, if no idea how he was going to reach it. Grega was right, though. There was no way in hell he was going to ask for help, even if the next day he would have to fess up to the whole event, in painful detail.

After he stepped onto the asphalt and watched the van drive off, therefore, he made himself comfortable leaning against his own car and began trying to reach the bottom of his right pocket.

CHAPTER TWENTY-SEVEN

Two days after leaving Maine, Joe sat alone in his Brattleboro office, in the middle of the night, with all the lights off except for his own desk lamp. It wasn't a rare event. He did this often enough, and often not alone, when a major case was being worked and a string of ten-to-twelve-hour workdays was simply not enough to stay ahead.

Of course, there was a major case on hand. Brian Sleuter's killer—be it Luis Grega or not—was still on the loose, after weeks of investigating. In addition to Joe's personal efforts, and Sam's and Willy's, dozens of other cops, from locals to the U.S. Customs and Border Patrol, to the Royal Canadian Mounted Police, had all been contributing with interviews, data checks, public service announcements, informant shake-ups, and even a couple of roadblocks. And, of course, an uncountable number of hunches. Every cop with a brain, it seemed, plus a few more with active imaginations, had put an oar in the water.

All to no effect, and all with a growing sense of futility. Most of them still believed that Joe had been the only one to meet the cop killer, and to let him get away. There were probably as many theories on how that encounter could have been turned around as there were concerning the next reasonable course of action.

The irony was, of course, that because of the weight of not knowing how to proceed, Joe was in fact alone at this time of night, quite possibly the only cop awake, still working this very active major case.

In fairness, he wasn't doing much. He had the unit's small TV perched on his desk, with the tape from Sleuter's cruiser playing on the machine's VCR. There was nothing to see here, of course, that he and countless others hadn't already seen before, but the tape had become, in the absence of anyone under arrest, a form of talisman—the source of it all, if only "it" could be defined—and thus something that a large number of people had consulted in the same vein in which true believers visit a holy shrine, hoping they'll be touched by inspiration.

The most revealing aspect of this ritual in Joe's case, however, was that while the tape was on and he was positioned to watch it, he was no longer seeing a bit of it. His eyes were focused on some middle distance, deep inside his brain.

Primarily, he was thinking about Lyn.

He hadn't told her about finding the boat on Beale's island yet. He would soon, of course. There was no way around it. It wasn't the sort of thing that simply went away.

But he wished it would.

After all, what did it in fact reveal? That father and son had survived the storm? If so, their fates were tied either to homicide or flight, and the latter didn't make much sense. From what would they have been fleeing? Family and finances had been secure at the time;

nothing untoward had surfaced later to tarnish their memories. That left the horrific but practical conclusion that they had both been murdered, which, in turn, created a slough of nightmarish possibilities that could only fester with time.

Wellman Beale had been of no help, naturally. Nor would he ever be, at this point, since he had finally stopped talking. Interviews of all his associates, including the ancient mechanic found on the island, along with his erstwhile sternman and cousin, had led nowhere. Either they had corroborated Beale's story that he'd merely found the boat on the water—empty, drifting, and two hundred miles from its home port—or they claimed to know nothing at all.

Time and effort might change things, of course. And people did talk eventually, when the right circumstances fell into place. But right now, none of that looked likely. And the Silva family, in the meantime, was going to be left to wonder, and wait.

As soon as Joe told them what he'd discovered.

"Not a good thing—a man like you watching late night porno."

Joe squinted into the darkness past the TV set, trying to see the owner of the voice. "Hey, Willy," he said. "Sam throw you out again?"

A shadow emerged from the surrounding gloom. "Up yours. Couldn't sleep. What're you watching?"

"The Sleuter cruiser tape."

Willy reached out, grabbed a spare metal chair, and dragged it around beside Joe's, settling down and propping his feet up on the desk beside the TV. "No shit? I thought you had that memorized by now."

Joe let out a brief snort. "Me and a hundred other cops."

"Not me," Willy admitted, staring at the screen. The action before them was about half played out. "I never seen it."

Joe picked up the remote from his lap. "Allow me." He hit Rewind, and they both watched the screen go snowy.

"Any news on Grega?" Willy asked as they waited.

"No," Joe said dourly. "That whole deal got so weird. I have no idea what the Mainers'll do about it—probably just wait for something to fall in their lap. That would be my plan."

"We don't really care, do we?" Willy asked. "He didn't do Sleuter."

Joe shifted in his seat and stared at him. "You believe that?"

"Sure—that's what he told you."

Joe laughed. "The man's a crook, for Christ's sake."

"Yeah," Willy retorted, "which makes him a businessman. What was in it for him to kill a cop? I take him at his word. He's got bigger fish to fry—like he said when he grabbed you. Which," he added with an approving nod, "I thought was a really ballsy move. Actually," he added as further explanation, "that stunt is what makes me think he didn't kill Sleuter—no bad guy in his right mind would've done that otherwise. He seriously didn't want that particular rap on him, for whatever reason."

Joe couldn't argue the point. He, too, had been impressed by Grega's determination, especially in the middle of a police department parking lot. "You may be right," he conceded. "Speaking of which, you remember that guy he mentioned I'd never heard of before? Alan Budney?"

"Claimed he was the one who killed the kingpin in Rockland," Willy answered. "Got that whole ball rolling."

"Right. Well, Kevin Delaney sent me an e-mail this afternoon. Nobody can find Budney, either. According to every snitch they've talked to, he was there one second and gone the next. His family's clueless, too."

"So?"

"I was thinking," Joe told him. "When Grega was talking about him, he referred to him in the past tense a couple of times and then made a point of telling me he'd be hard to find."

"Meaning he pinned the Roz killing on the poor slob and then knocked him off as both a smokescreen and a dead end," Willy filled in. "*That's* why he didn't want Sleuter on his tab. I like it. It allows all of them—the Canadian exporter, the finance lady with the guy's name, and all the rest to keep on ticking while the cops sit around with their thumbs up their ass. Cool."

Joe pointed the remote at the TV and hit Play. "You are a sick man. Here we go."

The screen stuttered awake to the image of a distant pair of taillights, accompanied by the rhythm of the cruiser's strobe lights bouncing off the quickly passing countryside. Standardly, onboard police cameras ignite whenever the emergency lights are switched on. Joe had seen this so many times by now—still, he couldn't shake the same ominous dread that hit him every time.

Willy abruptly swung his feet off the desk and sat up. "Rewind it."

"What?"

"Rewind it." He grabbed the remote from Joe's hand.

Joe looked at the picture. Behind the snow, he could just make out the Toyota getting smaller and moving away, and the oncoming car suddenly appearing to speed backward into the distance.

Willy hit Play, bringing everything back to normal.

"What did you see?" Joe asked.

Willy didn't answer, instead leaning forward in his chair, staring intently. Once more, the approaching vehicle grew larger, got almost abreast of the cruiser, and then froze as Willy hit Pause. He fiddled with the control, changing the image one frame at a time, until he found one where the police strobes acted like a flash to light up the driver's face.

"I'll be a son of a bitch," Willy said softly.

The approach Gunther chose for the arrest was unconventional. Generally, there would have been ballistic vests, an entry team, a backup team, an ambulance in reserve, and maybe—if the politicians got their way—even some journalists out of sight for the follow-up press conference. Finally cornering a long sought-after cop killer—a front page item for weeks on end—was supposed to be at least an opportunity for relief, closure, a little self-congratulation, and a lot of good PR.

Instead, although watched over by several tucked-away people with guns, all that appeared at the suspect's house two mornings after Willy's revelation were Joe and Willy himself. And Joe was there only as company.

But the plan proved well thought out. On a bright and sunny morning, with the sounds of summer building with the heat, Willy rang the bell, the door opened up, and Shirley Sherman stepped out before them, a dish towel in her hands.

Her expression settled between pleasure and calculation upon recognizing Willy.

"You're back," she said neutrally.

"Hey, Shirley," Willy greeted her. "This is my boss, Joe Gunther."

Joe nodded wordlessly. Shirley stayed rooted in place.

"We put it together," Willy continued. "We got you on Brian's cruiser tape, and we're gonna match the bullet to your .45."

She lifted her chin half an inch, as if warding off the slightest of long expected blows. "I was kind of hoping it would be you."

She glanced over their shoulders, as if surprised to see only the driveway and the fields across the road. She raised her eyebrows slightly. "You want to come in?"

"Sure."

She walked stiffly ahead of them, turning as Joe closed the door after issuing a quick thumbs-up to those covertly watching from outside. Both he and Willy were wired for sound.

"You want coffee?" she asked.

Willy hesitated, but Joe wanted her sitting down as soon as possible. "We're good, thanks." He made a sweeping gesture with his hand toward the assembled living-room chairs. "Be all right to talk here?"

She shrugged and chose a fake antique ladder-back near the fireplace. Paranoid about anything going wrong at this late stage, Joe scanned the area near her for any potential weapons. There were none. He and Willy perched on the edge of armchairs, roughly to either side of her.

"Shirley," Joe began, "I've got to advise you that you don't have to talk to us, if you don't want to."

But she'd already held up a hand in protest. "Don't worry about that. I know what I did. I can live with the consequences."

"So you did kill Brian Sleuter?" Willy asked formally.

"Yes," she answered, and then dropped her gaze to the rug. "I was driving home when I saw his blue lights. I didn't know it was him at first, of course. But I recognized him as I passed by. That's when it grabbed me."

In the following silence Joe asked, "The urge to kill him?"

She nodded. "I had the Colt with me. Don't know why—threw it in the car at the last minute. I do that sometimes, just for what-the-hell. Never know when you might see something to plink at."

"You didn't know he'd be on that road, on patrol?" Willy suggested.

"I knew he was out. I didn't know where. And I wasn't looking for him. I was driving back from Middlebury. I'd been at a bar down there."

She shook her head. "I don't know. Just seeing him. Something snapped. I didn't even think much about it. I parked over the rise, walked back with the gun, popped him where he sat, and left." She snapped her fingers. "Like that. Didn't even look at who was in the other car. I didn't care." She looked up at Joe. "I couldn't believe it when the papers started talking about drug runners and all the rest. That was all pure dumb luck."

"Why did you do it, Shirley?" Willy asked.

For the first time since he'd first met her, Willy thought she looked not only her age but older—almost hollowed out.

"I know it sounds weird," she said. "But Bri and I always kind of connected, in our funny way. I should've hated the guy, the way he treated Kathleen, but . . ." Her voice trailed off.

"You were lovers?" Joe suggested.

She tilted her head to one side. "I never liked that word. Sounds phony."

"Still," he pressed.

"Yeah—whatever."

"Anyhow, you had a fight?" Willy filled in.

She laughed bitterly. "He dumped me, is more like it. I knew he would. I mean, look at me." She placed her hands on her round thighs.

She gazed at each of them in turn before adding, "I'm not an idiot. I know what this is. But you don't know what he said to me. I hated him more for that than for what he did. He was just a man—they're all shitbags. But Bri was a mean man."

Wantastiquet Mountain is in New Hampshire, right across the Connecticut River from downtown Brattleboro. It is of classic rounded, ancient New England dimensions—and provides a backdrop for the town as tangible as the place's own history. It is also a favorite place for hardy hikers to climb, in order to look back and enjoy a view like that from a low-flying plane.

Joe was sitting on a large rock near the summit, but without eyes for the untidy urban sprawl below him. Instead, he was looking at Lyn, also adorning a rock, about ten feet away and slightly downhill so that he couldn't quite see her face. She was perched there like a slim schoolgirl, hugging her knees, and—he knew—not enjoying the view, either.

He had just finished telling her of what he'd found in Maine or, worse, what he hadn't. She'd taken the news quietly, numbness quickly replacing shock, and then had asked for a little privacy in order to gather her thoughts.

He wished her well there. Years earlier, she, like so many others hit with a family tragedy, had been able to make her peace and move on. She'd constructed a cubbyholed chest of emotional keepsakes and then sealed off a select few of its compartments.

He knew what damage he'd just done to that structure. What he didn't know was how she would cope with the resulting jumble.

He took his eyes off of her long enough to glance at the town that he'd called home for his entire adult life, and to which she had moved, in large part to be near him.

Two people were in jail—a woman scorned by a younger man, and Wellman Beale, for some minor drug charges cobbled together because he couldn't be touched for a double homicide. The others— Luis Grega and Alan Budney—remained enigmatic, because they either were lying low or were perhaps pinned down by weights at the bottom of the ocean.

A little justice, hampered by limitations, had been erratically meted out—by pure luck, by paltry legal finesse, or by vicious Darwinian selection.

The rest of it would have to wait, to fester with time, threatening to bring havoc at any moment.

Joe returned to watching Lyn, waiting for any sign to which he could helpfully respond, fearing—given his growing love for her and the nagging weariness dogging his meditations—that he might be left hanging for a very long time.

He could only trust that the wait would reward them both.

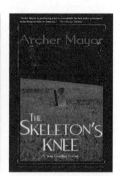

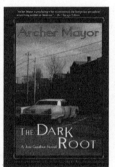

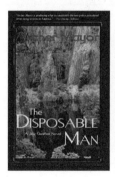

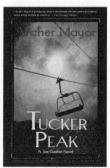